The Ema

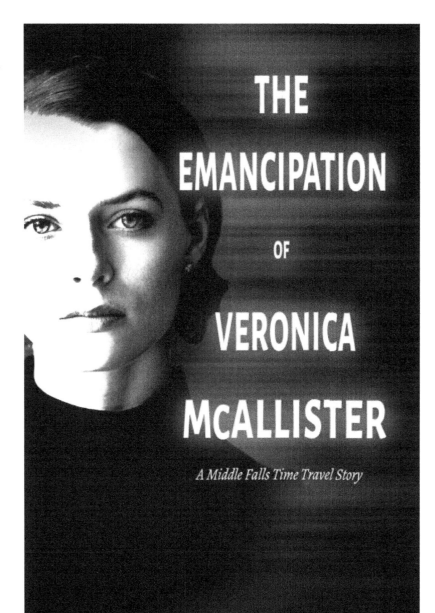

THE
EMANCIPATION
OF
VERONICA
McALLISTER

A Middle Falls Time Travel Story

SHAWN INMON

1

For my sisters

Chapter One
February 2018

Veronica McAllister was ready to die.

She peered into the deep blue eyes of the hospital janitor, then closed her own eyes for the final time in that life. His last words to her—"Know that you are safe. That you are loved. That you are perfect. That no harm can ever come to you."—echoed in her ears.

Exactly the kind of gooey-hooey I always hated. And yet. Coming from him, it felt different. As though he knew. Doesn't matter at this point. The die is cast. Soon, I'll know the answers to every question I've ever asked. No more uncertainty. Everything will be clear. Or completely dark. That's more likely, isn't it? An eternity of nothingness? And that's okay too.

Less than five minutes before, she had swallowed a deadly dose of secobarbitol and pentobarbitol, administered by her physician. She lay in the Critical Care wing of the Middle Falls Hospital, in Middle Falls, Oregon.

Her doctor hadn't been happy she had chosen to end her life, but she had invoked Oregon's *Death with Dignity* act. Her body was riddled with cancer, and there were only long days, weeks, and months of pain ahead of her, with the ending predetermined. As she looked back over her life, that description fit the last sixty years, as well.

I have been a failure in this life. I can't say I am sorry to see it go.

That was her final thought.

VERONICA MCALLISTER opened her eyes with a start. A book which had been sitting open on her lap, fell to the floor. She looked around in a panic.

Where am I? Wait. I'm dead, right?

She reached her hand out and felt the fabric she was sitting on. It was textured and felt completely real, not like a dream or hallucination at all. She looked around in a semi-panic. She was in a nice, middle-class living room in a nice, middle-class home she did not recognize. She sat on an orange, low-slung couch, with a matching chair beside her. An antique television sat between two matching wooden bookcases filled with knick-knacks and *Reader's Digest Condensed Books*.

Veronica put her hand against her chest. Her heart was beating a staccato rhythm against her ribs. She stood up and looked down at unfamiliar clothing. She was wearing a long, pleated skirt that went well past her knees, a gray sweater, and saddle shoes.

Did I fall into a costume party, and I came as a fifties girl?

Veronica picked up the book that had fallen. *Lolita*, by Viktor Nabokov. *I read that when I was a teenager. I remember I had to hide it from Mom.* She reached down and smoothed the skirt, then walked in a daze from the strange living room to a strange dining room, and then an equally strange kitchen.

I need to get a hold of myself. I died. Then, I open my eyes here, in a house straight out of a museum, but I have no idea where I am.

She stopped in the middle of the kitchen. The cabinets were painted butter yellow, and the flat surfaces were pastel blue.

"Oh my God. It looks like the Easter Bunny threw up in here. Who has a kitchen that looks like this?" Veronica leaned against the metal-rimmed countertop. She hadn't realized she was speaking out loud. "Okay, let's work this out. A minute ago, I was in a hospital bed.

I closed my eyes, then opened them here, in some odd retro museum. But," she said, looking again at her soft sweater and long skirt, "why am I dressed like I'm part of it?"

She looked at a clock on the wall. 12:32. She glanced at the darkness outside the kitchen window.

It's either noon, and I'm trapped underground somewhere, or it's half past midnight.

With a shock, she noticed her hands. Her fingers were long and slim, with neutral polish on the nails. Her skin, which had been paper thin, with blue veins mapping a route across her hands, was clear and smooth. Her fingers flew to her face. The sagginess of her jowls and cheeks, the bags under her eyes, were gone.

She fled from the kitchen and found a small bathroom. The pastel blue from the kitchen had spread to this room. All the fixtures—the sink, toilet, and tub—were the same shade of blue. She thrust her face over the sink and looked into the mirror.

Veronica goggled. Her hands flew to her face again, tracing an arc over her high cheekbones, her full lips, her plucked eyebrows.

"I'm ... young." Her hands traced the curve of her waist, her small, firm bust. She sat down hard on the blue toilet. "How is this ... what happened to me?" She stood and examined her face again. She raised her eyebrows as she examined her image in the mirror. "I thought I was ugly. What was wrong with me?"

She stepped out of the bathroom, still trying to get her bearings. The front door opened and a tall man in a jacket and tie entered, smiling, fresh off an evening out. He was followed by an attractive woman wearing a jacket over a floral dress. The man was tanned, with a good face and a quick smile. When the woman doffed her jacket, Veronica saw she was pregnant, with a cute little belly bump.

"Well," the man said, "how was he?"

"Wh—what? Who?" Veronica stammered.

"Zack. Was he a monster, like usual?" The man wasn't listening, but was instead walking around the house, inspecting for broken lamps or windows. He walked into the kitchen, opened the refrigerator and seemed to be taking inventory.

I don't know who these people are, but they see I'm in their house, and they don't care. They think I belong here. Curiouser and curiouser.

"Don't pay any attention to him, dear," the woman said, removing her jacket. "James, can you pay Veronica and give her a ride home, while I check on Zack?"

"Yes, dear." Vince reached in his wallet and pulled out a dollar bill. "Let's see, twenty-five cents an hour, plus fifty cents an hour after midnight, so that's ... " He looked up and to the left, calculating. "A dollar and seventy five cents. Let's round it up to two, shall we? Good babysitters are hard to find." He plucked out another dollar bill, and held both out to Veronica.

Automatically, she reached out and accepted them.

James noticed the book sitting on the floor in front of the couch and picked it up. He read the cover. "Lolita? I've heard about this. Pretty advanced stuff, huh?" He was smiling, but Veronica thought he might be looking at her differently.

What are you going to do? Tell my Mom? Oh my God, that might be exactly what he is planning! Is that where I am? Back in Middle Falls in, what, 1957? '58? That's not possible, is it?

James handed the book over to Veronica, which she accepted as numbly as she had the two dollars. "Did you have a jacket?"

Did I? I have no earthly idea.

James glanced at her blank face, then said, "Of course you did. It's still chilly in the evenings. Spring is here, but not after the sun goes down, right? I'll get it for you." He stepped to a coat closet by the front door and retrieved a tan jacket. "Here you go."

Veronica slipped it on, still in a daze.

James stepped to the staircase and said, "Anne? I'll be right back." He paused for a moment for an answer, but none was forthcoming. He shrugged, jingled his keys for a moment, then opened the door and walked toward the car. After a few steps outside, he noticed Veronica wasn't following. "Coming?"

"Umm. Of course. Yes." *What else am I going to do? I am a cork bobbing in an ocean I do not understand. I guess I'll move with the tide.*

Veronica walked out into a cool spring evening. There were still damp spots on the sidewalk from an earlier rain, and the air tasted cool, clean and fresh.

James opened the driver's side door of a large four door car. It looked new, in a way restored cars from the fifties never quite mustered. Veronica walked around the front of the car and opened the passenger door. She scooted in on the wide bench seat and automatically reached behind her for a shoulder belt, which was nowhere in evidence. She did find a lap belt though, and clicked it in place.

Guess no one is writing tickets for not wearing a seat belt, are they?

"Good girl," James said approvingly. "You can never be too safe."

Veronica glanced over and saw James hadn't bothered to buckle his.

As he pulled out of the driveway, she saw the name written on the mailbox: Weaver.

I swear, I don't know that name from Adam. I'm so confused. Veronica swiveled her head left, then right, then left again. *Everything looks vaguely familiar, but I can't put my finger on it.*

The AM radio began playing *Cherry Pink and Apple Blossom White* by Perez Prado. James Weaver hummed along as he drove down the quiet, tree-lined street. He looked at Veronica and said, "Oh, I'm sure you don't listen to this stuff, do you? Here." He punched a button beneath the radio, and Buddy Holly's *That'll be the Day* played. "That's what you kids listen to, right?"

Veronica had a hard time finding her voice, but nodded, and said, "Mmm-hmm."

Buddy Holly faded out and the announcer said, "This is Sudden Sammy Michaels, playing all the songs you want to hear on a Friday night on Middle Falls' own KMFR." A cheery jingle played—*KM-FR!*—then Sam Cooke's *You Send Me* started, and Veronica recognized where she was.

That's Whitfield Park. When I was a little girl, Ruthie and I rode our bikes over there and ... and what? What exactly did we do? I can't remember.

A few blocks later, James turned right onto Garfield Street.

No doubt about it. This is Middle Falls. But, it doesn't look anything like the town I left yesterday.

A moment later, James pulled smoothly to the curb and said, "This is right, isn't it?"

Veronica stared at her childhood home with her mouth ajar. *Who says you can't go home again?*

Chapter Two

Veronica managed a polite smile and unbuckled her seat belt, opened the heavy door, and stepped out onto the curb.

"Thanks again," James said.

Veronica shut the door and turned to stare at her house. In a neighborhood that mostly consisted of ramblers, the McAllister house was a proud two story. White, with brick accents at the front, and a two-car garage instead of a single.

"Nicest house on the block," as her father had loved to say.

She walked up the walk and took the single step to the tasteful red door, then suffered a moment of panic.

A key. I have no key. It's one o'clock in the morning, and I have no way to get inside. She thrust her hands deep into her jacket pockets, looking desperately for a key, but came up empty. She reached one tentative hand out and touched the door knob. Saying a small prayer, she turned it. The door swung open.

Didn't we even lock our doors at night? Or, did we only leave them unlocked when a daughter is out late babysitting?

She stepped inside and stopped cold. *That smell.* Pledge, mixed with the faint smell of her father's pipe that wouldn't be eradicated, no matter how her mother tried. The smell of home she had forgotten many years before. She closed her eyes and inhaled deeply. *No way to fake that. This is home.*

The small entry way opened to a sitting room on the right. It was filled with lovely but uncomfortable-looking furniture that rarely knew the touch of a human posterior. Straight ahead, a staircase led up to the second story. A short hallway went ahead to the kitchen on the right and the den on the left.

Bad feng-shui, to have the staircase leading directly to your door. Any Asian designer will tell you all your money escapes that way. For the first time since she opened her eyes here, Veronica allowed herself a small smile. *We weren't too worried about Asian esthetics in small-town America in the 1950s, I guess.*

She wandered back toward the kitchen. No matchy-matchy pastel colors, here. Just the solid, spic 'n span kitchen of her childhood. Signs of her mother were everywhere—the polished silver teapot that had once belonged to her great-grandmother, displayed in a place of honor in the china hutch. The perfectly alphabetized spices in the spice rack. *Not nearly as many spices as you would have had in another fifty years, but organized. Oh, yes. Organized.*

A tiny desk was built into one corner of the kitchen. The desk's surface was clear, except for one piece of paper—the beginning of a shopping list. Above the desk was a calendar with a picture of blooming daffodils. The page was turned to April, 1958.

Veronica stepped into the dining room. A five-light chandelier hung low over the oak table. Six chairs were tucked neatly into it. *One for Mom, Dad, Johnny, me, Barb, and one for company.* She ran her hand along the smooth, polished surface.

"Veronica?" A woman's voice.

"Eeep!" Veronica said, jumping guiltily, though she had been doing nothing at all.

"What are you doing?" The source of the voice, Doris McAllister, came around the corner of the kitchen. She was wearing a blue bathrobe over her night clothes. Her hair was in curlers. She raised her eyebrows at Veronica when she didn't get an immediate answer.

"M-m-mom?"

"Yes, of course. Who else? Mamie Eisenhower? What are you doing in here?" Doris glanced at the smudge Veronica had put on the table, sighed, and rubbed at it with the cuff of her robe until it disappeared.

Oh my God. I thought you were old, but you weren't. You were young.

"Umm. Nothing. I just got home from babysitting."

"I know that. I heard you come in like a herd of cattle." She looked pointedly at Veronica's saddle shoes. She sighed. "You know you're not supposed to wear your shoes in the house. They scuff my floors."

"That's right. I forgot. No shoes."

"Don't 'I forgot' me, missy. If I remind you once a day, I remind you ten times. Get up to bed, now. You've got work tomorrow."

"I do?"

Doris walked over to a calendar that hung over her desk. There were cramped, handwritten notes on every square. She pointed to a date Veronica couldn't see, and said, "V—Artie's, 12-8."

Artie's. My God, Artie's. The center of my world for so long.

Doris peered closer at the calendar. "You're only working two days during the week. Monday and Thursday. So, you should be able to get a lot done on your term paper. When you're ready to start typing it up, I'll bring the typewriter out of the office and set it up at the kitchen table for you."

Term paper. Veronica's stomach tightened. *Am I going to have to write a term paper?*

"Oh, your father is golfing tomorrow, so I'll have to take you and pick you up."

"I could drive myself, maybe?"

"In what, Miss Rockefeller? Did you earn enough babysitting tonight to buy a car?"

Veronica dropped her eyes. "No."

"Of course not. Come on, now, I'm tired, and I can never get to sleep until the last of you are home and in bed."

Veronica nodded, slipped her shoes off, and saw that Doris grimaced when she didn't untie them first. "Sorry," she mumbled. She dropped the shoes in the empty spot in a line of shoes by the front door and hurried up the stairs, moving lightly on her feet. *Mom is the same as she always was, but it is so good to feel young!*

She paused outside the door to her bedroom—*their* bedroom—as she shared it with Barbara. There were three bedrooms in the house. Johnny had always had one bedroom to himself. When he joined the army, Veronica thought she would get that room. Even though he had been serving in Europe since 1956, neither she nor Barb had taken it over. Instead, it had become her mother's sewing room, with a twin bed shoved in the corner for whenever Johnny returned home. She and Barb had lived for many years in a forced state of *détente*.

Veronica pushed the door open. Pale moonlight lay across the neat bedroom. Their beds were kitty-corner from each other. A single dresser stood against one wall with four drawers—two for each of them. A student's desk sat opposite the dresser with a small lamp and a few books stacked neatly in one corner.

She shut the door quietly behind her and walked with silent feet to Barb's bed. Barb was lost in sleep, her chest rising and falling rhythmically. A stray strand of her strawberry blonde hair fell carelessly across her face.

She looks like Haylie Mills. That's it, then. I'm really here. Seeing Mom and now Barb clinches it. I don't know how, or why, but I'm back in Middle Falls, in 1958. She looked at Barb and resisted the urge to sweep the hair from her face. *You really were a beautiful girl, weren't you, Barb? Or, are, I guess. I am so confused.*

Veronica moved to her bed, slipped off her skirt, sweater, and undid her bra. By some long-buried memory, she walked to the dresser and pulled open the bottom drawer. She pulled out a soft flannel nightshirt and dropped it over her head.

Don't think I can sleep, but I'll just lay down here and think for a bit. There's got to be a way to make some sense out of all this.

She slipped between the cool sheets, snuggled into her pillow, and was asleep almost instantly.

Chapter Three

"Veronica. *Veronica,*" Doris said, her voice sharpening with each syllable.

Veronica McAllister sat straight up in bed like a puppet master had jerked on her marionette's strings. "Huh? What?" Her hair fell in front of her face and her mouth felt fuzzy and tasted sour.

I was out. I never sleep that deeply. She looked up to see her mother standing at the end of her bed, holding her skirt and sweater and looking disapprovingly at her. *Other mothers say, "I'm not mad at you, I'm just disappointed." Somehow, Mom, you managed to convey both at all times. That's a talent.*

"Just look at your clothes, dropped in a heap like this. This is a good way to ruin your nice things."

"I folded them on the edge of the bed before I went to sleep last night, but I must have—"

"Is that what we are supposed to do with our clothes? No. If they need to be washed, they go in the hamper, if not, you hang them back up."

I've got to get over apologizing and making excuses for everything. That's part of how everything went wrong. I spent my whole life apologizing. She risked a glance at her mother's face, twisted in a sour knot. *Easy to say. Harder to do when faced with Doris.*

Veronica grabbed the covers and threw them back. She jumped out of bed, snatched the clothes away from her mother, and said, "I've got them, thanks," with a little more force than she had intended.

Doris took one step back, arching an eyebrow. One small dose of teenage attitude wasn't going to cow her. She was a veteran of these conflicts and remained the undefeated champion. She glanced at the small silver watch on her wrist. "You've slept until almost eleven."

"You're kidding. I never sleep that late."

Doris lowered her chin, an attitude that said, *Don't try to kid an old kidder.* "I have to pick up Barbara at noon, so I'm going to have to drop you off at Artie's a little early. Hurry and get ready, and I'll make you something to eat." She turned on her heel and was gone, leaving the room much less efficient.

Barbara's bed was empty and already neatly made. *She and Mom always were like two little peas in a pod. I never wanted to be in that pod, anyway. Now, what did I wear when I worked at Artie's?* She searched her brain but came up empty. Finally, she went to her closet and immediately recognized her uniform. It was a crisp button-down blouse with red accents at the collar and cuffs of the short sleeves. Her name was embroidered above her heart. When she pulled it off the hanger, she saw a straight gray skirt hanging beneath it.

Five minutes later, she was dressed, teeth brushed, and sitting at the breakfast nook in the kitchen. Doris had made her a bowl of oatmeal, which was essentially flavorless beyond a tiny sprinkling of cinnamon. *I've still got two dollars from last night tucked away upstairs. Maybe I can buy a burger and shake at Artie's this afternoon. Or, did they give us a free meal when I worked there. I've forgotten so much.*

The house was quiet, lifeless.

"Mom?" No answer.

"Mom?" Veronica asked, louder.

"What?" Doris said, opening the door from the garage.

"Where's Barb?"

"It's Saturday," she said, as though that answered all questions. She glanced at Veronica, saw there was no recognition on her face, and said, "Drill team rehearsal. Just like every Saturday. I swear, I don't know what I'll do with all my extra time when I don't have to chauffeur you two all over hither and yon."

Well, Mom, if you really want to know, you will spend that time searching for the bottom of a vodka bottle for a few years. Failing to find that, you will find God, sober up, and be the most insufferable type of Christian imaginable. That will get you through until a stroke will kill you in 1989. Barb will find you wrinkled and pruned at the bottom of your shower. But, that's all a few years ahead of you. There's still time to change the events of those Christmases future, as Dickens would say.

Veronica was swirling the oatmeal around more than eating it, when Doris whisked it away. She emptied it into the trash and washed it quickly, setting it to dry on the dish rack. She glanced at the clock. 11:30. "Come on, then, we're going to be late."

I feel like I might never catch up.

Two minutes later, they were in her mother's Mercury Monterey, rolling through downtown Middle Falls in complete silence. If the radio worked in Doris's cars, she would never know. She thought music while driving was an unnecessary distraction. Downtown looked much more familiar than the neighborhood she had been in with Mr. Weaver the night before. Things were different—where the Safeway was supposed to be was still a vacant lot. She didn't see any buildings taller than two stories, either, but the bones of the downtown area were similar. The marquee of the Pickwick Theater read that *No Time for Sergeants* was playing at 6:45 and 9:15. The Woolworth store, which had closed in the 1980s, was open and bustling on a Saturday morning.

Doris pulled into a corner of Artie's parking lot. It was the post-card-perfect image of a 1950s drive-in restaurant—a single story with a tall neon sign rising above the center of the building. The sign flashed "Artie's" in bright-yellow neon and "Burgers and Shakes" in red beneath that. There was a single walk up window where you could order if you were in a hurry. The inside seating area was small, but off

to the right was a long covered parking area with double-sided ordering stations. In the front and on the other side was a large parking lot
that could hold fifty cars. The whole place looked new and modern.
Futuristic, even, in the way the *Jetsons* would envision the future in a
few more years.

To the left of the parking lot was a tower with a square platform
on top. A hand painted sign read "KMFR, AM 1090, Broadcasting
LIVE every Friday and Saturday, 6:00 to 10:00 p.m., Easter through
Halloween."

*Oh, my gosh, I'd forgotten about the disc jockey up in the tower. We
thought we were pretty damn hip.* Veronica looked at a young couple
walk by holding hands, dressed like they had just stepped out of a
Sears and Roebuck catalog. *We* were *pretty damn hip. Or, are. I don't
know any more. We're going to need a new language if we're going to
time travel.*

Doris laid her hand on Veronica's shoulder, shaking her out of her
reverie. "Dad will be here to pick you up at eight. Don't keep him
waiting."

"Right. Okay. Thank you for the ride." Veronica got out of the car
and walked across the parking lot to the door that led into the inside
seating. A young boy behind the counter looked up at her, surprise
etched across his face. "Who are you, the queen of Sheba? You know
Zimm gets bent out of shape if we come in the front."

*Zimm. Zimm. Zimmerman. Perry Zimmerman. The manager,
that's right. He started at Artie's when he was sixteen and never left.
Ended up buying the place when Artie died. If this is 1958, then he's still
only about twenty-five now, though.*

"Oh, oops. Sorry." Veronica smiled and shrugged. *Of course that's
right. There's a back entrance for us.*

The boy flipped the countertop and beckoned her in. "Come on
through, just don't tell Zimm. He's already got me working all the

crap shifts, anyway. Thus, my presence here on the opening shift on a Saturday."

"Thanks," Veronica said, trying and failing to bring up his name in her mind. She scooted through the counter and thought to look at the name embroidered over his pocket. "Thanks, Dimitri."

The boy, who had his dark hair combed back in a reasonable imitation of an Elvis pompadour, looked at her like she had grown two heads. "Dimitri? Ronnie, are you feeling okay? Only my parents call me Dimitri."

Veronica stared at him, trying to force her reluctant brain to bring him better into focus. Cute enough, maybe trying a little too hard to be cool. Pretty blue eyes, though.

"Oh, right, of course," Veronica said, embarrassed. *I better get used to feeling this way. I'll probably step in it a dozen times today.*

"Hey, DJ," another boy called from the grill. "You gonna put these burgers together, or are you waiting on them to turn completely to charcoal?"

"Relax, I'm coming," DJ said. Turning back to Veronica, he said, "Grab a tray, I'll have an order ready for you in two shakes."

DJ. DJ. Why don't I remember you? There's so many things to try and remember, though. Veronica looked around in a slight panic, then saw a door ajar that led into a back room. She pushed through and saw a tiny alcove where coats were hung. She hung hers on a peg, straightened her skirt and blouse, and threw her shoulders back.

I can do this. I can do this. She let out a long, calming breath. *What choice do I have?*

Chapter Four

The first few hours of her shift were chaotic. She was a stranger in what had once been a familiar land. Her days as a carhop were six decades behind her, but as the day wore on, the routine returned to her as though it had been yesterday.

The Artie's menu was simple—hamburgers, cheeseburgers, shakes, and Coca Cola products. No fish or chicken sandwiches, no frozen yogurt, and no low-calorie options. *All we served was fat and calorie-stuffed meals, but look at the kids. There's got to be kids who could stand to lose a couple of pounds somewhere, but they're not around Artie's on a Saturday afternoon. Maybe it's because we didn't get to eat out too often, or maybe our parents just kept us moving.*

Veronica's job was to grab the baskets of burgers and fries hot off the grill and deliver them to the cars. The trays were designed to hook onto the windows. She also had to keep an eye on all the cars so she could pick up the trays when people were done eating. Between that and taking orders at the little eating area inside, the day flew by in a blur of buns and shakes.

She'd been at work for almost half her shift before she saw someone she recognized. She had a tray loaded down with two cheeseburger baskets and chocolate shakes to deliver to a wood-paneled Ford Country Squire parked in spot eighteen. When she got to the driver's side window, she almost dropped the food onto the parking lot.

"Danny!" she said, inadvertently quoting Olivia Newton John's line in Grease, a movie that wouldn't be made for another thirty years.

Danny Coleman had asked her to Prom her senior year, but she had already started going out with Christopher Belkins, whom she would eventually marry. She had regretfully told Danny she couldn't go with him, because she wasn't the kind of girl who went out with two boys at the same time. As life had unfolded, she had spent many years wondering how things might have been different if she had gone with him, instead of Christopher. Danny had gone on to own Coleman's Department Store right there in Middle Falls. He had always been kind to Veronica over the decades that followed. He wore his dark hair in a crew cut, which gave him a definite square-jawed, all-American look.

"Hi, Ronnie. How's tricks?" Danny said, casually.

Veronica glanced beyond Danny and saw Lisa Berry sitting beside him. *Wait a minute. If this is April 1958, Danny Coleman, you're supposed to be asking me to Prom. What are you doing here with Lisa?* She shook her head to clear the silliness of being unhappy over something that hadn't happened yet. "Oh, you know. Just work. Here's your order," she said, hooking the tray onto his window. "That'll be ninety cents." She leaned down slightly, "Hey, Lisa."

Lisa smiled and waggled her fingers at Veronica, but didn't say anything.

Danny laid a dollar on the tray. "Keep it, Ronnie. Thanks." He tipped her a wink and flashed a smile.

Hey, big spender! Veronica slipped the dollar inside her apron pocket, took a dime out of her change maker and dropped it neatly into her other pocket. "Later, gator." *That's what we said, right? Or am I just remembering old movies now?*

Back inside, Perry Zimmerman said, "Take your break, Ronnie. Evening rush'll be starting soon."

"Thanks, Perry." *Can't remember if we called him Zimm to his face or what.* Veronica reached into her tip pocket and pulled out a quarter and two nickels. She laid it on the counter and slid it toward Perry. "I'm starved. Can I get a burger and fries?"

Perry cocked his head at her like a dog that had heard a sharp whistle. "You know you get a meal, Ronnie. You've been acting passing strange today. Are you okay?"

Veronica did her best to laugh it off. "Oh, I know. That's your tip, right?"

"Yeah, right," he said, pushing the coins back at her. "Just let DJ know what you want, but hurry and chow down. I think we're going to be busy tonight."

Veronica went back to the large grill, where DJ and another boy she didn't know were standing . The grill had a full array of hamburger patties and buns. They stood like brothers in arms, spatulas in hand, staring at the sizzling food.

"Zimm said I could take my lunch. Can you make me a burger and fries, DJ?"

"Oh sure, now that you're hungry, *now* I'm DJ. When you come in through the front door like you're Cleopatra floating down the Nile, I'm Dimitri. " He shook his head in mock-disgust, and said, "Dimitri!" as if he couldn't believe the insult. Then he smiled and flipped the bottom of a bun up and deftly plucked it out of the air. He flipped a patty and caught it on the bun. He grabbed a dispenser which contained Artie's secret sauce and poured it on the burger. The secret sauce was just ketchup, mayonnaise, and a little vinegar, but it was delicious. He added two thin slices of pickles, no onions, and he flipped the top of the bun to land neat as you please.

He dropped the burger in the basket, scooped some fries in beside it and said, "Just like you like it, m'lady."

She had been serving Artie Burgers all day, but holding it in her hands, and realizing she hadn't had a good meal since 2018, made her stomach roll. She poured herself a small cup of Coke. There were no diet options, but she could have added a squirt of cherry, vanilla, or lemon flavoring if she had wanted.

The parking lot was busy, but the dining room was empty. No one wanted to be inside on a sunny day in early April. She sat at a table in the corner where she could look outside. She stared in the direction of the Country Squire wagon without realizing she was.

The hamburger was heavenly. *That DJ is going to make somebody a damn fine husband someday, if he can cook anything other than a burger.* She took a second bite before she had completely swallowed the first. *I don't remember anything tasting this good in fifty years. Is it because I'm young, or was food just better during this time? Maybe not so many preservatives?*

Some of her enjoyment drained away when she saw Lisa lean over and dab at the corner of Danny Coleman's mouth with a napkin, smiling and laughing. *They sure look cozy out there.* Veronica chewed slowly, swallowed, and put her burger back in the yellow plastic basket. *Well, I had my chance, and I made the wrong choice. Or, will I get another chance this time around? Is he going to dump Lisa in the next few days and ask me to Prom again? If he does, what will I say? And how odd is it that an eighty- year-old woman is acting like a flibbertigibbet about being asked to Prom?*

She sipped at her Coke. *Or, should I wait for Chris to come along again and ask me out and sweep me off my feet?* Her mind wandered back through the inventory of her marriage. Infatuation, first love, the wedding, the birth of her daughters. Happy memories. Then, she remembered Chris brutally kicking her out of their house so he could marry someone fifteen years younger. *But, if I don't marry Chris, Sarah and Nellie will never be born.*

That felt like a punch in the gut. She had come out on the short end of everything in her divorce with Chris, but the worst of it had been losing her connection with her daughters. Over the years, Chris and his new wife had become the new normal for Sarah and Nellie, and Veronica had been more of an afterthought. Something to work into their schedules as more of an obligation than a joy.

And I don't blame them. I was a miserable, wrung-out woman with no joy of any kind in my life. Why would they want to spend time with me? Now, I am on the horns of this dilemma. Marry a man who was unspeakably cruel, so I can have my daughters again, or wise up and ignore him, but face up to the fact my daughters will never be born. Tears formed in her eyes at the thought.

As she watched, Danny emerged from the car and walked inside with his tray.

Oops. Bad Ronnie. Bad carhop.

If Danny was put off, he didn't show it. He sat the tray on the counter, where Mary, another carhop, scooped it up with a "Thanks, hon."

Danny turned to go back outside, but stopped when he saw Veronica sitting alone in the corner.

Veronica froze. *He's not going to ask me right now, is he? He wouldn't do that with Lisa out in the car waiting for him, would he? He's not that kind of guy.*

If that was what Danny was considering, he showed no sign of it. He smiled at Veronica and nodded at her. "Thanks again, Ronnie."

Veronica did her best to answer, but her mouth was full of French fries and ketchup. She did her best to smile around the mouthful and gave him a little wave.

Danny climbed back into his car, which Veronica remembered now had been his parents', turned the ignition and backed out of the parking spot. As he did, Lisa scooted next to him and laid her head on his shoulder.

Veronica tossed the rest of her meal in the trash can and went back to work.

Chapter Five

As the sun set and the exterior lights around Artie's came on, everything came to life. A skinny young man with curly hair climbed the shaky ladder that led up to the top of the KMFR tower. He began fidgeting with equipment and making preparations for the remote broadcast. In the golden light of the setting sun, kids were cruising the strip in front of the restaurant. Artie's was at one end of the strip, with the bowling alley—Middle Falls Lanes—serving as the anchor on the other end.

Every Friday and Saturday night from spring through fall, kids drove endlessly up and down the strip. Even though the cars and pickups that cruised the loop were gas hogs, no one was going broke, because gas was twenty-five cents a gallon. Every car that had a working radio was tuned to KMFR, so the entire strip throbbed to the same rock 'n roll beat. The weekend cruise was as close as Middle Falls, Oregon, came to a cultural ritual.

The strip, which was plain old Main Street any other time, was the place to see and be seen. Cars full of girls flirted with pickups filled with boys stacked like cord wood in the back. Couples who were already paired up tended to sit comfortably in Artie's parking lot and observe the mating rituals of those still on the lookout. It was a scene played out all over America every weekend.

At the top of the KMFR remote tower, the loudspeaker crackled into life, broadcasting *The End of the World* by Skeeter Davis. When the record faded out, the skinny young man slipped a large set of headphones over his ears. He picked up his microphone and said, "Good evening, this is Scott Patrick, your musical host for another Saturday night on KMFR. I'll be here all night, playing the best music for cruising, necking, or crying, if you're all alone. If you're not on the strip right now, you're nowhere. I'll be right here, high above it all for the next four hours, spinnin' the hits and helping lonely hearts be just a little less lonely. If you've got a request, come on by the rockin' 1090 tower, drop it in the bucket, and I'll do my best to make your musical dreams come true. We'll kick things off tonight with *Come Go with Me,* by the Del-Vikings." The doo-wop a cappella intro of the song, played by the board operator back in the studio, began to play. It echoed from dozens of car speakers in the parking lot.

The last two hours of Veronica's shift flew by in a nostalgic haze, fueled by music, neon, and the fumes of a hundred internal combustion engines.

A few minutes before eight o'clock, Wallace McAllister pulled into the far corner of the parking lot. She recognized his sky blue Chevy Belair immediately. She thought he would sit and wait for her shift to end, but instead, he hopped out of the car and strode toward the front door. He looked oddly out of place, walking across the parking lot—an oasis of staid adulthood in the sea of teens.

Oh, Daddy, you're so young and handsome.

Wallace pushed through the door, smiled, and said, "Well?"

"Well?" Veronica said, lost as usual.

"Where's my ride-home-tax?" He took a dollar bill out and slipped it to Veronica.

When he saw that Veronica still did not understand, he said, "My burger and fries? You know your mother is always on me about my weight." He patted his middle, which had the slightest spare tire imaginable. "This is my only chance to get something that'll stick to my ribs."

Veronica smiled, nodded, and said, "Oh! Oh, of course! Sit down, I'll be right back with it." She ran to the back and asked DJ for a burger basket in a hurry, then turned to Perry Zimmerman and handed him the dollar. "For my dad's food."

Perry nodded. "Just put it in the register like always, Ronnie. You know I trust you."

Veronica did, retrieved the change and turned around to find DJ holding out the order. "One Daddy burger, made to order."

Veronica noticed that DJ held her eyes a moment longer than she would have expected. *Wait. Is this boy I don't even remember kind of flirting with me? Was I too caught up in myself to notice him?*

"Thanks, DJ."

"No problemo," DJ said, turning toward the door into the back. "My last burger for the day, thank God. I'll never get all this grease out of my pores."

Veronica dropped the change on the tray and hurried the food out to her dad, who had taken a seat at the only empty table. "Here you go, Daddy."

"Thanks, kitten." He didn't hesitate, but grabbed the burger and took a man-sized bite, then sighed. "Go on, finish up. I'll be ready to go when you are."

Really? Can you eat a hamburger and fries in the time it takes me to go get my purse and jacket? I doubt it.

Two minutes later, after collecting her things and saying good-night, she popped back into the dining room. She was surprised to find her father wiping his mouth with a napkin and tossing it into an empty basket.

"Daddy! You shouldn't eat so fast."

Wallace looked abashed, and said, "I know, but if we dawdle, I'll get the third degree from your mother when I get home." He reached in his jacket pocket and pulled out a roll of Spearmint Certs. He slipped one out, popped it in his mouth and offered one to Veronica. "What she doesn't know..."

"...won't get you in trouble," Veronica finished for him.

Wallace chuckled. "Right you are."

Wouldn't you have been happier if you could have found a way to just be yourself and damn the consequences, though? I guess not, since you let her run your life until the day you died. That thought, coupled with her father standing beside her, large as life, gave her a lump in her throat. She slipped her arm through his as they headed out the door, and laid her head against his shoulder. "I love you, Daddy."

"You know I love you too, Ronnie," he said, fishing his keys out of his pocket and handing them to her. "Here, you can drive home."

A few minutes later, Wallace and Veronica walked in the front door. They both remembered to slip their shoes off at the door, though Veronica noticed her dad didn't untie his shoes first, either. *Maybe I got more than just my DNA from you, Dad. We're both pretty relaxed, which makes us too easy to run over. No good.*

Doris sat in a small easy chair in the den, bathed in a pool of light from a floor lamp beside her. She still wore the dress she'd had on that morning—no relaxing sweats for moms in the fifties—and was working on a knitting project. Barb was stretched out on her back on the floor at Doris's feet, holding up a copy of *Teen* magazine with Elvis in an army uniform on the cover. The headline read, "Will the army change Elvis?" There was a television against one wall, but it wasn't turned on.

Wallace went into the kitchen and poured a glass of water. *Probably a good idea to wash down all that fat and sodium, Dad.*

Doris looked up from her knitting. "How was work?"

"Oh, fine. Just another day in the salt mines," Veronica joked.

Doris didn't crack a smile. "You'll get your paycheck next weekend. Just sign it and give it to me, and I'll deposit it in your college fund on Monday."

No wonder I don't have a car! I'll never get one if I have to keep putting every penny I own into the bank. Her hand brushed against her purse, still heavy with the mound of change she had gotten as tips that day. *Well, not every penny, I guess. It's going to take a mountain of nickels and dimes to get an old beater, even. Still, I hate to put all my money into a savings account for a college I'm not ever going to attend. Unless. Unless I decide to run like hell when I see Christopher Belkins again, which seems like the smart thing to do.*

Images of Nellie and Sarah danced across her mind, though, a reminder of the price she would pay for choosing her own freedom.

"I'm tired, Mom. I'm going upstairs."

"Don't forget to set your alarm. We have church in the morning."

Veronica's shoulders sagged. She hadn't been to church in decades. Dying and waking up as a young girl again didn't reinforce her belief in the idea of heaven and hell.

"No attitude, young lady. Be ready to go at 8:30."

I know when I'm beat. Veronica nodded, trudged up the stairs and sat down on her bed. *I wasn't lying. I really am tired, young body or not.* Beside her twin bed was a small table with a lamp and a bright red wind-up alarm clock. She wound it, wondered how long she needed to get church-ready, and set the alarm for 7:15.

Chapter Six

Sunday passed by quickly. Church was every bit as boring as she remembered it. In 1958, the McAllisters attended a non-denominational community church on the edge of their own neighborhood. The service may not have been exciting, but it was punctual, and the whole family was home relaxing long before lunch.

Barbara, who hadn't spoken a word to Veronica since she had been back, took off on her bicycle to her friend Audrey's house for the day. Of course, to Barbara, Veronica had been there all along.

Wallace McAllister turned on the television and turned it to CBS. He settled into his chair, pulled out his pipe, and sighed contentedly as the black and white broadcast of the final round of the Masters appeared. "I think Arnie Palmer's gonna win this darn thing," he said, to no one in particular.

"No one cares, dear," Doris said from the kitchen. She pulled a pork roast out of the refrigerator and turned the oven on to preheat. She looked at Veronica. "What do you have planned for the day? I've got a long list of things to do if you're at loose ends."

Hey, I'm only young twice. Well, at least twice. Think of something fast.

"I thought I'd hang out with Ruthie. It would be nice to see her."
Hmm. That sounds like an old lady instead of a teenager.

"Ruthie?" Doris's eyebrows shot up. "You haven't seen her in years. I thought you two had a falling out."

"Did we?" *I would think I would remember some of this stuff. Funny, the way memory works. It's like it plays our greatest hits over and over, but so much of our day to day stuff just filters away.* "Well, it's time for us to make up, then. Ruthie's been my friend since kindergarten."

Doris waved a dismissive hand at Veronica. "Fine, fine." She glanced at the clock over the sink. "Be home by 3:00, though. I'll have dinner on right after that. Change out of your good clothes first."

"Thanks, Mom," Veronica yelled over her shoulder as she scampered up the stairs and into her room. She ran to her closet and flipped through the clothes hanging there. *Skirt, skirt, dress, sweater, sweater.* She pulled one hanger out with a small piece of fabric hanging on it. *What in the world?* She had to stifle a giggle. *Oh, my God. It's a dickie. A dickie! Who in the world thought this was a good idea?*

At the back of the closet, she found a single pair of jeans. She held them up against her. *Can't believe I can fit in something this tiny again, but I'll bet I can.* She dropped her skirt to the floor and shimmied into the blue jeans. They were cuffed at the ankle and looked nothing like the ripped and bedazzled jeans of the twenty-first century. *These will do nicely. As long as Mom doesn't see me, that is. I'll bet she wouldn't be crazy about her oldest daughter running around Middle Falls on the Sabbath in blue jeans.* She found a warm sweater that looked comfy and put it on. She looked appraisingly in the mirror that hung on the back of the door.

Not bad at all.

Veronica slid silently down the stairs, slipped her shoes on, and went out the front door as quietly as she could. Once on the sidewalk, she looked left and right. *I don't have any idea where Ruthie's house even is. I wasn't about to be cooped up in the house polishing the silver or scrubbing the floor on my hands and knees, though.*

She turned right and walked quickly until she got a block away from her house, then slowed to a stroll. She turned her face skyward.

Not quite as warm as it was yesterday, but it's not raining, I'm young, apparently, and the whole world is my oyster. Now, I've just got to figure out what I want. College, and a career? Marry Christopher again, have the girls and split right after? Really throw myself into the marriage and see if we can make it work this time? I'm sure I contributed to our divorce in my own way. Will he love me at all, though, if he sees I'm strong? Was he looking for a partner, or a doormat to wipe his feet on?

These were questions with no easy answers. She let them roll around her mind, looking at each option from a different angle. She did not find a perfect solution. She paid no attention to where her feet were carrying her. She went straight or turned left or right apparently at random.

After a half hour's walk, though, she came out of her daze and looked at a familiar house right in front of her. *Ruthie's. I guess I did know where she lived, at least on some level. Maybe I just need to get out of my own way sometimes and let my subconscious help me find my way.*

The house where Ruthie Miller lived wasn't much. Her father had passed away when they were in the fifth grade. Her mom hadn't worked outside the house before he died, but she had to find a job as soon as she took off her black mourning dress. Mr. Miller hadn't left them anything in the way of life insurance or savings, so they always struggled to keep their noses above water. Poverty, mixed with losing her father, had left Ruthie bereft.

I think she wasn't much fun for a few years after that, and instead of being the friend she needed, I let her drift away. Veronica squared her shoulders and marched up to the small porch. She knocked three times and stood waiting to see if anyone was home.

The door opened and a small, matronly woman said, "Yes?" A pause, then, peering over the top of her glasses, "Ronnie? I haven't seen you in forever. Is everything okay?"

Veronica smiled. *You always were a kind lady.* "Yes, everything's fine. I just woke up missing Ruthie this morning and wanted to see what she was doing."

"How nice. I'm sure she'll be thrilled to see you. Come on in, I'll get her."

Veronica stepped inside. There was no entry way in this house, just a small living room and a kitchen with a tiny two-person eating area on the right. There was no television in sight, but a black and white picture of Mr. and Mrs. Miller in their younger days sat on top of a silent radio. A pot boiled on the stove in the kitchen.

After a few minutes, Veronica realized it was taking quite some time for Mrs. Miller to retrieve Ruthie. *Maybe she's not all that thrilled to see me after all.*

Finally, Mrs. Miller reemerged with an apologetic smile. "Sorry. She was napping, and I needed to wake her up. She'll be right out."

You're not a good liar, Mrs. Miller. She didn't want to come out and you had to threaten her to get her to agree. What kind of a heel was I to Ruthie? And why? She was never anything but sweet.

"Can I get you some tea, dear?"

"Oh, no. I can't stay. I was out for a walk and realized my feet carried me here, so I thought I'd better stop in and say hello."

"Hello, Veronica."

Okay. Not Ronnie. Veronica.

"Hey, Ruthie. How are you? It feels like I haven't talked to you in forever."

"That would be because you haven't. What do you want, Veronica?"

Oof. So, it's like that.

Veronica glanced at Mrs. Miller. It was impossible to be out of earshot in the small space. Still, she was doing her best to be preoccupied with something in the kitchen and pointedly ignoring them.

"Can we go in your bedroom for a minute. I just want to catch up with you."

Ruthie hesitated. Then hesitated some more. Finally, without looking up, Mrs. Miller said, quietly, "Go on."

Ruthie shrugged and turned back toward the room she had come from. When they walked into the room it was obvious this wasn't Ruthie's room. It was Ruthie *and* her mom's room. The house only had one bedroom. Nonetheless, it still looked like a teenager's room. There were pictures of Ricky Nelson and Elvis thumbtacked to the wall, and her bedspread was fluffy and pink. Stuck into the other corner was the second bed.

Ruthie sat on her own bed, crossed her arms, and said, "What do you want?"

Veronica sat on the other bed and her knees were almost touching Ruthie's. *Slightly claustrophobic in here. I'll never complain about sharing with Barb again. What if I had to share with Mom? Perish the thought.*

Veronica looked at Ruthie. When they were young, she had been a pigtailed little tomboy, but now she was a little too skinny and looked lost in the shapeless, oversize sweater she wore. Her hair hung lankly around her face, which was framed by brown, cats-eye glasses.

"I don't want or need anything. I promise. I haven't been a good friend, especially when you needed one. I'm sorry. You were never anything but my best friend, and I know I've let that slip away."

"Slip away? Sure. Whatever you need to tell yourself. You turned your back on me. You acted like you didn't know me in the hallway. I don't know what I ever did to you." Ruthie's eyes filled with tears.

"I wish I could give you a good reason, but I can't." *I mean, I really can't. I honestly don't remember. Why would I have done that?* "I don't expect you to just say 'halleluiah' and suddenly, we're best friends. I know life's not like that. I do miss you, though. Hey, I've got my tips from working at Artie's last night," she said, patting her small purse.

"Wanna walk down to the bowling alley and get a Coke? My treat. I figure I owe you about a thousand Cokes for acting the way I have."

Ruthie didn't respond immediately. She squinted one eye closed and tilted her head slightly, trying to figure what had caused this sudden change. She shrugged and said, "I'll have to ask my Mom."

"Great!"

Two minutes later, they were outside, walking toward the bowling alley. At one point, Veronica went straight when Ruthie turned left. Ruthie stopped and looked over her shoulder. "Don't tell me you've forgotten where the bowling alley is?"

Veronica laughed and ran back to Ruthie. She slipped her arm through Ruthie's and laid her head on her shoulder. "I really am sorry, Ruthie," she whispered.

The next few hours passed easily. It wasn't that Ruthie and Ronnie were immediately best friends again. But, as time wore on, some of the well-worn grooves of their friendship were found once again. They avoided speaking of the previous years, which Ruthie found distasteful and which Veronica didn't remember. Eventually they found some common ground to stand on. Mostly Elvis, who Ruthie loved, and who Veronica had listened to right up to the end of her life.

After they had drained two Cherry Cokes each, Veronica looked up and noticed the clock on the wall.

"Oh, heck. Look at the time! Mom told me I had to be home by 3:00. Am I going to be late?"

"If you walk home with me first, yes. But not if you walk straight home from here."

Veronica looked at Ruthie, calculating. *Two bad choices. I don't want to strand Ruthie here, but I don't want Mom getting on me when I get home, either.*

Ruthie saw her indecision and said, "Don't worry about it. It's no problem."

Veronica nodded. "Okay." She hugged Ruthie. "Thanks." She hustled toward the door, then turned and looked back at her.

Ruthie stood, looking at her, a little dazed at the sudden turn her Sunday had taken.

Chapter Seven

Veronica managed to slip unnoticed through the front door. *Got to change before Mom catches me wearing pants outdoors.* The smell of her mother's pork roast cooking was enticing. *Mom always was a good cook. Now's the time to take advantage of my young metabolism and eat whatever I want.* She ran up the stairs. Once she got far enough up that she knew her mom couldn't see her, she yelled, "I'm home, Mom! I'll be right down!"

"No need to yell," Doris said. "I'm right here." Her mother was standing at the linen closet at the top of the stairs, putting away freshly-folded sheets.

"Eeep!" Veronica said, attempting to jump right out of her skin. *Mental note. If there's a place Mom can catch me doing something I'm not supposed to be doing, she's going to be standing in that place.*

Doris looked at Veronica appraisingly. Flushed cheeks, windblown hair, and of course, her jeans. "Is it appropriate to be sneaking out of the house dressed like that? And, on the Sabbath?"

Mom, wait until you see how girls are going to dress in another few years. Micro-mini skirts. Bikinis. Free love. You're not going to like it one bit. Eventually, I'm going to have to start standing up to you, or you're just going to keep running over me.

"Mom, I'm eighteen years old. I'm graduating high school in a couple of months. There's nothing wrong with wearing a pair of jeans to go for a walk."

Doris quietly contemplated that. "I won't have any back talk from you. While you are living in my house, you will conduct yourself like a lady, and that does not include cavorting around town in jeans." She raised her eyebrows, tilted her head forward a bit. "Are we clear on this?"

Maybe I'll pick something more important to take a stand on. "Yes, ma'am. Sorry."

Another child-rearing crisis averted, Doris headed downstairs. "Change and then come downstairs to dinner."

Veronica did just that.

Dinner at the McAllister house was a quiet affair. Doris and Barbara sat next to each other and talked about a project Barbara was doing for girl scouts. Their voices didn't quite carry to the other end of the table, where Veronica and Wallace sat. Wallace never said a word during the entire meal. He chewed his food and acted like the king of the castle that Doris allowed him to pretend to be.

Veronica looked at her mother and Barbara, heads nearly touching.

What if I'd made more of an effort? Could I have been part of that little coffee klatch?

Doris said something and Barbara giggled.

I don't think so. Oil and water. She glanced at her father. *And what about you, Dad? Was this a good life for you? Or, did you just put your shoulder to the wheel and push it ahead, one day at a time, until it ended with a heart attack in 1985?* She jerked her head up at a sudden thought. *Wait. When you died, Dad, did this same thing happen to you? Are you somehow a young man back in Salem, reliving your life? Or is there something special about me? If you did go back, would you marry Mom again to make sure that Johnny, Barb and I are born? Or would you look for a more suitable match? Too many questions on a full stomach.*

Veronica dabbed at the corners of her mouth with her napkin, and said, "May I be excused, please? I'll do the dishes as soon as everyone's done."

That grabbed Doris's attention. "Of course. Make sure you're all ready for school tomorrow, first. Why don't you curl your hair tonight? You always look so pretty like that."

School. High school. A sudden knot appeared in Veronica's stomach. *And curlers. Curlers that will poke me and keep me awake.* She nodded. "Okay, Mom. I'll go get ready now, then come back down and do the dishes."

Doris nodded, satisfied at this toeing of her line. She would accept nothing less.

Upstairs, Veronica went through her closet and picked out a skirt and sweater to wear to school the next day. She put them together on the same hanger and hung it on the door knob to her closet.

School. The last time I was in this school was sixty years ago. I'm going to be lost. How do I get through it? Fake amnesia like a soap opera star? Don't think that will work. Ask Ruthie? How do I explain that, exactly? Her eye fell on a small stack of books and notebooks on her bedside table. She pulled a book off the top of the stack. *Men and Nations: A World History.*

Hey, how about Women and Nations? No? Welcome to the fifties. She sat the book on her bed and picked up a spiral notebook. On the first page, in her own young handwriting, was written, "First Semester 1957-1958." *I always was an organized student. I guess I got something from Mom.* There was a list of all her classes, including the teacher and the room the class was held.

She turned to the second page. Across the top of the page was, "Second Semester 1957-1958." Again, below that was all her classes, teachers, and which room each class was in. *Organization to the rescue! Thank you, younger Veronica for making this easier for me.*

She took a deep breath, held it, and released it. *I guess I'm about as ready as I'm ever going to be.* She went back downstairs to do the dishes, which her mother or Barbara had helpfully stacked next to the sink. Her mother had returned to her knitting, and her father was working on the crossword puzzle from the Sunday paper. Barbara was upstairs taking a bath.

All in all, a pretty good weekend. Artie's is as wonderful as it ever was, I got to see Ruthie again. Home might not be the most loving place, but there are certainly worse places I could be. It's all felt a little like a vacation to Fifties Land, though. The glory of the whole thing might wear off a little when those curlers poke me in the scalp all night.

Chapter Eight

Veronica sat down to a bowl of Cheerios and toast. Her hair was curled and she had on a skirt so tight at her calves she had to adjust her steps as she walked down the stairs. *This time has some things going for it, but there are drawbacks, too. I miss my pantsuits. Or, better, my comfy sweats.*

Doris looked her over and must have decided she passed muster, because she nodded once. "Don't forget—you're on at Artie's from four to eight tonight. I have bridge this afternoon, so I won't be there to give you a ride. You'll need to get on Mr. Harrison's bus #12. I'll call the bus garage and let him know he can drop you off at Artie's." She nodded again, another item from her infinite to-do list checked off.

Small-town America—where you not only know your child's bus driver, you know all the bus drivers.

"Okay, Mom. No problem."

"Dad will be there to pick you up at eight." She turned away, then paused, and turned back around. "Oh, and don't give him a hamburger tonight. He really does need to watch his weight."

Veronica opened her mouth to deny any knowledge of forbidden hamburgers, but thought better of it. "Okay, Mom."

"He thinks popping a Certs gets rid of a hamburger with onions on it, but I know better."

It would be nice to have a mother who isn't half Sherlock Holmes, but, there we are.

Barb came bounding down the stairs, stood in front of her mother and smiled. Or, rather, she bared her teeth at Doris, who examined her closely. She reached up and swept one stray curl into place, then gave her an approving nod.

Veronica picked her books and the small grocery bag with her Artie's uniform up off the corner of the kitchen table. She hustled past her mother at double time, worried she might have a stray Cheerio stuck on one of her teeth.

Outside, she and Barbara walked half a block to where a small group of neighborhood kids were gathering. Boys and girls, ranging from first graders on up to high schoolers, were waiting. Two young boys had scratched out a circle and were shooting marbles for "keepsies" while they waited. Everyone else seemed content to stand still and pretend like they were still home, tucked into their beds.

Barbara didn't seem to have anybody special to stand with at the bus stop, and there weren't many other high schoolers, either, so they stood together. Veronica looked at her sister. "You look cute, today."

"Thanks," Barbara said, nodding in agreement.

Good to have self-confidence, and Barb always had that.

The bright-yellow bus came around a corner and stopped in front of them with a squeal of brakes and the strong smell of diesel. Barbara and Veronica were the last ones on, but there were plenty of seats. Barbara stopped midway back and sat down next to a young dark-haired girl. They immediately fell into deep conversation.

Veronica looked ahead, hopeful she might spot someone she remembered, but it didn't happen. She moved all the way to the second to the last seat and sat down.

Going to be a long day, I think. But, it's April, so I'll be done with school in another couple of months. I can make it through that.

No one spoke to her the entire trip to school, and Veronica was content to be ignored. She got off the bus and looked around for Ruthie, but she was nowhere in sight. *First problem. How do I get in my locker? I don't remember where my locker was, let alone what the combination was. I guess there's only one thing to do—ask.*

Middle Falls High School wasn't huge, but it did act as the central school for several other smaller communities in the area. That meant there were a little more than five hundred students enrolled. It was a stone structure that was obviously well built, because it was still being used as the local high school in 2018. To Veronica's eye, everything looked fresher—the lawn greener, the stone structure cleaner—as she walked up to it.

She entered the hustle and bustle of the high school and moved with the crowd along the main hallway. It all seemed familiar, but dimly so. Eventually, she saw an opening in the middle of the school. There was an office with an open window facing out to the crowded hallway. There were two boys lined up there, and Veronica got in line behind them.

Both boys had notes excusing previous absences that they turned in. They were quickly dealt with. Veronica found herself face to face with a large woman with hair like steel wool. She wore a blue dress with small golden stars on it, and had a pair of half-glasses perched on the end of her nose.

"Good morning, Veronica. What do you need?"

"Oh! Um, good morning." Veronica didn't even attempt to remember this woman's name. *I don't know why I thought I'd be completely anonymous here. Of course people are going to recognize me. Just because I don't remember them doesn't mean they're not going to have seen some other version of me here yesterday.*

The woman was impatiently tapping her pencil on the counter.

"I'm having a little trouble getting my locker open, and I'm afraid I'm going to be late to first period. Is there anyone who can come see if it's jammed?"

The woman nodded, turned and opened a file drawer. She pulled out a file, then looked through it for the right piece of paper. She stepped to an intercom system and pushed a button. "George? Are you there?"

"Yah," a tinny voice answered back.

"Can you meet Veronica McAllister at locker 426? She's having a hard time getting it open."

"Damned things are always getting stuck," the tinny voice said.

"Language, George, if you please."

"Sorry, Mrs. Harris, sorry. What's the combination?"

"22-8-31"

"Tell her I'll meet her there in five minutes."

Mrs. Harris turned back to Veronica. "Go on, then. George will be right there."

Veronica turned away, repeating *426, 22-8-31* over and over until she could get to a place where she could write the numbers down.

Well, that was easier than I thought. I feel a little bad about making George come all the way over for nothing. Nothing to be done about that, though. Now, to find locker 426.

Veronica rejoined the crowd of students moving through the hallway. She moved to the side, where she could see the locker numbers until she found the 400s. Eventually, she came to locker 426. She looked at the locker. *Nope. Not familiar at all. Just like a thousand other lockers I walked by.*

"Morning," a gruff voice said, making her jump. "If you'll scoot a bit, I'll see what I can do." He held his left hand up and squinted at it, trying to make out the numbers he had written on there, but they seemed to have gotten smeared. "Damn it," he swore under his breath.

"It's uh, 22-8-31," Veronica offered.

"Oh, right. It's your locker. I should have figured." He turned and spun the knob, which moved easily, stopped at the 22, went past the 8 once, then stopped, moved it to the right to 31. The locker popped open, easy as you please. George let out a grunt of surprise.

"It's always like that, isn't it?" Veronica said. "Take your car into the mechanic, and it won't make that funny noise it's been making?"

George didn't say anything, but as he turned and walked away, Veronica thought she heard him mumble something about "damned kids today."

The inside of her locker was neat and organized. The top shelf held a few pencils, a pink eraser, and a metal compass with the stub of a pencil in it. *Oh, no.* She picked up the compass like it was a foreign object. *Please, please tell me this was for a class last semester. If I have to use this today, I'm going to flunk out for sure.*

The bottom half of the locker held a small bag that had a change of clothes for PE—a modest jumper—a few text books, and a small hairbrush. *Boring, boring. I have to face it, I was a boring, good girl.*

Veronica slipped the textbooks she had brought from home to the bottom of the locker. She grabbed *Men and Nations: A World History* because that was her first class.

Room 246, so, upstairs somewhere.

The first bell sounded, giving her five minutes to find her room. The crowd in the hall was thinning, and she found her room with more than a minute to spare. She slipped into a seat in the back, hoping there were no assigned seats. Just before the second bell rang, a young man with a crew cut and an ill-fitting suit hurried in. He sat a briefcase down on the teacher's desk at the front.

Oh, my God, he doesn't look old enough to have graduated from high school, let alone be teaching at one. She recognized him with a shock. *That's Mr. Burns! I remember when the school honored him with a retirement dinner. When? Sometime in the mid-eighties. And here he is, a young teacher, just starting his career.*

Mr. Burns smiled at the class. "Good morning. Please turn to page 148 in your textbook. Today, we're going to discuss the tensions in the Middle East and look at some of its historical roots."

Veronica perked up. *Did we really talk about interesting things like this in class? I remember being bored most of the time, and only doing the homework to get the grades to keep Mom off my back. School is so often wasted on the young, including me, apparently.*

Veronica leaned forward on her desk, put her chin in her hands and listened to Mr. Burns' lecture. She got so caught up, she even raised her hand and asked a salient question. She was rewarded with a smile and a "Good question, Veronica."

The hour went by quickly, as did the rest of her first day back to school. She survived, thanks mostly to her own notes from long ago that told her where she needed to be.

Veronica did her best to catch up with Ruthie in the halls, but she didn't quite have the hang of navigating the crowds between classes. She did manage to sit with her at lunch, although she noticed another table of girls looking at her. *Did I usually eat lunch with them? Well, if they want, they can come over here and join us.*

Chapter Nine

V eronica emerged from Middle Falls High, into an overcast afternoon, feeling much more confident than when she had arrived in the morning.

And now, I get to go to Artie's. I guess it's a little weird to look forward to going to work, but Artie's is so cool.

Veronica walked along the buses lined up, looking for Bus 12. Eventually she found it and stepped up. Mr. Harrison flashed a quick smile and waved her on. "Heard from your mother already."

Of course you did. Veronica sat at the back of the bus again, more comfortable this time, because she didn't normally ride this bus, and so wouldn't be expected to know anyone.

Unless she was.

A dark-haired girl with a turned up nose acted like she was going to walk right by Veronica, then faked her out and slid in beside her. She bumped her with her shoulder. "Hey, stranger."

Oh shit. I know you. I know you. But, what's your name? Wait! Alice. Alice ... Alice ... Gregory! Alice Gregory.

"Hey, Alice, how are you?"

"We're feeling formal today, aren't we? She lowered her voice, drew her chin in and mimicked Veronica, "Hello, Alice, how are you?" Then, she laughed, though, and everything seemed fine. "What are you doing on my bus? Gotta work today?"

Veronica grinned and nodded, glad to be back on steady ground.

"You are so lucky to have gotten on there. So many girls applied last year. Me too."

"I think my Dad put in a good word for me. He knows Artie from his job." *Huh. That's right. I haven't thought about that for years, but he did. Daddy helped me get on at Artie's. He may not rule the roost at home, but he always got things done outside the house. I need to remember to thank him, because I probably didn't. I was so self-absorbed.*

"So, I saw you eating lunch with Ruthie Miller today. Are you abandoning us?"

"No, of course not. But, Ruthie was my best friend forever. It feels like I've lost touch with her."

"Sure," Alice said. "I understand."

The way you said it makes me think you don't understand, but I don't care.

"Oops. Gotta get out here," Veronica said, standing up and scooting by her as the bus pulled to a stop right in front of Artie's. "Bye, Alice." She walked to the front of the bus without looking back. She said "Thank you, Mr. Harris," as she hopped down the stairs.

She remembered to use the employee entrance in the back, stepped into the small bathroom in the back room and changed into her uniform. She dropped her school clothes into the bag and hung it on a hook. At 3:30, she walked into the grill area, smiled and said, "Veronica McAllister, reporting for duty."

"Well, aren't you chipper?" Perry Zimmerman said. He glanced up at the red Coca Cola clock in the dining room. "You don't start for half an hour. Ask DJ to make you something if you want." He turned back to writing something in an order book.

Hasn't been that long since lunch. But then, who am I to turn down an Artie's burger? I've still got my youthful metabolism working in my favor. Veronica glanced back at the grill area. Unlike Saturday, DJ was the only one working the grill, and it wasn't jam-packed with patties and buns yet. Only a few were sizzling away.

"Hiya, DJ."

"Artie's answer to Annette Funicello puts in an appearance!"

"I'll take that as a compliment."

"As it was intended," DJ said, flipping three patties over smoothly. "What can I do to bolster your strength for another strenuous Artie's shift?"

"Mmmm. How about the usual?"

"One Ronnie burger and fries, coming up." DJ glanced at her, and the familiarity of the conversation, combined with the intensity of his glance, made her tingle, just a little.

What's wrong with me, suddenly crushing on every cute teenage boy I see. I'm almost eighty years old and feel like a schoolgirl. Hormones are a powerful thing. No wonder we don't handle them well when we're young.

Veronica stood and chatted with DJ while he made her burger basket, then took it out to the dining room, which was empty once again. High school kids, loosed momentarily from the shackles of their education, were trickling into the parking lot. Veronica looked at each of them, but didn't recognize very many. She had been surprised to find she remembered more of her teachers than she did kids at school.

A few minutes before 4:00, Veronica stood up, dropped the grease-stained butcher paper from the basket into the trash and went to work. *Mom said I only work two days this week after school. Too bad. I'd like to come every day.*

Much like drive-ins in small towns all around America, Artie's was a social center in Middle Falls. It didn't matter the day of the week, or the season—at dinner time, it got busy. By 5:30, DJ was as busy as one person could be on the grill, the green and silver double milkshake machines were humming, and Veronica was hustling to keep up.

Man, I love this. It feels like I could do this forever, but I don't know if I'll feel that way when I'm forty again, still slinging burgers and fries.

As it started to get dark, Danny Coleman's Ford Country Squire pulled up to one of the ordering speakers. Veronica was delivering another order on the other side of the parking lot, but saw him pull in. She tilted her head a bit to see inside the car and noticed that today, Danny was alone. *Which of course, doesn't mean a thing.*

Unless it did.

Veronica went on working, delivering food with a smile, chatting with everyone she came into contact with. It was much easier for her to be relaxed and easygoing with people she didn't know. Her only real concern was that she would treat someone she was supposed to know like she didn't. *I'll burn that bridge when I get to it.*

Eventually, she picked up the tray that went to Danny. She took it out to him and placed it on the window. "Are you so rich that you can come eat at Artie's every night?"

"Well, no," he admitted. "It is where the prettiest carhops work, though." When he smiled, she noticed how white his teeth were.

Veronica smiled, and asked, "Where's Lisa?"

Danny stuttered a little bit, but Veronica's attention was pulled away by the car that pulled in right beside Danny. A silvery-blue 1956 Ford Thunderbird convertible. She didn't even need to look inside to know who was behind the wheel. Christopher Belkins, her ex-husband, who she had not met in this life yet. Her smile faltered, then faded altogether.

"Hey, Ronnie. You okay?" Danny asked.

"Yes, I'm fine. Sorry. I've got to go back in and pick up some more orders."

"Can you come back in a minute, when things slow down a little? I want to ask you something, but I can wait."

"Sure," Veronica said, not even thinking.

She turned and walked back inside. "Hey, Zimm? Can you cover for me? Nature calls."

"Sure, go ahead. I'll keep an eye on things. Be sure to wash your hands!"

Veronica nodded and headed for the door that led to the small restroom. She pushed the slide lock into place and sat down on the toilet. Her hands were trembling, her stomach in knots. She tried to take deep breaths, but had a hard time calming down.

I thought I had time to figure things out, to decide what was next, and now here he is. It's not like he's going to ask me to marry him today, but it didn't take long. We met in April and got married in August that same year. I moved straight from Mom and Dad's house into his. What am I going to do? Just seeing him makes me sick. But.

Veronica felt tears forming and reached for a few squares of toilet paper to blot at her eyes.

But, if I ignore him, or rebuff him, Sarah and Nellie will never be born. What right do I have to do that to them?

She stood and looked at herself in the mirror, dabbing at the corners of her eyes again.

But, I have a right to a life, too, don't I?

She leaned against the sink and stared straight into her own bottle-green eyes. *It's decision time.* She nodded at her reflection. *I know what I'm going to do.*

Chapter Ten

Veronica emerged from the ladies' room to find several trays lined up, ready to be delivered.

"Just in time to save me from myself," Perry said. "Tag, you're it."

Veronica nodded and did her best to swallow the lump in her throat. She grabbed the first of the trays, checked the ticket and hustled out to deliver it. She delivered three more trays before she returned to find a burger basket and Coke with a slip that had "17" written in a circle.

Veronica picked up the tray and walked in what felt like slow motion to the Thunderbird. Veronica remembered that Christopher had bought the car and the little two bedroom house he owned, thanks to an inheritance from his grandmother. Some kids would have blown it on beer and parties, but not Christopher. He always had an eye on the future.

She approached the car and waited for Christopher to roll his window down so she could put the tray on it. When he did, he said, "Would you mind not attaching the tray? It's a new car, and I don't want to scratch the window."

Veronica glanced down at the rubber-coated tips on the tray, designed specifically to not cause any damage, and said, "Of course."

Christopher took the Coke off the tray and put it between his legs, then claimed the basket.

I'd say you have a much better chance of messing up your interior by dropping ketchup all over it than you ever did of scratching your window. But, what do I know?

Veronica leaned over and said, "Forty cents, please."

When she leaned over, her face moved closer to Christopher and he stopped dead, right in mid-reach for his wallet. A moment later, he smiled a little self-consciously and said, "Sorry." He grabbed his wallet, fished out a dollar and handed it to her. "Has anyone ever told you that you have the most amazing green eyes?"

Veronica managed to say, "Has anyone ever told you that is a lame pick up line," but she couldn't help but notice his own hazel eyes. *He always did have beautiful eyes.*

Christopher laughed a little, then said, "Just give me two quarters back, if you would."

Veronica put the dollar in her order book, clicked two quarters out, and handed them to him. "Is there anything else you need?"

He leaned toward her. "Yes. I need you to go out with me."

Veronica's eyes grew wider. "Oh, Artie's carhops are not allowed to date customers. That could get me fired."

"I promise I will never eat here again. You have my word."

I know what your word is worth, Christopher Belkins.

"C'mon. Whadya say? Dinner and a movie on Friday?"

"I say that I will be right here, delivering delicious Artie burgers on Friday night."

"Saturday?"

"Ditto."

"I don't give up easily. There's a Sunday matinee playing at the Pickwick. After church, but before it gets too late."

"I'm still in high school."

"Congratulations, I'm just out of college. Just went to work at Crimmins and Holder Accounting. I expect it to be Crimmins, Holder, and Belkins accounting before too long."

You never did lack for confidence. And, damn you, you're exactly right, that's what happened.

"Just out of college and driving a beautiful car like this? How'd you swing that?" She knew the answer, but wanted to see if he'd answer truthfully.

Christopher shrugged. "Good things happen to good people, right?"

Well, that's not a lie, exactly, but most people wouldn't call their grandmother dying a 'good thing.' That was always his talent—to tell the truth in a slanted way that made him look better.

"Hey, Ronnie! We're getting backed up in here," Perry Zimmerman called from behind her.

"Sorry, Zimm. Be right there." Veronica turned to leave, but Christopher reached out and grabbed her hand.

"You didn't give me an answer. Sunday? I can come pick you up at your house at 1:00. Deal?"

I already made up my mind. Might as well go ahead with it.

Veronica wrote her address on a slip of paper from her order book. She hesitated. *In for a penny, in for a pound.* She jotted her phone number as well and handed it over. Christopher released her hand, but it still tingled a bit where he had held her.

"You better call me on Thursday night and speak to my folks. I don't think they're going to like me going out with someone already out of college, and I don't want you to waste a trip on Sunday."

"Will do. I am happy to speak to your parents. I have honorable intentions." He glanced down at the paper with her address and phone number. Christopher gave her his best Pepsodent smile, and said, "Thank you, Ronnie."

Veronica's eyebrows arched up in an excellent imitation of her mother's. "No, no. Veronica to you. You don't know me well enough to call me Ronnie yet."

Christopher chuckled a little and nodded. "Yes, ma'am. Veronica. I'll call on Thursday, and see you Sunday after church, then. "

Veronica turned and hustled away. She didn't notice that Danny Coleman had his passenger window down and had followed the whole conversation.

Christopher saw him, though, and waggled his eyebrows at him with a rakish grin, then held up the paper like a trophy.

Danny put his parents' station wagon in reverse and slowly drove away.

VERONICA SPENT THE rest of her shift in a daze. The quiet satisfaction she had started the day with faded away, replaced by a sense of impending dread. *When you make a decision, you stick to it and take the consequences, right? Besides, it's not like he asked to marry me, and I said yes. It's just dinner and a movie.*

Still, deep inside, Veronica felt a growing conviction she had set her feet on a path she wouldn't be able to step off.

Once again, a few minutes before her shift ended, Wallace McAllister parked in the far corner of the parking lot. He strolled in with his hands in his pockets and an expectant look on his face.

"Hello, Daddy," Veronica said, coming out from behind the counter and kissing him on the cheek. "Just a warning. Mom knows you grab a hamburger when you come pick me up."

"Oh, I always figured she did."

"You don't care?"

"No, not really. You'll understand someday when you get married. I still get to have my own life, but ... " he trailed off, not knowing how to complete that sentence.

"But, it's within the confines of a loving marriage, so some sacrifices of complete honesty have to be made?" Veronica guessed.

THE EMANCIPATION OF VERONICA MCALLISTER   55

Wallace beamed. "Couldn't have said it better myself!"

"Sit down, Daddy. I'll get your basket. Maybe I'll ask DJ to leave the onions off tonight, though. The retsin in those Certs isn't doing the job."

His smile faded.

"I know, you love the onions. Okay. I'll have DJ leave the onions on and damn the consequences."

Wallace dug in his pocket and pulled out a dollar bill and offered it to her.

"My treat tonight. It's been a good tips day."

"My little girl is almost all grown up.

You have no idea.

Chapter Eleven

The next day at Middle Falls High, in between second and third period, she saw Danny Coleman in the hallway. He made a point of turning his back and not seeing her.

It's for the best, anyway. Of course, I thought the same thing last time, and how did that turn out?

It was only her second day back at school, but she was already growing more confident. She was sure she would be able to fake her way through and get her diploma.

If it goes like last time, Christopher and I will move quickly from dating to going steady, to him wanting me to get married. At least if I do that, I can cash in my college fund and buy myself a car. I still don't know what I want after that, though. After the girls are born, then what? I guess that will be up to how he acts. And, if he lets his mother run our life like she did last time. I can't put up with that any more.

Third period was English, the source of the term paper Doris had been reminding her about off and on. Today, as she sat in class, she searched through the notebook marked "English" she had found in her locker. She flipped halfway through and was rewarded with a complete outline for a term paper on the impact television was having, both on entertainment and education.

Hmmph. Pretty good. I can write that, with a little research on Google, of course. She smiled to herself. *Or, I guess, the 1958 version of Google, Ye Olde Public Library.*

She flipped hopefully past the outline, but the pages were all blank.

Oh, past Veronica, you organized young woman. Why didn't you go the extra mile and write this in advance for me, so I don't have to? Can't have everything, I guess.

Miss Deakins was leading a discussion on Mark Twain's *The Stranger*, when the loudspeaker in the corner clicked on.

"Attention, teachers. This is a drill. Please execute duck and cover now."

Students around the room groaned, but Miss Deakins waved her hands to quiet them down. "This is important, class. In case of an actual nuclear attack, it has been estimated that executing duck and cover could reduce fatalities up to 60%. Girls, you don't need to try to get under your desks. Just kneel beside them and cover your heads. First row, by the windows, move further in."

Oh, my God. Duck and cover. It seems unlikely the Soviet bloc would have been interested in bombing Middle Falls. Seattle, home to Boeing, maybe, but that would give us weeks to get ready to die before the radiation reached us, right?

Some of the girl's skirts were so tight around their calves that they had trouble kneeling down modestly. The boys happily plunked down under the desks and several kept a shark's eye out for any illicit leg that might be accidentally flashed.

Sorry, boys, no free burlesque show here.

Veronica kneeled down and dramatically put her hands over her head and made her mouth a perfect "O" of exaggerated fear. Several of the boys noticed and laughed. Miss Deakins sought out the source of levity and zeroed in on Veronica, overacting to the hilt.

"Miss McAllister, I expect a more serious response from you."

Veronica lowered her hands and her normal expression returned. *Maybe this feels so ridiculous because I know nothing is ever going to come of it. No bombs will drop. No child will ever be saved by kneeling under her desk.* A sudden realization dawned. *Or will it? No bombs dropped when I lived this life last, but does that mean none will this time, either? Or can things change? Ever since I've been here, I've been doing things a little differently than I did the first time. Small changes can make big ripples. What if one of those ripples splashes up against something else, and something else, and the Cuban Missile Crisis goes a different way? I guess I better get over the idea that I'm all-seeing when it comes to the future. Maybe Mom won't become an alcoholic and die in her shower. Maybe Kennedy won't be assassinated in Dallas. Maybe Christopher won't leave me this time.*

The speaker in the corner of the room crackled again. "Thank you for your diligence and attention. This drill is complete."

The kids stood, the girls dusted themselves off and straightened their skirts before sitting back down.

But if all that is true, what if I go through with marrying Christopher again, and then Sarah and Nellie aren't born? What if I don't get pregnant at the exact same time? Will I recognize them the moment they are born, or will I think they might be a little stranger? Veronica drummed her pencil thoughtfully on her desk. *There's only one way to find out, and that's to live through it, I guess.*

THE REST OF THE WEEK flew by for Veronica. She worked another shift at Artie's, and waited nervously for Christopher to call on Thursday.

Veronica went to the library after school and spent some time relearning how to use the microfiche and Dewey Decimal System. Eventually, she was able to locate a number of newspaper and magazine articles highlighting the dangers of the growing popularity of television. Those risks were especially great to the fragile minds of America's youth.

Doris had dragged the heavy Underwood typewriter out and set it up on the kitchen table as promised, and Veronica was flipping through her notes when the phone rang. There was only one phone in the McAllister house, and it was in the kitchen. When it rang, it was so loud Veronica jumped and let out a wordless exclamation.

Doris said, "Never mind, you keep working on your paper. I'll get the phone." She put down her *Good Housekeeping* magazine and crossed to the kitchen.

"Hello, McAllister residence." She paused, then said, "Yes?" Her inflection rose slightly at the end of the word. Then, again. "Yes." A statement this time.

Doris was quiet for quite some time, but did glance over her shoulder at Veronica with one eyebrow slightly raised. Finally, she said, "Well that's all very interesting. I'll have to talk to my husband, of course."

Oh, come on, Mom. You never asked Dad for his opinion until after you'd given it to him. I don't even know what I'm rooting for. Do I want Mom to shut him down, or Christopher to charm her completely?

"Why don't you come by for lunch on Sunday, and we'll see how that goes, shall we?"

A moment later, "Fine, then. That's fine. See you Sunday." She hung up the phone and turned to look at Veronica. It was an appraisal. A reconsideration. New information had been introduced and needed to be considered.

"Did you say you would go out with a man named Christopher Belkins?"

"Umm, kind of? I told him he needed to call and ask you and Daddy first." *That's kind of true, right?*

"Do you think it's appropriate for you to be seeing someone so much older? He said he had already graduated from college."

"I didn't know if it was appropriate. He seemed nice. He has a good job."

"I'll see what I think, once I meet him.

Chapter Twelve

The McAllister house had the feel of a holiday dinner that Sunday. It was the first time anyone had ever come asking to court one of their daughters. Johnny had dated through high school, but boys were not as protected as girls. By the time he brought a girl home for dinner, everyone had already met her a number of times. Having a complete stranger drop in, wanting to take Veronica out, was exotic and exciting.

Doris asked Barbara to set the table. As she did, Barbara sang, "So, you're sure he's real?" "He's not imaginary?" "He's really going to sit and eat with us? Not like Santa or the Easter Bunny?"

After the fourth or fifth verse, Veronica passed by Barbara and accidentally bumped her into the table so hard the good china rattled.

"Mom!" Barbara yelled.

Doris shot Veronica a look, but it wasn't too severe. She was getting a little fed up with the whole line of inquiry as well.

Finally, precisely at noon, the doorbell rang and Barbara sprinted past her mother's objections to answer the door. She swung the door open dramatically and said, "Whoa," under her breath.

Christopher Belkins looked like he had stepped right out of a movie. His short hair was combed. He was wearing a herringbone sports coat over a white shirt and blue tie. In his hand was a large bouquet—daisies, carnations, and baby's breath—a bouquet designed for a mother, not a date.

Christopher smiled, and said, "Is Veronica here? I think she's expecting me."

"You're really here for *Ronnie*?" Barbara asked in amazement. Then, "Mom! You can come look at him now!"

Doris quickly came around the corner, a strained smile on her face, put a hand on Barbara's shoulder and firmly pulled her behind her.

"Hello, Mr. Belkins, I'm Doris, Veronica's mother."

Some suitors might have gone in for the kill too quickly, underestimating Mrs. McAllister's keen nose for bull manure. An anxious suitor might have said, "Really? I thought you were her sister." That anxious suitor would have been scuttled amidships before stepping foot inside the house.

Christopher Belkins was a natural salesman, with the unerring instinct of what works and what does not in a given situation.

"Hello, Mrs. McAllister. Thank you for the invitation to dinner today. I live alone and can barely boil water, so a home-cooked meal is a treat."

Barbara managed to get off one final shot. "Better not marry Ronnie, then! She can't cook either!" before being scooted forcefully off to the living room.

"Come in, Mr. Belkins. Can I take your coat?"

"Yes, thank you," Christopher said, shucking his jacket off and handing it to Doris, revealing a nicely ironed shirt underneath. "These are for you," he said, handing the spring bouquet to Doris.

"Oh, how lovely. Come on in and have a seat in the parlor. I'll just go and put these in some water. I'll have dinner on the table in a few minutes." She called over her shoulder, "Veronica, why don't you show Mr. Belkins in to meet your father."

Veronica appeared around the corner of the kitchen, pushing a stray lock of hair behind her ear.

"Hello, Christopher. Come in and meet my dad." *I guess that's the meanest thing I can think to say to a young man coming to pick up a father's daughter for the first time. I wish Daddy was a little more intimidating.*

Christopher raised his eyebrows for a moment, blew a sharp breath out and flashed a quick grin. "You know how to scare a guy, don't you?" he said, quietly.

When they walked into the parlor, Wallace McAllister looked as intimidating as a kitten in a cardigan. He had been happily dozing in his chair with a *Mechanics Illustrated* open across his lap. Now, he looked like a guilty professor who fell asleep mid-lecture. He plucked his reading glasses off his nose, and stood with his hand out and a slightly apologetic smile on his face. "Sorry, you might have caught me dozing off."

Christopher shook his hand and said, "A man's home is his castle, and the king sleeps when he wants, right?" Again, unerring.

"Right you are. That's what I've always said."

Daddy, Mom would never let you think that, let alone say it.

"Gentlemen, ladies, dinner is served," Doris said.

Everyone filed into the dining room.

"Christopher, why don't you sit on this side, next to Veronica."

"Yes, ma'am. Beautiful table." He pulled out Veronica's chair as naturally as could be.

Christopher Belkins, you are on your best behavior. This is the man I fell in love with the first time. You're going to have to work much harder to convince me this time. I've seen how you can change.

The table was spread with a baked ham, mashed potatoes, asparagus, and a lime Jell-O salad with bits of carrots in it.

"I hate that," Barbara said, pointing at the jiggly green Jell-O.

Doris didn't even bother to respond, but gave her two full seconds of the death glare. Barbara quieted.

"So, Mr. Belkins, what do you do?"

"I just started with Crimmins and Holder Accounting, over on Spring Street."

"Oh, yes, good outfit. Jake Holder and I golf occasionally," Wallace said.

No braggadocio about how it will be Crimmins, Holder, and Belkins soon? You know how to play to your audience, don't you Christopher. I've got to get over it, and accept that this is who you are. She glanced at him from the corner of her eye. *He does look handsome today. I can overlook some of the other, less-pleasant aspects of his personality. It's just a date.*

The rest of the dinner passed in a blur of polite conversation and exclamations over how good everything was.

After everyone had their fill, Doris said, "Let's go into the parlor and sit for a while. I've got a pot of coffee percolating. Do you drink coffee, Mr. Belkins?"

"I do, and Mrs. McAllister, it would be great if you would call me Christopher. Mr. Belkins is my father."

"All right. Christopher, then. How do you take your coffee?"

Black, like his soul.

"Black is fine. Thank you."

The men moved into the parlor while Doris poured coffee into delicate china cups which sat on equally delicate saucers. She pointed to them and said, "Take the coffee in, but give your father his, first."

Veronica rolled her eyes. *I feel like I fell headlong into an episode of Downton Abbey. Every phrase is weighted and protocol reigns supreme.* "Fine," she said, picking up both saucers.

Soon, the four adults were sitting in the parlor, staring at each other.

"Mr. and Mrs. McAllister, thank you for having me over. It's very kind of you. Now, if I'm not being too forward, I'd like to ask your permission to take Veronica out to a movie this afternoon. *South Pacific* is playing at the Pickwick, and I'd like to take her."

Veronica found herself holding her breath.

Doris looked at Wallace and gave him the slightest of nods.

Wallace cleared his throat. "Ordinarily, we wouldn't be in favor of Veronica dating someone so much older, but you seem like a fine young man. Where is your family from?"

"Right here, in Middle Falls. We've lived here three generations now."

"Fine, fine, that's fine. With the understanding that Veronica is still in high school, and living at home, we'll give you our permission to take her out. Her curfew will remain the same, though. She has to be home by 8:00 on school nights and 11:00 on the weekends."

Christopher beamed. "Well, that's swell. Thank you for trusting me with your daughter. I'll take good care of her."

Veronica stared at Christopher, chewing the side of her cheek, uncertain if that was true.

Chapter Thirteen

As Christopher and Veronica drove through the quiet Sunday streets of Middle Falls, a misty rain fell. This meteorological phenomenon is a western Oregon specialty—not really mist, but not heavy enough to actually rain. Small drops managed to almost hang in the air and wait for you to walk into them.

The Thunderbird had a nice sound system, or as nice as an AM radio in a car had in the late fifties. Christopher had it tuned to 1090 AM, KMFR. A commercial was playing for the local Ford dealer.

Christopher glanced at his wristwatch. "We've got forty-five minutes until the movie starts. I was ready for some fresh air, though. Do you want to drive through town for a little while?"

"Fresh air, huh? I think you were just ready to get out of the house, and I don't blame you. It's hard being on your best behavior for so long."

"Hey, hey! What did I do to deserve this?"

Fourteen years of transgressions, that's what. I'm not being fair, though. It's not like you're Eddie Haskell. Veronica smiled to herself. *Would you even understand that reference yet? Is* Leave it to Beaver *even on yet? No idea.*

"Just teasing. Sure, we can drive around a while. I don't mind."

"Okay, good." He drove on for a few blocks, then glanced at Veronica. "I think maybe you just like teasing me."

"Not just you," she teased.

"You really know how to hurt a guy."

Christopher drove out past the edge of town, to where the falls that gave the town its name tumbled over the rocks.

Christopher pulled over into the small viewing area. He turned the windshield wipers off and the view out the front window immediately faded into raindrops. "I like you, Veronica."

"You don't even know me yet."

"That's true, mostly, but the little sliver I do know," he held his thumb and forefinger a quarter inch apart, "I like."

That made Veronica laugh. She held her hands a foot apart. "Let's see if you still like me when you know me this much."

Christopher nodded. "That kid sister of yours is a pistol, isn't she?"

"Oh, Barb's used to being the center of attention. She and Mom are tight. She didn't know what to do when the world didn't revolve around her for a few minutes. She's a good kid."

"Sometimes, you sound a lot older than you are, you know."

"Do I? Maybe I'm just mature for my age." *And, maybe, being an old person in a teenager's body, I can be more of a match for you this time around.*

They drove back to town, found a spot half a block down from the Pickwick, and Christopher said, "Hang on." He jumped out of the car, opened the trunk and came around to Veronica's side and opened her door. He opened an umbrella with a flourish and held it above the door.

"You really can be sweet, Chris."

"Hold on now," he said, helping her out. "If I'm going to be Chris to you, you've *got* to be Ronnie for me."

"No, *you* hold on there, cowboy. Not so fast."

Christopher looked slightly downcast, and it struck her as such a sincere emotion that she snuggled up against him under the umbrella. They strolled together to the theater box office. The ticket seller was an older man with silver hair, neatly parted on the left side. He was dressed in a maroon uniform, complete with a cap perched on his head at a jaunty angle.

"Two, please," Christopher said, holding out two dollars.

The ticket seller reached through the opening in the glass and plucked a single bill from him. "Matinee pricing, sir, two tickets for a dollar. Specials on popcorn in the lobby, too. Enjoy the show."

Inside the theater, they both decided they couldn't imagine eating anything after the way Doris had stuffed them, so they found seats in the front row of the balcony.

Christopher looked around the empty theater, leaned over to Veronica and said, "I see why matinee tickets are cheap. I guess they're not big sellers."

"Still, it's kind of nice. Like we rented out the whole place, just for ourselves."

Eventually, a few more couple wandered in, the lights dimmed, and a newsreel came on that showed Princess Margaret on a tour of Canada.

I have no idea why we would be expected to care about that. Maybe it's because the Korean War is over, the Vietnam War hasn't started yet, and with no shooting to show, this is what they had to resort to.

Next up was a Woody Woodpecker cartoon. Finally, the 20th Century Fox logo came on, and *South Pacific* started. Veronica had seen the movie, but it had been so long ago, it was almost like new to her. Very soon, she was sucked in to the exotic locale, the songs, and the romance. By the time Mitzi Gaynor sang *I'm Gonna Wash That Man Right out of My Hair,* she was entranced. She leaned her head against Christopher's shoulder and felt oddly happy.

When the movie let out, they walked out in the early evening twilight. The rain clouds had cleared, and a few rays of golden light lit the western horizon.

"This was nice, Christopher."

"Uh-oh. Christopher again. I liked it when you called me Chris earlier." He opened her car door, then hurried around to his own side. Once inside, he said, "What do you say? Want a piece of pie?"

"I always want a piece of pie, but I think we better head for home. This has been a nice day, but Mom will have her eye on the clock. She probably called the theater to see what time the movie let out."

"You're likely right. This has been better than a nice day for me. I guess I didn't want it to end."

"But if we go home early, my parents are more likely to let us have more nice days like this. Besides, I still have a term paper to work on."

He started the Thunderbird's engine and the smooth purr filled the interior of the car. The radio came on, playing Gogi Grant's *The Wayward Wind*. "What's your term paper about?"

"Something completely boring. Please don't make me tell you about it."

Christopher smiled, nodded, and pulled the car away from the curb. Five minutes later, they were home.

"Can I walk you up?"

"Mom would probably shoot you if you didn't. But, just to warn you, Barb will be spying on us from upstairs, and she'll tell Mom everything."

Christopher held his hands up in front of him, the picture of innocence.

Once again, he came to Veronica's side and opened the door for her. As they walked up the sidewalk to her front door, she slipped her arm through his.

Why does this feel so right?

"When can I see you again?"

"It's another busy week. Three shifts at Artie's this week, and you've promised never to eat there again, so I know I won't see you there."

"Oh, please tell me you're not going to hold me to that. I love Artie's burgers."

"I know. Everyone does." She hesitated, then said, "Okay, fine. You can come by once in a while." When she saw his eyes light up, she repeated, for clarity: "Once in a while. But, we've got to be discreet. Promise?"

"Discretion is my middle name."

"I thought it was Allen," Veronica said, playfully.

A strange expression crossed Christopher's face. "How in the world would you guess that? I've never told you my middle name."

Damn it. Come on, Veronica, don't get all swept up in this teenage romance stuff and lose your head, now.

"Didn't you? I thought I remembered you mentioning it. How else would I know?"

Christopher considered this, then shrugged, and said, "I don't know!" He smiled, slightly baffled. "You are a strange and interesting girl, Veronica."

Glad to be back on safer ground, Veronica leaned forward, whispered, "You can call me Ronnie now." She kissed him lightly on the cheek, then ran inside.

Chapter Fourteen

The wedding was held in the McAllister backyard on August 9th. They had talked about a church wedding, but Christopher didn't attend a local house of worship, and it became more than they had wanted to deal with. Instead, the prospect of a wedding inspired Wallace McAllister to finally add on to the deck in the back yard and build the pergola he had dreamed about for years.

Veronica could have told them it would happen that way, but she had learned to not count on events transpiring exactly like they had in her first life. She was already noticing that certain things were different, especially as she moved farther away from the path of the life she had already lived. For this major event in her life, though, it had played out almost exactly the same.

It was a small wedding, with fewer than two dozen people attending. A few of Christopher's relatives had driven down from Portland, and two of Veronica's old maid aunts had come up from Medford.

There were whispered asides in the crowd. A few wags asked if they "had" to get married. Another joked about where the shotgun was. The truth was, they just wanted to get married. Christopher was already doing well at the accounting firm, and believed it would help him to be a settled-down married man. It wasn't really such a calculated decision—he had truly fallen in love with Veronica.

One change from her first wedding was that Veronica asked Ruthie to be her maid of honor. She had vowed to stay in touch with Ruthie in this life. Christopher's friend from college, Andy, had served as best man. The bride wore white, and Doris made Ruthie's maid of honor dress so she didn't have to buy one.

It was a lovely, low-key ceremony. Doris McAllister was made for moments like this and rose to the occasion, pulling the whole thing off with military precision.

There was an equally small reception and barbecue in the back yard, then the newlyweds were off on their honeymoon. That night, they drove to Portland, where they spent their first night as husband and wife. Part of the reason Christopher had pushed for a quick wedding was that he was determined they wouldn't sleep together before they were married. Even in the more Victorian fifties, such dedication to the cause was unusual, but it was encouraged by the stern visage of Doris McAllister. Christopher had no interest in finding out what she would have done to him in the case of an accidental pregnancy. Thus, the hurried wedding.

Their first night of lovemaking was somewhat awkward, with Veronica much more experienced, but unable to show it, and Christopher all pent up frustration and fumbling uncertainty. It had been more than forty years since Veronica had had sex. It was every bit as anticlimactic as she remembered it.

She lay under Christopher's arm, her head on his chest. He kissed the top of her head.

"Well? Did you?" he asked.

She wasn't cruel enough to ask, "Did I *what?*" so she snuggled closer up against him, laid a hand across his chest, and said, "Mmm-hmm." *Some lies are necessary. There are more important things in life than sex.*

The next morning, they had breakfast in a small café off the lobby of the hotel they had stayed in. They had tickets to ride a ferry, the *Princess Marguerite*, from Seattle to Victoria, Canada, on Monday. The trip to Victoria had been a wedding gift from Christopher's parents. Mr. and Mrs. McAllister had been a little more practical with their gift—a complete set of Wearever pots and pans to fill Christopher's empty kitchen.

The fact that the *Marguerite* didn't sail until Monday, gave them time to dawdle on Sunday, since Seattle was only a few hours north of Portland.

As they sat in the little café, lingering after their pancakes and sausage, Christopher read *The Oregonian*, and Veronica people-watched. Even four months into her new life in 1958, she was still endlessly fascinated by comparing and contrasting this time with what she remembered from 2018.

More conversation at the tables. Not a smartphone in sight, obviously. That's a plus. People seem to be more polite, maybe more thoughtful here. Why would that be? Because most people in this café were raised by the rod? When kids smarted off, it was their rear ends that were smarting?

"Hey, honey, look at this," Christopher said, folding the paper and turning it around. The paper showed a black and white image of a boat racing across the water, throwing a huge spray of water behind it. "Isn't that something? They call them thunderboats, because they make so much noise, that's what they sound like."

Veronica started to dismiss this with a, "That's nice, Chris," but then looked at his face, alight with boyish excitement. Instead, she said, "Are you interested in those boats?"

"Hydroplanes," he said, knowledgeably. He shrugged. "I mean, it's not like a life-long dream of mine or anything, but I've always thought it would be pretty nifty to see them, yeah."

"Are they somewhere around here?"

"Well, kind of. They're racing up in Seattle today. On Lake Washington."

"What time?"

"According to this," he said, tapping the paper, "it goes on all day."

"We've already got a reservation to stay up there tonight. Why don't we go?"

"Really?"

"Yes, really." *Another major change. I certainly never saw whatever these boats are called in the last life. I think that's good, isn't it? It will get awful boring if I'm just watching reruns for another sixty years.*

Christopher smiled, and said, "I love you, Ronnie. You're the best wife ever."

Keep thinking that way, Christopher Allen. "I love you too. Let's pay the bill and get out of here."

Christopher dropped two dollar bills on the table and five minutes later they were on US 99, heading north.

Chapter Fifteen

It was a warm August day and they drove with the windows down, tuning in whatever AM radio stations they could after KGW in Portland faded away.

"Days like this, I wish I'd sprung for the convertible model," Christopher said.

Veronica laid her hand on Christopher's knee and shook her head. "Not many days like this in western Oregon. Most days, we're glad to have a solid roof over our heads when we're driving."

They drove through small towns like Longview, Centralia, and Olympia, which was the state capital, but wasn't much of a city, especially in 1958. Once they got to Seattle, they didn't have any idea how to find the races. They pulled off at a gas station, and the attendant happily sold them a city map for a quarter and marked the route they needed to take.

Soon enough, they found a neighborhood where people were selling parking spots on their lawn. They held up cardboard signs that said, "See the Thunderboats!" or, "You're here, time to park!" They pulled into one such jam-packed lawn.

"How much to park?" Christopher asked, getting out of the Thunderbird.

"Only one dollar, and I'll babysit your car like it's my own child," the man said.

Christopher looked over the man's shoulder and saw a ragamuffin child drawing in the dirt. He almost left, but just then, an echo of a powerful motor reached his ears. "Man," he said, a faraway look in his eyes. "Is that one of the boats?"

The man grinned. "Yes sir, ain't that something? If you're right there on the banks, you can feel the ground shake under your feet. They're running the preliminary heats right now. The final heat is at 4:00."

Christopher grabbed his wallet, handed over a buck, and said, "We'll be back before then."

The man laughed. "It's an unusual man that can see the big boats run and leave before they're done, but either way, you're good. This is my last spot, and you can stay here until tomorrow, if you want."

Christopher leaned down, said, "You might want to grab your hat, honey. It's a scorcher, and I'm not sure where the race actually is. I don't want you to get sunburned." He turned back to the man and asked, "Where do we go, exactly?"

He pointed down the street that ran alongside his house. "Just walk down here. Before too long, you'll start to hear the crowds, and for sure you'll hear the boats. Walk toward the thunder."

Veronica grabbed her sun hat off the floor, and said, "Veronica Belkins, ready for duty." She snapped off what she thought was a jaunty salute.

"I like the sound of that," Christopher said, giving her a quick peck.

They walked a mile or so down the road, then heard one of the boats fire up.

"Whoa," Christopher said, raising his eyebrows.

"Yes, 'whoa,' Veronica said, laughing, enjoying Christopher's excitement.

They hurried a little further along the street, and found themselves in the middle of a small crowd of people, all walking the same direction. The road turned slightly left, and the view opened onto an immense, crystal blue lake. The sunlight reflected off small whitecaps frothed up by the speedboats.

"Holy cow, look at this place," Christopher said, amazement tinging his voice. A log boom formed a barrier in front of them, and stretched as far out onto the lake as he could see. Hundreds and hundreds of pleasure boats were tied up to it. They ranged from decent-sized yachts, to a small rowboat that contained two bare-chested young men and a cooler full of beer.

"If I hadn't seen that article in the paper, we never would have known this was going on! Look! There's the buoys that mark off the race course." Tens of thousands of people lined the banks of Lake Washington and alcohol flowed freely, but everyone seemed in a good mood.

Christopher and Veronica picked their way down toward the lake. Everywhere, people were sitting in lawn chairs, on blankets, or sitting on the grassy bank. At that moment, five of the great boats fired at once and headed out onto the course.

"Do you know what we're looking at?"

"Other than the fact it's a boat race, I don't have a clue!"

Christopher laughed. "Well, you're not alone. I don't have a clue either, but isn't it a sight?"

The brightly-colored boats made their way out onto the oval race course and began maneuvering around, jockeying for position. In the middle of the race course was a huge clock that had an immense second hand counting down the seconds.

"First hydro race?" a sunburned man in a trucker's hat asked, seeing Christopher's open-mouthed expression. He had to shout a little to be heard over the boats, even though they were on the other end of the course.

Christopher didn't answer, but nodded.

He offered his hand. "Walt Lewis."

Christopher shook his hand and said, "I'm Christopher. This is my wife, Veronica."

Well, that was nice, introducing me as Veronica, instead of Ronnie. He knows I don't like it when people I don't know call me that.

Lewis pointed to the large clock in the middle of the course. "That's the start clock. It's right at the start/finish line. What they're trying to do—" he paused and held up his hand while the boats thundered around the corner in front of them and waited for them to pass. "What they're trying to do, is hit that start line at top speed, and preferably with inside position. Then, the race will be on."

"Thanks," Christopher said, and bent to try and tell Veronica, but she mouthed, "I've got it."

Veronica looked around at the incredible mass of people spread out in front of her. *To me, this is much ado about nothing, but I guess it must mean something to all these people. Or, more likely, it's a good excuse to come out on a sunny day and have a party. That works, too.*

A moment later, the boats came toward them again, this time at a much faster speed.

"Here we go!" Lewis shouted happily.

All five boats hit the start line at the same time, rocking back and forth on their plane, shooting a huge plume of water out behind them. Christopher pointed, but couldn't be heard above the thunder of the boats. He put his arm around Veronica and pulled her close. He stood on his tiptoes and craned his neck so he could see them as they rounded the corner at the far end of the course.

Christopher leaned over and shouted in Veronica's ear, "They were right! Feel it in your chest!"

The boats approached the first corner in front of them, racing deck to deck, huge roostertails pluming out behind them. The boat in the lead, painted a vivid red and white, suddenly veered in front of the other boats, just missing them. It headed directly toward Christopher and Veronica at an incredible speed. It swung right again and rammed directly into a Coast Guard cutter with a mighty crash.

Screams echoed everywhere, from the log boom, from up and down the race course. Everyone around them jumped to their feet and peered out at the water, thousands holding their breath as one.

The other boats continued on, but a yellow flag was raised and they all slowed, then returned to the pit area.

"What happened?" Veronica asked. "That's not supposed to happen, is it?"

Christopher looked at Walt Lewis, who shook his head, as perplexed as they were. "This is my fifth year watching this race, and I've never seen anything like that before!"

"Are they okay? Is everyone all right?" Veronica asked.

They watched, slack-jawed, as the Coast Guard cutter turned bottom up and followed the red and white hydroplane beneath the waves of Lake Washington.

Lewis had his binoculars out, trained on the scene of the accident. "I see some Coasties floating in the water. They look all right. They're not panicking." He swept the binoculars around the area. "Wait. There's Muncey! That was the Miss Thriftway, and I can see Muncey floating out there. He's signaling he's all right. Oh, man!" He looked at Christopher and Veronica. "I can't believe it. You guys get here five minutes ago, and see something people will be talking about for years!"

Christopher and Veronica looked at each other. Their five minutes of boat racing experience didn't give them any perspective on how to handle a catastrophe like this.

"Thanks for letting us know they're all alive," he said to Walt Lewis. "I think we're going to head out, now."

"Oh, they'll have a restart for the heat in a few minutes. Sinking one little Coast Guard ship isn't going to stop the Gold Cup!"

"Thanks. I mean it. But, we're on our honeymoon, and I think that's enough boat racing excitement for us."

Chapter Sixteen

They were more somber walking back to their car than they had been heading the other direction. Seeing people escape death by inches does that to a person. They got back to the spot where they had parked the car, and found the same man was sitting in his lawn chair. He was as good as his word. He babysat their car with the same attention he gave his own child. He was dozing.

A small transistor radio sat on the arm of his chair, a cord leading up to an earpiece stuffed into his right ear. He jerked awake when they approached. He took out the earpiece, and said, "Oh, you guys left too early. You missed an incredible crash!"

Ah. Maybe that's why some people go. In case something like this happens.

"No, no, we saw it. It happened right in front of us," Christopher said.

"Oh, you lucky SOB! Come on, tell me about it."

Christopher did his best to describe what he had seen, egged on by the man in the lawn chair. Christopher glanced at Veronica and saw that she was shifting from one foot to the other. "Well, sorry, but that's all the news that's fit to print. We've got a reservation to get to."

The man raised his Olympia beer in salute, muttering something to himself.

Once they were back in the car, they did their best to retrace their route back to 99, then turned toward Seattle proper.

Veronica sat back and enjoyed driving through this version of Seattle. She had been to what was then called The Emerald City a number of times in her previous life, but it had been later, after the Space Needle was built, and skyscrapers dominated the downtown skyline. Today, the tallest building was still the Smith Tower, which would eventually come to look quaint next to the other behemoths. Even without the Needle or the skyscrapers, Seattle was a jewel, nestled into the curve of Elliott Bay. Christopher dropped down along the waterfront, then found a parking garage on 4th Avenue and University, right next to the Olympic Hotel, where they were staying.

They retrieved their bags from the Thunderbird's trunk and strolled through the lobby of the Olympic. The lobby wasn't immense, but it was the elegant face the grand old hotel showed the world, filled with fine wood, thick carpet, and a marble reception desk.

"Chris! Can we afford someplace like this?"

"No, probably not, but you only get one honeymoon, right?"

Well, that depends, I suppose.

"It was twenty-seven dollars for the night, but Mom and Dad paid for the rest of the trip, so I thought it was okay."

They checked in at the reception desk—cash or check only—and were escorted to their room by a bellhop in a full uniform.

When they got to their room, they both decided the splurge was worth it. A queen bed with a comforter so thick it looked like a cloud sat against one wall. A writing desk and phone, a fainting couch, and a television console completed the furnishings. The bellhop placed their bags in the closet, then dramatically opened the heavy drapes, showing a view of the Seattle skyline, 1958 version. If they leaned to the right, they could even catch a glimpse of Elliott Bay.

The bellhop neatly pocketed the two quarters Christopher slipped him, and said, "Just call the front desk if you need anything at all," then was gone. The room seemed quiet. Veronica sat on the bed, which was so tall, her feet dangled. Christopher stood at the window, looking at the view.

"I wonder if it's too late to walk down and see the Pike Place Market? I've always heard about it, but never seen it."

Veronica looked at the small gold watch Christopher had given her for a graduation gift. "It's almost five, and a Sunday. I'll bet it's closed, or will be before we can get there."

"You're likely right."

Another four years, and we could ride the monorail over to the Space Needle, but not yet.

Christopher returned to staring out the window. There was a small television tucked into the corner, rabbit ears pointed skyward. Neither of them wanted to turn it on, though. This was their honeymoon.

After two full minutes of silence ticked slowly by, Veronica said, "Hungry?"

"Yes!"

I can't tell if he's actually hungry, or just glad to have something to do other than stare out the window.

"Good idea. Let's see what Seattle has to offer," Christopher said, grabbing his sports coat off the end of the bed.

Veronica suggested that since they had splurged on the room, they should eat a little more modestly. Christopher smiled his agreement, and they walked a few blocks until they found a small restaurant. It was likely filled with downtown workers during the week. It sat deserted and quiet on a Sunday evening.

When they returned to their quiet room, Christopher gave up and turned the television on. They kicked off their shoes, sat on the edge of the bed and watched The Steve Lawrence and Eydie Gormè Show for an hour before bed. The Marguerite sailed at 8:00 a.m., so they turned in early.

Veronica expected another round of her marital obligation, but the combination of the trip, the boat race, and the big meal, had done Christopher in. He was fast asleep by the time she came out of the bathroom.

She found the paperback she had packed, turned on the small lamp on her bedside table, and read until she fell asleep.

Chapter Seventeen

The ship Chris and Veronica boarded the next morning was technically *The Princess Marguerite II*. The original *Princess Marguerite* had been requisitioned into the war effort and sunk by a German U-boat in 1942. Locals called her *The Maggie*, and she made the triangle run between Seattle, Victoria, and Vancouver, British Columbia, every day. For people in the Pacific Northwest, it was an inexpensive way to travel internationally.

The Maggie was officially classed as a "miniature luxury liner" but she was a fairly spartan vessel. There were plenty of viewing areas, though, and lots of private cabins fitted with wooden benches if the weather got blustery. There was even a snack bar where you could get a hot dog for ten cents, or a cup of hot chocolate for a nickel.

The Maggie pulled in to the inner harbor of Victoria a few minutes after noon, announcing her arrival with long blasts on the steam whistle.

"Oh, Chris, look, it's beautiful!" Veronica said as they stepped off the gangplank. "If I squint a little bit, it almost looks like we left Seattle and ended up in England!"

Chris smiled. "Do you see that?" he asked, pointing off to the left at a massive brick structure right on the edge of the harbor. "Looks like it was picked up from London and dropped down right here, doesn't it?"

"Yes!"

"Well, I have a reservation for us to have high tea there," he said, imitating holding a delicate tea cup, pinky extended, "at 3:00."

"Really?"

"Oh, yes, so we had best get on to our room and get unpacked."

Their hotel was a nice, solidly built establishment called *The Carriage House*. It wasn't as fancy as the Olympic in Seattle, but the location was ideal. They threw their bags in their room—no bellhop to tip at *The Carriage House*—and walked around the magnificent inner harbor of Victoria. There were tourist attractions and many small shops where you could stop and pick up a pennant or a souvenir magnet of your trip. But, there were also old ivy-covered buildings that made them feel like they were far from home.

High tea at the Empress Hotel was an event, and Veronica immediately wished she had changed out of her breezy sundress and into something more formal. The maître d' who seated them did not give her a second glance. He sat them at a table covered in a thick linen table cloth, with a small bouquet of fresh flowers in the center.

Seconds later, a woman in a black servant's dress arrived at the table, all smiles and menus.

"Oh!" Veronica said. "I didn't know I would have to choose. I thought we just came in and sat down, and you brought us tea."

The server smiled. This was a story she had heard many times before. "No," she said, "afternoon tea is a bit like an extra meal stuck between lunch and dinner. Long ago, people often didn't eat their supper until 8:00 or later. So they would have a small meal late in the afternoon to get them through."

Veronica looked at the menu uncertainly. A dozen types of tea were listed on the first page. *I don't know if I've ever had a tea that wasn't Lipton or Constant Comment. I might be out of my element here.* She glanced across at Christopher who was doing his best to not appear confused, and failing miserably.

The server leaned in and spoke quietly to Christopher. "Would you like me to just bring you a variety of things I think you'll like?"

Relief lit Christopher's face. He nodded. Once the waitress departed, he leaned in and said, "I took care of ordering for us."

I'm eighteen again, Christopher, nothing wrong with my hearing or vision, you know.

Minutes later, they had two pots of tea. Veronica had no idea what it was, but it was much better than Lipton. They also had a feast of scones, finger sandwiches, clotted cream, and other delights she honestly didn't know how to identify. It was all delicious, though.

After tea, they walked to what would eventually be called The International District, but in 1958, it was called Chinatown. Chris bought Veronica a red silk kimono with intricate designs stitched in gold. "You can model it for me later tonight," he whispered.

"With nothing under it," she promised.

Veronica talked a big game, but it was a bluff. Through all of one lifetime and this part of another, she'd had only one lover. She was also concerned about pregnancy. She knew the exact night she had gotten pregnant with Sarah, because by that time in their marriage they hadn't been intimate often. She had caught on their fourth anniversary, August 9th, 1962, and Sarah had been born on May Day, 1963.

Well, I didn't get pregnant for four years last life, I guess I have to hope we play out the same way again. In a few more years, the pill would be available, and I could control this a bit better. We had it tougher before that. It's not like I can tell him I don't want to have sex on our honeymoon, or ask him to use protection, either. That would cause a huge ruckus. So, I will cross my fingers, instead of my legs.

They spent their last day in Canada touring the Butchart Gardens. Neither of them was particularly excited to see the gardens, but Betty Belkins, Christopher's mother, had included two admission tickets with the rest of the trip. They didn't want to waste that, and both knew Betty would expect a full report when they got back, so they dutifully trundled off to see the gardens.

As in so many situations, diminished expectations led to an even greater appreciation. All of Victoria was beautiful, but the Butchart Gardens are an oasis of pristine natural beauty. August is not the best month to hit Butchart, but the master gardeners there know how to plan a garden. Something—dahlias, flowering maples, hydrangeas, and Zinnias in this case—is always in bloom.

They spent four hours wandering around the grounds and found a vendor selling boxed lunches with sandwiches and macaroni salad. They ate sitting on a hillside looking down at a magnificent fountain.

Christopher polished off the last bite of his sandwich, then laid his head down on Veronica's lap. "Ready to go home?"

"No." She paused and soaked in the beauty around them. "And yes. This has all been wonderful, and I will remember it always." *Somehow, this honeymoon turned out much better than our last one. When we tried to drive to Lake Couer d'Alene in Idaho, the T-bird broke down halfway there, and we ended up turning around. Maybe this bodes well for us.* "But still, this has all been like a fantasy. It's time for us to get on with real life now."

Chapter Eighteen

Real life came, and it swallowed them whole. In her first life, Veronica had been oblivious to the changes in their marriage, sometimes purposefully so. This lifetime, she was watching for signs, and she saw them everywhere. In her first life, she had been a naïve eighteen-year-old girl. She hadn't known what she had a right to expect. This time, she did, but it didn't change the outcome. In fact, if anything, that knowledge sped the process up.

It didn't start immediately on their return from their honeymoon, or even in the months immediately following. The honeymoon itself was over, but the honeymoon period lasted for at least a few more months. Christopher worked hard at the accounting firm, trying to get ahead. Veronica focused on turning Christopher's house into a home where they could build a family.

The day after they had returned from Victoria, they had driven to the McAllister house to move Veronica to the marital home. This was one job the Thunderbird was not built for, so they borrowed her father's car and were able to get everything she needed in a single load.

And isn't that kind of sad? But, how much of your childhood do you need when you are a married woman?

Christopher's house—now Christopher and *Veronica's* house—was on the other side of Middle Falls. Close to his parents, but far from hers, so far as Middle Falls goes. It was a two bedroom, one bath rambler in a modest neighborhood. Veronica had been to the house before the wedding, of course, but she had never been there when it was also ostensibly *her* house, too.

The following Monday, Christopher went off to work and Veronica sat at what passed for a kitchen table in the small kitchen. Really, it was a card table, with folding legs, rubber top and all. *This is a clear memory from my first life. I woke up on the Monday after our honeymoon, Chris was gone to work, and I sat here feeling like a stranger in my own home. I had no idea what to do, so I pulled the sidewalks in after me and hid. That didn't work very well. Time for a new plan.*

Veronica walked into the living room and dialed her mother.

When Doris answered, Veronica said, "Mom? This place doesn't feel like anybody's home, but especially not mine. I don't know what to do."

Briskly, Doris rose to the challenge. "Here's exactly what you do. Make yourself some breakfast, if you've got anything there to cook with. Some coffee, if you don't. By the time you finish with that, I'll be there. We'll figure it out together."

Veronica sat back down in wonder. *Was that all it took? Mom was a few miles away, wanting to help, and I just never gave her a chance?*

Thirty minutes later, Doris pulled into the driveway and opened the trunk of her car. She was dressed in jeans and one of Wallace's old shirts, with a bandana wrapped around her hair. Veronica's mouth fell open. Doris pulled a mop, a bucket, and a cardboard box full of cleaning supplies out of the trunk and set them on the ground. She looked at Veronica, standing uncertainly on the porch and waved. She was in her element.

Veronica ran to her and hugged her, catching Doris totally by surprise, but she hugged her back warmly. "Look in the back seat. I brought some extra pillows, tablecloths, and a few other little extras I've been keeping in the garage just for you."

Veronica nodded, but knew she didn't dare speak, or she might start to cry.

Christopher was not a slob. But, he wasn't obsessive about his cleaning, either. Doris McAllister was exactly that. They started in the kitchen, scrubbing every surface with Ajax, Pinesol, and Murphy Oil Soap. While they cleaned, Doris told Veronica stories about how her grandmother had taught her to clean when she was a little girl.

They moved from the kitchen, to the bathroom, to the living room. They dusted, vacuumed, and cleaned as they went. Doris told her stories of her own girlhood that Veronica had never heard. By mid-afternoon, the house sparkled, and Doris and Veronica had successfully made the transition from mom-and-teenager to mom-and-adult.

Doris and Veronica took off their aprons and patted their brows.

"Now," Doris said. "Let's run down to the store and pick up a few things to throw together a good dinner. No man wants to come home, tired and hungry, and find a cold kitchen. We'll get a few things today, and tomorrow, I can come over and help you plan out a menu, and we can go shopping for real." She hesitated. "Um, if you want my help, of course. If not—"

"I want your help, Mom." *I know how to do these things, of course. But I never had this with you before. Girl talk, and stories, and advice. I thought you only wanted to give that stuff to Barb. Was it you, Mom, or was it me pushing you away all along?*

HER FIRST FIGHT WITH Christopher was a few days later. It started at dinner two days later, when Veronica said, "I'm going to call Zimm tomorrow and tell him he can put me back on the schedule."

Christopher looked up, surprised. He stared at her thoughtfully for a few seconds, then returned to his dinner. "No, you're not."

"Pardon me?"

Christopher cleared his throat, as though perhaps Veronica had simply misunderstood him. "I said, 'No, you're not.' I don't want you working."

Oh my God, 1950s alpha male on full display in his natural habitat.

"I wasn't asking permission."

Now Christopher looked at her sharply. "Veronica, I make plenty of money for us. Well, maybe not *plenty* yet, but I've only been with the firm a few months. It won't be long. For now, I'm making enough for us to get by." He waved his hand expansively around the tiny kitchen. "After all, I paid cash for this place, so we don't even have a mortgage."

"It's not about us needing the money. I need to get out of the house sometimes. I can't just sit here, polishing silverware and planning menus out every day."

"Go see your friends. I'm sure Ruthie will be glad to see you."

"Ruthie is working too." She set her jaw. "I'm calling Zimm tomorrow."

Christopher picked up his knife and fork and went to work cutting his cube steak much more vigorously than was necessary.

In the end, Veronica won that first skirmish, and went back to work during the day on weekdays. She agreed to tell Zimm she couldn't work weekends any more. She also promised she would do her best to be home when Christopher got there. He hated coming home to an empty house.

It was their first fight, but not their last.

Chapter Nineteen

The first two years of the 1960s weren't all that different from the late 1950s. The turn of the decade brought an energetic young president to the White House, but fashions and hairstyles remained much as they had been during the Eisenhower era. Elvis had fired the first shot across the bow of adult supremacy. The real invasion was still eighteen months away, when the mop-topped Liverpudlians touched down in New York.

In Middle Falls, Oregon, Veronica sat on the edge of the bed in the same house she had shared with Christopher for four years. If asked, she would have admitted it wasn't really a home any more. She and Christopher were more like roommates who occasionally shared a meal than they were husband and wife. She had hoped that showing a little backbone and being a more active partner in the marriage would help. Instead, it had only sped the dissolution of their relationship. They had been married twenty years in Veronica's first life. She wasn't sure if they would make it to their fifth anniversary this time

One thing I know for sure. If I don't do something, then I'll have wasted these last four years.

She straightened her spine, wiped the tears off her face and went to the small bedroom closet. She pushed her clothes all the way to the right and at the back, she found what she was looking for. The red kimono with gold inlay hung limp and almost forgotten. *It's not exactly sexy lingerie, but I don't have any sexy lingerie, so it will have to do.* A small, bitter laugh escaped her lips. *Why would I bother with lingerie,* anyway? We haven't had sex in six months. When it does happen, it's a quick tumble in the middle of the night when he gets back from a night out with the boys. I knew Christopher wasn't romantic, but I didn't expect this life. Not this time. Fool me once, shame on you. Fool me twice, I must be Veronica.*

She pulled the kimono down and held it against her. *I haven't gained a pound since our honeymoon, so it will still fit.*

After things had started to fall apart, she had considered giving up. Maybe going home to her mother and father's, or getting on a bus to who-knows-where and starting over somewhere else. *I'm more than eighty years old. I have a pretty good idea what's coming over the next fifty years. I should be able to provide for myself.*

Every time that appealing idea began to take root in her mind, it was replaced by thoughts of Sarah and Nellie, all blonde curls and smiles, and she pushed it away. *I have to keep my eyes on the prize. Once they are born, then I will be free of him. The girls and I can go anywhere we want. Life will be worth living again.*

She laid the kimono across the bed, then went to the kitchen to check the pot roast baking in the oven, surrounded by potatoes and carrots. Barbara had been right when she had said Veronica couldn't cook, that first night Christopher had shown up for dinner. But, that was then.

Since then, Doris had taken Veronica under her wing and showed her a thousand small tricks. She might not be Julia Child, but she could hold her own with any of the young brides in the neighborhood. Her dishes at the company picnic always came back licked clean.

I don't know if Christopher even remembers it is our anniversary. This is not the day to leave anything to chance.

She went to the living room, picked up the handset of the heavy black telephone and dialed Christopher's work number. When the receptionist answered, Veronica said, "Can I speak to Suzie, please?"

She had learned that asking for Christopher while he was at work was an exercise in frustration.

When Suzie came on the line, Veronica said, "Hi, Suzie, it's Veronica. Can I leave a message for Christopher."

"Of course, hon. Shoot."

"Will you ask him if he can be home for dinner by six tonight? It's important."

"Sure. You bet. Bye."

Okay. Dinner's on to cook. Table's set. Candles are ready to light. Time for a quick shower, then I can sit around for another hour or two, wondering if this is all in vain.

CHRISTOPHER DID NOT make it home by 6:00, but he did come through the door, rumpled, sleeves rolled up, and jacket slung over his shoulder, at 6:30. Veronica didn't care. He could have come in at midnight, and she wouldn't have said a word.

Christopher hung his coat up in the hall closet, then said, "Suzie said it was important that I be home as early as I could. What's up?"

Veronica was dressed in one of her normal house dresses. She didn't want to overplay her hand. "I'd like to talk to you about something."

"Oh, Christ," he said, wandering into the kitchen. "When a wife says she wants to talk about something, it's never good news, is it?" The roast was sitting on top of the stove. He lifted the lid, inhaled and said, "Mmm." He opened the refrigerator, slung one arm over the door and leaned into the cool air. "Hey, you got me a six-pack. Thanks."

He stopped and looked first at the roast and then at the beer in the fridge. A look flitted across his face, but he shrugged and pulled a

Heidelberg out and uncapped it. He took a deep swig and said, "Better already."

He returned to the living room to find Veronica sitting on the couch waiting for him. He sighed deeply, then said, "Okay, let's get this over with. What?"

Veronica said, "Let's eat dinner first, shall we?"

"What are you softening me up for here? Whatever it is, let's get to it. If we're going to have a fight, I'd like to get it over with, so I can go to bed."

"Okay. At least come sit down with me here," she said, patting the couch.

When Christopher was settled and had another swig, he gave her an impatient "let's go" motion with his right hand.

All right. Let's see what every ounce of pride I've ever had tastes like on the way down.

"I know I haven't been a very good wife."

"Well, it's my fault too. I didn't do a very good job of finding out what kind of wife you were going to be."

Veronica lowered her eyes and stared at the couch until the flare of anger in them faded away.

"I deserve that." *You unspeakable bastard.* "We haven't been doing well, and I know it's my fault."

"Amen to that," Christopher said, toasting her with his beer. Then, he softened a little. "Ah, hell, Ronnie. I just never thought you would be as difficult as you are. You're just a kid, though, and I know that." He reached out and touched a lock of her hair, the first time he had touched her in weeks. "Your red hair should have given me the first clue. And, I admit, I should have done a better job in helping you figure out how to be a better wife, so it's part my fault, too."

Dear God, please give me the strength to get through this without burying a butcher knife in his sternum.

"But, it's not too late, is it? I can still be a good wife." Veronica batted her beautiful green eyes and reached for Christopher's hand. "Tell me it's not too late."

"Where there's life, there's hope."

Veronica leaned over and kissed him like she meant it. "Come on, I've got a special dinner made for us."

While Christopher got another beer out of the refrigerator, Veronica dished up dinner.

When they sat down, Christopher looked down at the roast on his plate, raised his eyebrows at Veronica and said, "Ketchup?"

She jumped up and quick-stepped to the fridge for the ketchup bottle. *How good would it feel to smash this bottle right into his smug face?* When she set it down beside him, she said, "Sorry, honey. I forgot."

The best that can be said of the rest of the dinner is, Veronica made it through without committing murder.

After dinner, she got a third beer for Christopher and suggested he sit on the couch. She hurried into the bedroom, took off all her clothes, and slipped the kimono on. She let her hair down so it was loose around her neck. She stopped in the bathroom and spritzed on the perfume Christopher had gotten her on their first anniversary.

She walked self-consciously back into the living room, her bare feet sensitive against the carpet. She stopped and adjusted the kimono so it showed a bit more cleavage. Christopher had turned the television on. *Dr. Kildare* was playing, but Christopher wasn't watching. He was staring at the floor, rolling his beer bottle back and forth contemplatively.

Veronica walked quietly into the room. Christopher stared at her for several seconds as if he didn't recognize her. Then, he jumped slightly and nearly dropped his beer.

Veronica sashayed in front of him, turned off the television and clicked on the stereo. The tone arm dropped, and after a hiss of static, Elvis Presley's *It's Now or Never* played.

Five minutes later, they laid across the mussed sheets of their bed.

Christopher fell immediately into a contented sleep. Veronica, contented as well, smiled into the darkness.

Mission accomplished.

Chapter Twenty

There were no home pregnancy tests in 1962, but as soon as Veronica missed her next period, she was sure. Nonetheless, she scheduled an appointment with their doctor the next week to confirm. She did not tell Christopher about the appointment.

After the doctor took the blood sample from her, he asked, "Shall I call you with the results?"

"Is there any way I can wait?"

"Why don't we do this," he said, consulting his watch. "It's almost noon. I'll turn this in to the lab at the hospital on my way to lunch and ask them to put a rush on it. Then, I'll pick the results up on my way back. If you come back around 1:30, Nancy will have it for you at the front desk."

"Wonderful. Thank you, doctor. We've been so anxious, I appreciate it."

"This baby would be good news, then?"

"The best."

Veronica left the clinic and noticed she was in the same part of town as Artie's. *I haven't had an Artie's burger in years. When I find out I'm pregnant, I'll have to start eating healthier, so let's have one last splurge.*

She climbed into her blue Volkswagen Beetle and drove the half mile to Artie's. Their first fight had been over whether she could continue to work there. She had won that battle, but lost the war.

Christopher had been so angry about it, she had put in her notice a few months later. She had rarely been back.

Artie's was nearly unchanged. The only difference she noticed immediately was that the KMFR tower had been taken down. A car had backed into it while Scott Patrick was broadcasting on Halloween night, 1961. He came down like Humpty Dumpty, but in this case, the doctors were able to put him back together again.

She parked the VW and decided to eat inside. She walked up to the window and was happy to see Zimm himself behind the counter, taking orders. "Still here, huh Zimm? You're going to be a lifer."

"I feel like I've already been here several lifetimes. What can I get you, kiddo?"

"Kiddo, huh? What are you, five or six years older than me?"

"I was once. Every year behind this counter ages me ten years, though, so, you do the math."

"Poor Zimm. DJ isn't here today, is he?"

"DJ?" Perry Zimmerman scratched at his cheek. "No, he left not long after you did. Haven't seen him for years."

"I guess it's just you for old timers' day, then. I am dying for an Artie burger, fries, and a Coke, please." She opened her purse and took out her pocketbook.

Zimm held up his hand. "It's on the house on old timers' day." He winked at her, said, "You look good, Ronnie," and disappeared toward the grill.

Veronica nodded and smiled at the young carhop who came through the door with a tray of food, headed for the parking lot. *That girl looks so damn young. I know I'm still young, too, but this life, this living a lie, is wearing on me. I feel ten years older. It will all be worth it when Sarah gets here, though.*

This last sentence was like a mantra to her, repeated dozens of times each day.

Zimm himself brought her food out to her. "Glad to see you, Ronnie. You should stop in more often."

"I might be along, asking for my old job back one of these days."

"All you've got to do is ask."

Veronica realized she was sitting at the same table she had been at right after she had woken up in 1958. That day, she had been jealous over Lisa Berry being out with Danny Coleman. Then, Christopher Belkins pulled up the next day and changed everything.

I haven't had too many happy days since then. Sitting here, with Sarah inside me again, I can say that I am happy. Everything is finally falling into place. It's going to be a challenge being subservient to Christopher for another two years until I get pregnant with Nellie, but it will all be worth it.

She sucked on her straw until it rattled her ice, looked down and saw she had cleaned the entire basket. *Guess I was hungry. Pretty sure I'm eating for two, even though one of us is only the size of a walnut.*

She glanced at her watch. Almost 1:00. The thought gave her butterflies, and she hurried to her car. She arrived back at the clinic in two minutes, so she sat in the car, nervously tapping a rhythm against the steering wheel while she waited.

When she couldn't wait any longer, she hurried inside.

A woman was standing ahead of her at the counter, filling out papers. When the lady behind the counter saw Veronica, she asked the first woman to sit down to finish the paperwork. When Veronica stepped forward anxiously, the woman said, "Mrs. Belkins?"

"Yes."

"Doctor said you might be anxious for this. She handed Veronica an envelope that said, "Middle Falls Medical Clinic" in the upper left hand corner. Her name had been typed in the middle.

"Oh, that's very official," Veronica said, giggling a little bit.

She walked back to the car on shaking legs. She sat behind the wheel, holding the envelope and said a little prayer. "Please Lord. I am trying so hard to do the right thing. Please, please, bring my Sarah back to me. I know I let her down last life, but if you look inside my heart, you can see how I feel." She hesitated, looking for more words, but settled for, "Amen."

She blew a puff of air up toward her bangs, then slid her finger along the sealed envelope. Inside was a piece of onion skin paper with a small note attached. She skipped the note and pored over the onion skin. There were dozens of possible tests, but finally her eyes fell on the one she sought.

Pregnancy. Beside that single word, there were two check boxes—positive, negative. An X was typewritten just off center of the "positive" box.

She finally looked at the note. It was in Doctor Graham's almost illegible handwriting, but she finally puzzled it out. "Contact Nancy at your first opportunity and we'll get you in for a full exam."

Exhilaration coursed through Veronica. *Thank you, thank you, thank you.*

Chapter Twenty-One

V eronica sat in the VW, unsure what to do next. Everything she had worked for since she had woken up in 1958 had pointed toward this moment. Now that it had arrived, she didn't know what came next.

Not much I have to do, I guess. She rubbed her hand across her stomach. *Grow this beautiful little girl, but that happens on its own. When do I tell anyone? Who do I tell? Not Christopher. I'll tell him when I'm ready. Ruthie, maybe? Mom?*

She backed out of the parking lot and drove straight to her childhood home. It was midday, so Wallace was at work and Barbara was at Middle Falls High. Doris's car sat in the driveway, though, so Veronica pulled in beside it.

She walked into the house without knocking, saying, "Mom?"

"In here!" she said from the kitchen

"Sorry to drop in so unexpectedly," Veronica said. She clutched the test results in her hand.

Doris laughed. "You know you never need to call ahead. Want something to drink?"

Veronica shook her head. Doris took one look at her face, and said, "Is everything okay? What's going on?"

In answer, Veronica held out the paper.

Doris accepted it with a frown, then reached for her reading glasses she wore on a silver chain around her neck. She peered through them at the paper for twenty seconds, trying to make sense of it. Finally, she saw the result. Her eyebrows shot up.

"Really?"

"Yes. Just had the test this morning."

Doris threw her arms open and enveloped Veronica. "Oh, a baby! How wonderful." She held her out at arm's length. "Is it wonderful?"

Veronica nodded, a brilliant smile breaking out on her face.

"I know you and Christopher have had some problems. Marriage is never easy, and a baby won't fix a bad one, but it will certainly make for fun holidays for us! Who have you told?"

"Only you, Mom. I'm on my way home from the medical center right now. I'm not going to tell anyone else yet, so don't tell Dad or Barb, okay?"

"I understand. That's smart." She glanced away, then reached for Veronica's hand. "I never told you, but I lost a baby when I was three months along."

"Oh, Mom! I never knew."

Doris nodded. "I know. I don't like to talk about it. But that's why it's a good idea not to shout it from the mountaintops so early. It makes things easier if something terrible happens. There's plenty of time for announcements and baby showers in a few months." She looked Veronica over from top to bottom. "You're so thin, honey. You're going to look like a rope with a knot tied in it. I'm going to have to fatten you up a little. You don't know your due date yet, do you?"

"No, I need to make an appointment to go in for an exam soon. Maybe they'll give me a date then." *I could tell you this beautiful little girl will arrive in our lives on May first, but I think I'll keep that to my-self.*

Doris hugged her again. They had almost never hugged when Veronica lived at home, but everything was more comfortable between them now. "Thank you for trusting me. Don't you worry, we'll take care of everything."

You always do, Mom.

THE NEXT FEW MONTHS passed quite happily for Veronica. She had gotten adept at pretending to be a Stepford housewife around Christopher, and he had responded predictably. That was, after all, exactly the marriage he had always envisioned. He came and went when he pleased, and Veronica did her best to always have a hot meal ready for him whenever he came home. She spoke when spoken to, no matter how it galled her.

She let Ruthie in on the secret one Saturday when Christopher was off playing golf. They were sitting at the kitchen table, which actually was an honest-to-goodness kitchen table now.

Ruthie was working as a lunch cook at Middle Falls Elementary. She still lived at home with her mother, and didn't have a lot of prospects for anything else. After she saw how Veronica's marriage with Christopher had evolved, her own single life seemed perfectly fine. They were drinking tea and looking out the kitchen window at the maple leaves blowing around the yard.

Ruthie squinted at her in the way she always did when she knew something was up, but she couldn't quite put her finger on it. "Something's going on with you. You seem a little too happy. Did your doctor prescribe some of those happy pills for you?"

Veronica put a long-practiced expression of complete innocence on her face.

Ruthie's eyes flew wide. "You're pregnant!"

Veronica's mouth fell open. "How did you know?" She glanced down at her stomach. "Am I getting fat?"

"Hardly. You were trying so hard to look innocent, that I knew you weren't, and it popped into my head." Ruthie looked around, though she knew they were alone in the house. "Does Christopher know?"

"If I don't serve it to him on a plate or pour it out of a beer bottle, he doesn't see anything."

Ruthie looked thoughtful. "So ..."

"So, nothing. I'm having a baby at the end of April or beginning of May. I'm thrilled."

Ruthie shoved her glasses up the bridge of her nose and stared keenly at Veronica, who looked placidly back. "Huh. Okay. A baby then. That's exciting, right?"

"It is. I can't tell you how long I've been waiting for this."

QUIETLY, VERONICA HAD begun using a tiny bit of her grocery money to buy a few things for Sarah—a rattle, a teething ring, a bib. She kept them at the back of her underwear drawer, but took them out to look at them several times a week. It helped her get through the months of waiting for Sarah to arrive.

EVERYTHING CHANGED on the second Tuesday of November. Veronica woke up with a pain in her abdomen. *Uh-oh. I've completely avoided morning sickness, just like I did the first time I had her. Is this the start of that, or did I eat something I shouldn't have yesterday?*

Christopher was already up and in the bathroom, getting ready for work. Typically, she got up and made him his breakfast, but on this morning, she didn't feel up to it. When Chris came back into the bedroom, she held up a hand in warning and said, "I think I might be catching something. Better not get too close to me. Can you make your own breakfast this morning?"

Christopher took half a step back and held his breath. "Sure. I'll grab something on the way to the office." Like a flash, he was gone.

Veronica lay back down with a groan, closed her eyes, and slept. When she woke up again a few hours later, she felt better. *Whew. Good. No idea what that was, but I'm glad I'm on the other side of it.* She slipped out of bed and padded into the bathroom. Sitting on the toilet, she noticed a small amount of blood in her underwear.

Veronica's hand went automatically to her mouth. *That's not good.* She pulled her pajama bottoms up and hurried in to the living room. She called her mom. As soon as she answered, she said, "Mom, I'm spotting. How bad is that?"

A few seconds of silence stretched out. "It doesn't necessarily mean anything. Some spotting can be normal. I did with Barbara, but not with you or Johnny. Maybe we should take you into see Dr. Graham?"

Veronica considered. "No. Let's wait. I feel better now. I think it's probably nothing."

"Let's do this. I've got a casserole in the freezer I can bring over. I'll toss together a salad for you, and you can have that for Christopher's dinner. That way you can rest today."

Veronica thought about resisting, but decided against it. "Thanks, Mom. I think I'll do exactly that."

"You rest, I'll be there soon."

An hour later, Doris walked in to find Veronica lying on the couch. She took one look at her, put the casserole in the refrigerator, and said, "We're going to the hospital."

"Mom, I don't need to. And, I'm still in my pajamas."

"Hospitals see people in pajamas every day. You're not going to shock them." As she said this, she put her arm behind Veronica and helped her to sit up, then stand up, albeit shakily. "Where are your slippers?"

"In the bedroom."

Doris glanced down the hall, then looked at Veronica, judging the likelihood that she would be able to stand on her own. She let Veronica sit back down, then hustled down the hall, returning moments later with her slippers.

"I miss when the magic used to move me."

Doris looked into Veronica's eyes, but she didn't seem feverish.

"What do you mean, Ronnie?"

"Like when I was a kid, and I would fall asleep in the back seat of the car, or on the couch, while I was watching a movie. I would get sleepy, fall fast asleep, and then the next morning, I would wake up right in my own bed, safe and sound."

"That was just Dad and I carrying you, sweetie."

Veronica nodded. "I know, I know. I just miss it."

Doris put her slippers on, put an arm around her and helped her to her car, then on to the emergency room.

Chapter Twenty-Two

Six hours later, Dr. Graham stood with Doris McAllister, outside the hospital room Veronica shared with an old woman who was recovering from bladder surgery.

Dr. Graham wore a serious look. "I'm sorry, Mrs. McAllister. I ran a blood test. She's no longer pregnant."

"Oh, oh no," Doris said, looking over the doctor's shoulder at Veronica.

"She's still young. A single miscarriage is nothing to be concerned about."

Doris closed her eyes for two seconds, then impaled Dr. Graham with a stare. "That is easy to say, coming from a man who will never suffer through one." She dismissed him. "Thank you, doctor."

Graham disappeared as quickly as he could.

Doris stepped inside the hospital room. Unlike a twenty-first century hospital room, filled with electronic equipment, monitors, IVs and breathing machines, this room was simply immaculately clean, quiet, and bright. Although Doris walked on cat's paws, Veronica sensed her presence and turned toward her.

The terrible question that she did not want to ask was answered silently by the expression on Doris's face. Veronica closed her eyes tight and turned away for a long time. When she finally forced her eyes open again, Doris, the hospital, and the truth she didn't want to face were all still there.

At that moment, Christopher appeared in the door. He burst into the room. "What's going on here," he asked in a stage whisper that was too-loud in the still room.

Doris grabbed him by the elbow and led him into the hallway and down a few doors. They had an animated conversation that didn't reach Veronica's ears, and she was thankful for that.

Now what? Every single thing I've done since I've woken up here was to bring Sarah and Nellie back, too. I did everything I could. Planned everything. And now, she's gone. If she's gone, I'm sure that means Nellie's gone, too. They're gone forever, and I know I will never see them again.

Hot tears streamed down her face.

Something was against this. That's why it's been like trying to push a piece of string uphill. Why, though, God? Do You hate me? Did You put me back here to test me, and somehow I've failed You?

She shook her head vehemently.

No! I did everything. She turned her head to look at Christopher, who turned his head at that exact moment and met her eyes. *I hate you, Christopher Allen Belkins. I never want to see you again.*

Christopher and Doris, still deep in conversation, walked down the hallway, moving further away from her.

I don't want to be here anymore. I won't be. She stood, ignored the pain she felt in her abdomen, shucked off the hospital gown and stood naked in the room, not caring that anyone passing by could see her. She stepped to the small closet, retrieved the pajamas she had arrived at the hospital in, and put them on quickly. She grabbed her house slippers and put them on too.

While Christopher and Doris were distracting each other, Veronica turned the other way, hurried down the stairs at the end of the hall and immediately got lost. She turned down one corridor, another, and another, but finally found a door that led outside. She walked around the side of the hospital and toward the busy street.

She wanted to run and run and never look back. She rushed onto the hospital's circular drive and directly into the path of an ambulance. The ambulance driver jumped on his brakes, but there was no way to stop in time. It hit Veronica on her right side, knocked her out of her slippers and threw her thirty feet away, where she landed with a sickening thud on the pavement.

She lay on her back, staring up into the gray sky, trying to understand what had happened to her, when the pain from her broken bones broke through her shock.

Oh God, oh God. Please take me away from here.

Chapter Twenty-Three

Veronica McAllister opened her eyes with a grimace of expected pain. A paperback book fell from her lap. Her hands flew to her face.

It took her two full beats to realize she was no longer lying on the pavement in front of Middle Falls Hospital in 1962.

I'm here again. I started over. Same place.

Low-slung, orange couch. A television set that no longer looked so retro to her eye. Two bookshelves filled with knick-knacks and *Reader's Digest Condensed Books.*

Is this it for me, then? Am I doomed to live my life over and over, starting in this same spot each time?

She reached down and absently picked the book up off the floor, setting it on the couch beside her. There was no need to make an investigative tour of the house. She knew exactly where and when she was.

What does this all mean? If I have to live this life over and over, I will go crazy. Will the universe even care, or will I just continue to live the same life anyway?

Veronica leaned back against the couch. The physical trauma of the miscarriage was completely gone. The emotional impact lingered. *So. No matter what I do, no matter what sacrifices I might be willing to make, Sarah and Nellie are lost to me.* She put her hands together as if to pray, and touched them to her lips. *Wherever you are, I pray you will find a mother who will love you as I do. Please forgive me.*

She gathered herself, walked to the hall closet and grabbed her coat. She sat back down on the couch and slipped the paperback into her coat pocket.

Every damned thing I did for these last four years is gone, then. Mom. You and I are going to be right back at square one again, aren't we? This time, though, I know the secret to unlocking that sticky lock. You want to be needed, and to help.

Headlights briefly illuminated the inside of the living room as a car pulled into the driveway.

And you, Christopher Belkins. If I see you again, I will tell you exactly what I think, you pompous, overbearing—

The front door opened, interrupting her mini-rant. A smiling man and attractive woman walked in, fresh, once again, from an evening out.

"Well," the man said, "how was he? A monster like usual?"

"Oh, you," the woman said, lightly batting his arm. She turned to Veronica. "Don't pay any attention to him, dear. "James, can you pay Veronica and give her a ride home, while I check on Zack?"

"Sure, sure. No problem," he said, although he was only half-listening. He walked around the living room, inspecting, then went into the kitchen. Veronica followed a few feet behind him and saw that he was counting the beer bottles.

No sir. I don't believe 1958 Veronica would have drank any of your beer, and I know that third-time-around Veronica didn't either.

James Weaver came back into the living room, pulled out his wallet, and said, "Let's see ... "

"Twenty five cents an hour, and fifty cents after midnight, so $1.75," Veronica said.

James raised his eyebrows, chuckled a little bit. "Right. Right you are, Miss McAllister. Let's round it up to two dollars. Good babysitters are hard to find."

Things start out essentially the same, but I can change whatever I want, and the ripples will spread out from there. I can be anyone, or anything I want.

James handed her two one dollar bills and said, "Ready?"

Ten minutes later, James dropped Veronica off at the curb in front of her childhood home. It didn't have the same awe-inspiring impact it had the previous time this scene had played out. She had seen this house just a few days before.

Well, I'm here. I have a feeling that if I found another ambulance to step out in front of, I'd be right back here again. I might as well figure out how to do things the best I am capable of.

She pushed the door open quietly and slipped her shoes off. She tiptoed back to the calendar she knew was hanging over her mother's small desk. *Work tomorrow. That's just as well. It will be good to see everyone again. I need to stay busy.*

She walked quietly to the stairs and put her foot on the first riser when she sensed she was being watched. Her mother stood at the top of the stairs, her old blue robe covering her night clothes. Her hair was in curlers.

Unexpectedly, the sight of her mother caused the deep well of grief she was trying to suppress, bubble up. *Oh, Mom. I acted selfishly, and too quickly. Did I leave you back at the hospital, looking for me, then finding my broken body in the drive? I'm sorry. I was in such pain.*

Veronica stepped quickly up to the second floor. She didn't say a word, but enveloped her mother in a hug and laid her head against her neck. She whispered, "I'm sorry, Mom."

Doris held her at arm's length. "Sorry? Sorry for what? Are you all right? Did something happen?"

Veronica felt tears welling, but did her best to smile through them while shaking her head. "No, nothing, Mom. Everything's fine. I've just been thinking a lot. I know I've got to work tomorrow, but on Sunday, after church, would you maybe show me a few things in the kitchen? I really want to learn how to cook." *Disingenuous, maybe, but it will be nice to be with her, even if I already know the things she's teaching me.*

In the semi-darkness of the hallway, Doris's eyes went wide. "Well, of course. Is there anything in particular you want me to show you?"

"Everything. I love you, Mom. Goodnight."

Veronica slipped into her once-again familiar bedroom, took off her clothes and got her pajamas out of her bottom drawer. She looked at her skirt, then hung it up, but dropped her sweater into a small hamper. She set her alarm clock for 9:00 a.m. and slipped into bed.

It's a fresh start. Let's make the most of it.

A moment later, she was asleep.

Chapter Twenty-Four

The alarm clanged to life at 9:00 a.m.. Veronica fuzzily threw an arm out to shut it off, but instead knocked it to the floor. It danced and vibrated shrilly. She picked it up, shut it off, and rubbed her eyes.

What is it about being reincarnated, or time traveling, or whatever I'm doing, that makes me sleep like that? She cast her eyes upward. *Hey, God, if you're up there, I sure could use an instruction book. Right now, I'm kind of stumbling along without one.*

She jumped in the shower to clear her head, got dressed and headed downstairs to find Wallace McAllister heading out the front door, golf bag over his shoulder.

"Bye, Daddy. Have fun golfing. Knock 'em dead, or break a leg, or whatever it is you're supposed to do." She kissed him on the cheek then walked into the kitchen.

"Ronnie?" her father asked.

"Uh-huh?"

"Nothing," he said, shaking his head. "Just not used to seeing you quite so chipper on a Saturday morning. Your mom will give you a ride to work, but I'll come get you when your shift's over."

Veronica smiled at him. "Don't worry. I won't forget. I'll have your special delivery waiting for you."

Wallace ducked a little and looked around the corner for Doris, but she was still upstairs. "Shh!" he said, but he was smiling. "See you then, kitten."

"Oh, and Daddy. I don't know if I ever remembered to thank you for getting me the job at Artie's. I love working there."

"Sure, Ronnie, glad to have done it." He shook his head a bit, as if he didn't recognize this new being in front of him.

Veronica poured herself a bowl of Cheerios, splashed some milk in.

She had finished eating and was washing her bowl, when Doris came into the kitchen. She seemed to be stepping into an unfamiliar situation.

"Good morning?"

"Morning, Mom. Do you want me to give Barb a lift to school for her drill team practice? I'm sure you have a million things to do, other than chauffeur us around."

Doris's eyes narrowed as she ran this through her brain, looking for any possible reason for this strange behavior. When none came, she nodded. "And, you have to be at work by noon?"

"Yes, ma'am. I thought maybe you could drop me off at Artie's on the way to pick up Barb when her practice is over. We'll have to leave a few minutes early, but I don't mind."

Doris nodded numbly. She was being out-efficiented by her daughter. That was unprecedented.

"Okay, great," Veronica said, drying her hands on a dishtowel. "I'll go check on Barb and make sure she's ready to go. We've got to be there by 10:00, right?"

Another numb nod.

Veronica stepped to her mom, kissed her cheek, and said, "Why don't you relax and have another cup of coffee, Mom. You look like you could use it." Veronica whistled to herself as she went upstairs to get Barb.

VERONICA'S FIRST DAY back at Artie's was less stressful than in her last life. It had only been a few years since she had worked there, instead of six decades. She remembered what her job was, who everyone was, and managed to called the fry cook "DJ" instead of "Dimitri."

In the middle of her shift, Danny Coleman pulled in again in his parent's wagon, Lisa Berry once again by his side. *I feel for you, Lisa. You're in the passenger seat today, feeling snug and happy, but you'll be tossed out soon enough. It's the way of the world.*

Veronica delivered the tray to Danny and Lisa, then took her break. DJ made her another "Ronnie Special," and she sat in the dining room, eating her burger basket and drinking her Coke. Just as she had done the previous life, she watched Danny and Lisa. They were listening to music, laughing and eating.

What do I want in this life? Knowing what I don't want—Christopher—only goes so far. Do I want to be alone? Make it on my own? Blaze my own path? Or would someone like Danny be a good partner to have? He has always seemed sweet, I know he's got a good career ahead of him, and that's a good start. That's jumping way ahead, but stranger things have happened. I think I can make it happen, if I put my mind to it.

She noticed that Danny and Lisa were done, so she hopped up and tossed her own leftovers in the garbage, then retrieved their tray. *I remember this day so clearly from last time through. Now, everything is close to the same, but slightly different. It's like an echo returning from a distant canyon.*

THE NEXT DAY, SHE GOT up early and went to church with her family, then hung around the kitchen for a few hours, getting pointers from her mother. She learned how to season and care for a cast iron frying pan. How to make her secret marinade for chicken—beer was the secret ingredient. How to make perfect-every-time pie crust. The fact she already knew these things didn't detract from her joy in having her mother teach them to her again.

After she and Doris had the kitchen cleaned up, Veronica said, "I'm going to walk over and see Ruthie. I'll make sure I'm back in time for dinner, though."

"Ruthie? I haven't seen her in so long. I thought the two of you must have had a falling out. She was always a sweet girl. Say hello to Mrs. Miller for me."

I guess we did have a falling out, in a way, but I made up for it once, and now I've got to start making up for it again. I want to make sure all the things I fixed last time will stay fixed this time.

The scene with Ruthie played out essentially as it did the first time. Mrs. Miller was pleased to see her, Ruthie wasn't, but by copping to her past sins, she and Ruthie began to rebuild the bridge of trust.

As she walked home from Ruthie's toward a homemade dinner she had helped prepare, she had time to think.

I learned a lot last life. I just needed to give some people a chance. Mom wanted to help, but didn't know how to go about offering it. I don't know what drove Ruthie and I apart, but whatever it was, she was willing to forgive me. She shoved her hands deep in her jacket pockets. *But then, there are people like Christopher. There's no saving people like that.*

She turned left on McGillicuddy, toward her house.

If there was a way to make things work with Christopher, I couldn't find it. Is it that we're incompatible, no matter what? Or was he so infected with that privileged image of a 1950s male ideal that he would only accept a partner he could control? I don't know, but I'm not going to worry about it again. If he can't help me bring Sarah and Nellie back to life, he's useless to me.

She opened the door to home, and the smell of a pork roast filled her nostrils.

No matter what, I'm starting to figure things out.

Chapter Twenty-Five

V eronica's first day at school was also easier this third time around. She was frustrated she didn't remember her locker number, or her combination. She had to go through the whole charade of pretending it was stuck again.

This time, when she got the numbers—Locker 426, combination 22-8-31—she vowed to memorize the numbers and tuck them deep into her memory. *If I'm going to have to go through this life again and again, I've got to make it easier on myself. The only thing I take with me when I go back is my memory, so I've got to get better at remembering things. Especially things I need to know, like my locker combination. Maybe other things, too.*

She was walking toward first period, but stopped dead in her tracks. *For instance, what if I learned how to read the stock pages in the newspaper. I could figure out what stocks are going to be the very best every year, and make smart investments. I won't be able to memorize too many, probably, but maybe one or two for each year might be enough. It won't help this life, but if I'm stuck doing this over and over, it would be nice not to have to worry about money.*

She floated through the rest of the day, listening to lectures and doing schoolwork she had already done a few years before. *School would actually be fun, if I was learning something new. I was never all that interested in college before, but I think I want to do that now. If I learn something, I'll get to take that with me too, if I start over.*

At lunch, she stopped by the school counselor's office. The solid wood door was half-open and had a small sign on it that said, "Mr. Harris." The inside of the office was somewhat dark and dingy, with the overhead fluorescent lights turned off. The crowded desk was lit only by a goose-necked desk lamp. Veronica knocked on the half-open door. "Mr. Harris? Do you have a minute? Can I ask you a few questions?"

Charles Harris was also slightly dingy, in his worn sweater vest and pince-nez glasses. He was bent over a file, reading something, but looked up and peered at her owlishly. "Of course. Come on in. What can I help you with?"

"I haven't filled out any applications for college, yet, but I want to go. What can I do about it now?"

"It's getting pretty late in the game. Colleges have been accepting people for months, now." Harris stood up and turned to a three-drawer filing cabinet behind his desk. He looked at Veronica with a blank expression, then snapped his fingers and said, "McAllister, right? Okay, let me see where you are."

He riffled through a drawer, shut it, and then moved to the drawer below it. A moment later, he pulled a file folder out and returned to his desk. He opened it and ran his finger along several columns.

And there it is. The legendary permanent record. Dum dum DUM! I wonder if it has that time I got in trouble on the playground in third grade. Veronica wiped a hand across her mouth to try and keep from smiling too broadly.

"Well, your grades are fine. Not great, but good enough. Through last semester, you had a 3.25 grade point average. If you were to get all A's for this semester, you might bump that up a bit. What do you have for extracurricular activities? Have you held any student government offices?

"No."

"Any clubs that you were an officer in?"

I have no idea. Not that I remember.

"No."

Harris turned in his chair and looked at Veronica. "Let me ask you. What do you want to do?"

"I'm honestly not sure yet."

"Nursing? Teaching? Maybe accounting? Companies are always looking to hire a good bookkeeper."

"Is that it? Is that the full spectrum of choices for me? What if I want to be a doctor, or an attorney, or start my own business?"

Harris gave a small shoulder shrug. "If you wanted to be a doctor, I would expect better grades than this."

"And for me to be a man."

"Not absolutely, no. But, I'm going to be honest with you. For you to get into a college with an aim toward medical school, you would have to be better than the boys who are trying to get in. I don't see that here."

Veronica nodded. *I don't think the ceiling was made of glass in 1958. I think it was reinforced concrete. But, I haven't helped myself, either. If I wanted to go to a great school, I would have had to work a lot harder than I did. I needed grades that were better than just 'keep Mom off my back.' I have to take responsibility for that.*

"There is another avenue you could consider. Middle Falls City College is a good school. You could go there for two years and get an Associate's Degree in something you're interested in. Then, if you studied hard and got good grades while you were there, you could go on and finish up at a four year school."

That is not a terrible idea. I'm sure Mom and Dad would let me stay with them while I was going to school. I could keep working shifts at Artie's to pay for things, then I could decide in a few years what I want to do.

"Do you have an application for that?"

"Of course." He opened the top drawer in his desk and pulled several pieces of paper that were stapled together out and handed it to Veronica. "You won't have any trouble getting in, though. They'll be glad to have you."

"Thank you, Mr. Harris."

On the way back to her locker, she saw Danny Coleman, talking to some friends outside the boy's bathroom. He was the very picture of a fifties-era high school dream. He was tall and well-built, his dark hair in a crewcut, wearing his red and black letterman's jacket, adorned with patches for football, baseball, and track.

As she passed the group of boys, she veered slightly to brush right by Danny. She said, "Hey, Danny," in a low voice.

Danny's head snapped around and he watched her continue on down the hall.

"Hey, Danny," one of the other boys mimicked, and the others laughed.

"Whatever, doofuses. Are pretty girls walking up to you to say hi?"

They had to admit, they were not.

Chapter Twenty-Six

Veronica rode the #12 bus to Artie's after school, went in through the back entrance, and changed into her uniform.

When she walked into the grill area, Perry Zimmerman saw her and said, "Gosh, is it that late already? How time flies when you're having fun." He glanced up at the Coca-Cola clock, and said, "Grab something quick, then you're on. We're a little shorthanded today. Lilly called in sick."

"Sure, Zimm. Do you want me to start now?"

Perry looked at the mostly-empty parking lot, and said, "No, go ahead. I'll need you at full strength before the night's over."

"Aye aye, Cap'n," Veronica said, and wandered over to the grill where DJ had just a couple of buns and burgers on.

"Well, if it isn't Middle Falls answer to Susan Hayward."

Veronica blushed slightly, then dropped the smallest of curtsies.

"What's new with you, DJ?"

DJ began to work his magic on a burger for her. "Just trying to live up to the heavy responsibility that comes with being Middle Falls' greatest fry cook. Hey, did Zimm say Lilly isn't coming in today?"

"Sure did. Why?"

"No reason."

There's obviously a reason.

Veronica tilted her head to the right, then reached out and tickled DJ right in the ribs.

"You should know better than to try and lie to me, DJ."

DJ handed her the basket. A slight panic was on his face.

Reality dawned. "Oh, my gosh. You're sweet on Lilly. Well, I don't blame you. She's a wonderful girl."

With a hint of desperation, DJ leaned in close, and said, "Don't tell her, K?"

"I won't, but you should. If you don't, some rich guy in a convertible will come in and scoop her up one of these days." *Since that's exactly what I remember happening.*

Veronica took her meal out to the dining room and looked at it.

So simple. A burger and fries. And yet, I could eat this every day. Every day. At least until I get a little older and the middle-aged spread starts in earnest.

She gulped the meal down much faster than her mother would have approved of, then hustled off to work. The parking lot was filling up.

Just before the sun set and the whole drive-in was lit by the golden light of a fading spring day, Danny Coleman pulled in and parked. When Veronica saw him, she waved and smiled as she went about her duties.

A few minutes later, she delivered his food.

"Thanks, Ronnie. And, thanks for saying hi at school today. That was nice."

"I heard your friends giving you a hard time. Sorry."

"No, nothing to be sorry about! Busting on each other is what we do."

"Oh, good. I didn't want to be responsible for it." She turned to go back inside.

"Hey, Ronnie?" he said to her retreating back.

Veronica slowed and looked over her shoulder. "Yes?"

"What time do you get off?"

"I was supposed to get off at eight, but Lilly called in sick, so I'll bet Zimm's going to want me to close. Thanks for reminding me. I better call my Dad and tell him not to come pick me up until then."

"Umm," Danny said. He had the look of an eight year old boy asking for a cookie, not the starting quarterback on the football team. He squinted at her. "I could give you a ride home, if you don't want to make your dad come out so late."

Veronica considered this. *Would Mom be okay with that? Would Dad be okay with missing his bedtime burger?*

"I'll have to call home and check. I'll let you know before you get done with your food."

Veronica hustled off and found she was several orders behind already. "Hey, Zimm. Are you going to need me to close tonight?"

"I hate to ask you. I know it's a school night, but do you think you could?"

"Can I use the phone to call home and see if it's all right?"

"Sure, sure. Take these orders out, then you can use the phone in my office."

Perry Zimmerman's office had once been a janitor's closet that Artie had converted into a space where Perry could do his paperwork. Veronica slipped behind the tiny desk, picked up the phone and dialed home. *If Zimm ever gains a few pounds, he won't be able to get behind his own desk.*

When Doris answered, Veronica said, "Hey, Mom? We're down a carhop, and Perry asked me if I could work until about 9:15 instead of 8:00. Is that okay?"

"How much homework do you have?"

"I had some Geometry, but I got it done in sixth period."

"That's fine. I'll have your father come by then."

"Mom, do you remember Danny Coleman? His parents are Stan and Eve, and his brother was friends with Johnny? He and I are friends, and he's here right now. He said he can give me a ride home, if that's all right."

"Friends, huh?" A few seconds of silence, as Doris weighed her options. "I suppose that will be all right. You're almost ready to graduate. I want you home by 9:30, though, understood?"

"Sure, Mom, if it's going to be later than that, I'll call."

"Don't call. Just be home by 9:30. Understood?"

"Yes, ma'am."

Veronica hung up the phone and on the way to pick up new orders, she saw Perry. "Mom said I can stay, Zimm."

Perry flashed a quick smile and a thumbs-up as he took an order at the window.

The next order was a delivery right next to where Danny was parked. *Perfect. I can tell Danny he can give me a ride home at the same time.*

She grabbed the tray and went first to Danny's station wagon. "My mom said I can get a ride home with you ton—" she cut off in mid-sentence when she saw the new Thunderbird sitting next to Danny's car.

"Ronnie? You okay?" Danny asked.

Veronica had momentarily lost the power of speech. *I knew I would see him eventually, but I wasn't ready for it.* She remembered she had been in the middle of a sentence. "Yeah, I'm fine." She shook her head a bit. "Do you still want to give me a ride home?"

"Yes. What time?"

"We close at 9:00, but it takes me a few minutes to go through the closing procedure. Maybe 9:15?"

"Perfect. Okay, I'm gonna head for home, then, but I'll be back." Danny put the wagon into reverse and backed out. When he did, there was nothing between Veronica and the Thunderbird. She realized she was still holding Christopher's tray.

He rolled the window down and started to speak. Before he could, Veronica said, "Let me guess. New car, so you don't want the tray on the window."

Christopher looked slightly abashed, but smiled, and nodded.

"That's fine. Here's your food," she said, handing it through the window. "That's forty cents."

Christopher looked at her a little strangely, caught off guard by her abruptness. Nonetheless, he reached for his wallet, pulled out a dollar and handed it to her. "Can you just give me back two quarters?"

Veronica handed him his food, accepted the dollar, and clicked out two quarters and a dime and handed them to him.

"Here," he said, handing her back the dime. I meant for you to have this."

"I don't want anything from you, Christopher Belkins. Not now, not ever." She turned and left a confused young man in her wake as she went to deliver the rest of the orders that were stacking up.

WHEN 9:00 ROLLED AROUND, Perry Zimmerman turned off the neon overhead sign. That was the signal to all denizens of Middle Falls that they would have to wait until at least 11:00 a.m. the next day to get their hamburger fix.

It had been a long, long day for Veronica. First day back at school—again—a meeting with the guidance counselor, flirting a little with Danny, and finally, telling Christopher off. *Even if he was completely confused by it, it still made me feel better.*

Veronica moved around the small dining room with a round tray that had containers of salt, pepper, and ketchup, filling the smaller containers on the table. There were no plastic ketchup dispensers at Artie's—only real glass bottles, so she also carried a small funnel to fill them. She was halfway through the task when she noticed Danny's station wagon pulling up. She gave him a wave.

"Is that your ride?" Perry asked.

"Yep."

"No Dad tonight?"

"No, my slave driver boss made me work past his bedtime, so I had to rely on the kindness of strangers."

"Funny girl."

Veronica finished setting everything up for the next day. She wrote her time down on her time card—*Don't want to miss out on that extra dollar!*—and said goodnight to Perry and DJ. They would be there for some time, counting down the till and cleaning the grill, respectively. She went out the front door and found that Danny had pulled his car around so he was waiting right outside the front door.

As soon as he saw Veronica, he hopped out of the driver's side and opened the passenger door. He didn't make a show of it, like Sir Walter Raleigh laying his cape across a puddle. He just did it.

"Thanks, Danny."

A few seconds later they were at the edge of the parking lot. They idled for a few seconds, then Danny leaned his head slightly toward Veronica. "Which way?"

"Oh! Right! You don't know where I live."

"Nope. My brother Jack was friends with your brother, but I never knew where he lived."

"Turn left here. I'll give you directions."

Danny put his blinker on and checked both ways again, even though there hadn't been a car along in several minutes.

My Mom would love you.

A few minutes later, he pulled to the curb in front of Veronica's house. He looked appraisingly at the house, then at the neighborhood. "Nicest house on the block," he said.

Dad's gonna love you, too. Are you just too perfect, Danny Coleman?

Danny didn't turn the car off. He looked straight ahead for a few seconds, then said, "Can I ask you something, Ronnie?"

Veronica glanced at her watch in the glow of the dashboard. "Sure. I've got to make sure I'm inside in the next five minutes, or Mom will come out here and drag me inside."

Danny chuckled. "I won't take long, I promise. Prom is in three weeks. Will you go with me?"

You telegraphed that one, Danny boy.

"What about Lisa? You two looked very cozy on Saturday. Why aren't you taking her?"

"Honest?"

"Honesty is always better with me."

"I was going to ask her. We've kind of been going out, but nothing too serious. She's a nice girl, and all, but we broke up yesterday morning. Plus, I've always liked you, ever since freshman English, when you sat beside me and helped me with my papers."

Way to go, first-time-around Veronica.

"I think that was an honest answer. Thank you. Yes, I will go to Prom with you."

Danny's face lit up. "Great! Okay, we can talk about it at school tomorrow, then?"

"Sure. 'Night, Danny." Veronica leaned over and kissed him on the cheek, then ran up the walk to her house.

Chapter Twenty-Seven

Things proceeded apace in this third pass through the late 1950s for Veronica McAllister. She and Danny did go to Prom together. The theme that year was *Middle Falls – A Garden Paradise*. Because both she and Danny had jobs that kept their schedules full, Prom turned out to be their first date, and both were a little nervous. Danny picked her up at home. It wasn't the social occasion that it had been when Christopher had come to dinner, but it was still a rite of passage. Danny nervously pinned her corsage on the dress her mother had made, and Wallace took pictures with his Viscount Coronet camera.

They both had a good time at Prom, hanging out with Danny's friends, because Ruthie hadn't been asked. Of course, they didn't have *too* good a time. Doris McAllister had volunteered to chaperone the affair. It didn't take long for three wayward boys to discover there would be no shenanigans on her watch. One sly attempt at spiking the punch had landed three of them in Prom jail.

The time between Prom and graduation was a blur. Still, Danny and Veronica found a few stray evenings to spend together. It was a challenge because of her job at Artie's and his baseball games and working at his parents' store. Veronica found Danny to be many things that Christopher had not been. Even though he was an athlete, he was gentle and kind. He was also so honest, she learned not to ask him a question if she didn't want to know the answer. He was also quiet, stolid, and a little unimaginative. Like all of humanity, he was a mixed bag.

There were clouds on the horizon for the young lovers-to-be, as well. Danny had been accepted into the University of Portland, where he planned to study business. Portland was only a few hours north of Middle Falls, but it was much too far for him to drive every day. That meant he would be staying on campus. Veronica, meanwhile had been accepted at Middle Falls Community College and would be staying at home.

That left them two options—to break up before they got started, or attempt a long-distance romance.

One evening in the dog days of late August, they went for a drive. Veronica packed fried chicken and potato salad into a picnic basket and they found a quiet spot near a small country church outside of town. She spread a checked tablecloth and got the food and two bottles of Dr. Pepper out.

"Hitting the hard stuff, huh?" Danny said when he saw the pop.

"This is the downside to dating an athlete—no beer on dates."

Danny raised his eyebrows. "Would you rather have a beer?"

"No, silly boy. Just teasing you. If I was left alone for a week in a beer factory, I would still wander around and look for the pop machine."

"Ronnie. I need to talk to you about something. I leave for college in a few weeks. I'll still be coming home on some weekends, and on holidays, though."

"Right," Veronica said, handing him a paper plate with chicken and potato salad with a plastic fork stuck in it.

"I know it's hard, but I don't want to see anyone else when I'm away at school. I like you, and I don't want to lose you."

"You are the sweetest boy, Danny Coleman. I like you, too. It's easy to get swept up in things and get overwhelmed with it while we're here, so close to each other."

Veronica dished up her own plate, then set it down in front of her. She looked at Danny and reached out to stroke his hand.

"But, when you get away from Middle Falls, I think things might be different. You are the most honest person I've ever met. I know you wouldn't do the wrong thing, but I don't want to put you in that position. The truth is, I think we might have a future together. But, I think we'll mess it up if we try to do it straight through. I think sometime over the next few years, you'll meet someone up there. It will seem so tempting to go out with them, but you won't. That's the kind of person you are. But, it will make you resent me, eventually, and then we'll have a fight one weekend when you're home, and we'll break up."

Danny opened his mouth to object, but Veronica held up a hand. "Just a minute, then I'll listen to whatever you want to tell me, okay?"

Danny nodded.

"I don't want us to break up, now or then, but I don't want you to feel frustrated and unhappy, either. So, just know this. While you're away, I want you to do whatever feels best to you. If you want to wait for me, that's great. If you don't, though, that's great, too. No guilt either way. In four years, you'll be done with college, and you'll come home to run the store. When you do, let's get together and have dinner to celebrate. During dinner, we can talk about our future if you want. Does that sound fair?"

"Sure, I guess. What does that mean for you? Are you going to wait for me?"

"I can't tell you, because I don't know. Maybe. I might. But same thing—no guilt either way, right?"

"I'd still like to see you when I come home. What about that?"

"As long as you call me each time you get home, we'll keep seeing each other."

Danny stuck his lower lip out and nodded. "Hard to find anything to argue with."

"I know, I got an A in Debate."

"Okay. You've got a deal. I'll keep calling you when I get home from school."

DANNY WAS AS GOOD AS his word. He called Veronica on each of his weekend visits home all through his freshman year. He came to dinner at the McAllisters, or had Veronica over for dinner with his parents. They ate out at Artie's, or went to whatever was playing at the Pickwick, or just went for a drive. They were happy and contented.

Two months into his sophomore year, Danny came home for a weekend visit.

He didn't call Veronica.

Chapter Twenty-Eight

Veronica enjoyed her classes at City College. They were interesting enough, but not terribly challenging. About a month after she had last seen Danny, her mom mentioned she had seen him at the gas station. Veronica knew what that meant. Even though she had been preparing for that eventuality, she was still a little down, because she had grown to care about him. She hadn't exactly been sitting by the phone, waiting for him. She still had her job, but she got lonely from time to time. That loneliness was exacerbated by the fact that, in one way, she truly was alone. There was no one she could ever completely let her guard down with—not even her Mom, or Ruthie.

Veronica rang in the end of the fifties with Ruthie and her family watching Guy Lombardo play *Auld Lang Syne.* Doris even let the girls each have a small glass of champagne, even though they weren't quite twenty-one yet.

In June, Veronica graduated from Middle Falls City College with an associate's degree in accounting. After graduation, she went to a celebratory dinner at Burl's Steakhouse, once again with her family and Ruthie. Life was quiet, but as Veronica knew, quiet wasn't the same as bad.

In mid-July, 1960, Veronica found a job as a bookkeeper for a family-owned chain of tire shops. Neither the work nor the product were glamorous, but the people were wonderful and the paycheck was steady.

The full-time job at the tire shop meant she had to finally give her two weeks' notice to Zimm at Artie's. As he had been in her previous two lives, he was sorry to see her go.

As soon as she got enough money saved up, she bought a car and found a small, one-bedroom apartment.

The first night in her own place, she sat on the second-hand couch in the quiet apartment. She didn't even have a radio yet, let alone a television set. As she sat, she took stock.

My own place? Check. Learned a new skill? Yep. Boyfriend? Nope, and none on the horizon. So, then, is this what life is? A perfectly-good, but not exciting job, hanging out with Ruthie on the weekends, and saving up to buy a television to help me pass the time? There's got to be more to this life than this. I've been given a second, and then a third chance. There's got to be a reason. I have no idea what it is, though. I need to decide what I want.

As time passed, both customers and the guys who worked at the tire company asked Veronica out. She was too pretty to never be asked, but too remote and unattainable for anything to ever come of it. She would go on a few dates, find the spark of a wet sponge, and both sides would decide to move on.

This is starting to feel a lot like my first life. Work, home, work, home.

Her good work at the tire shop was recognized, and after a year, she was given a promotion and a raise that went with it. She decided to splurge by finally getting rid of the ugly, uncomfortable couch that had been hers since the day she had moved in.

She called Ruthie. "Want to go pick out a new couch with me?"

"The excitement of our life never fails to amaze me. The saddest thing is, this will be the highlight of my weekend. Where do you want to go?"

"There's only one place in town. Coleman's."

"Hoping to run into Danny?" Ruthie teased.

She knows how to ring my chimes. "Hoping *not* to run into Danny, thank you very much. Not much chance of that, though. He's still away at school. I think we'll be safe."

An hour later, Veronica had picked Ruthie up at the small house she still shared with her Mom, and they pulled up in front of Coleman's Furniture. It was a two-story brick building right in the middle of downtown. There were no crazy slogans painted on the windows in bright colors, just nice, solid furniture groupings that would appeal to the nice, solid citizens of Middle Falls. Camelot might be blooming in Washington D.C., but Middle Falls was still stuck in the Eisenhower era.

They walked in and were slightly overwhelmed at the size of the place.

"I think it's bigger on the inside than it is the outside," Ruthie whispered.

They wandered past the upper-end living room displays that all featured price tags Veronica couldn't dream of paying, even with her new raise. Veronica saw a young man dressed in a short-sleeved shirt and a tie. He had a black name badge clipped on his shirt pocket that said, "Todd." When he saw the two young women wandering, obviously lost, he smiled and approached them.

"I know, it can be a little overwhelming, can't it? Almost too many choices, I think."

Veronica plucked a price tag on a green couch beside her, and said, "It's more the prices that are overwhelming. I thought I could afford a new couch, but now I'm not so sure."

Todd nodded. "I understand. Coleman's always likes to put its best foot forward, so these are our best pieces at the front of the showroom. We do have some more modestly-priced couches back this way, if you'd like to follow me."

"Modestly-priced couches, for modestly-priced girls," Ruthie leaned in close and whispered.

Veronica shot her a look, and they followed Todd as he wound through one set of furniture after another. *Designs are changing, but I can't say it's for the better. Oh, well, gotta stay up with the times, no matter how tragic the fashion of those times might be.*

Finally, Todd arrived at an area of the store where the ceiling was dropped down a bit, giving a feeling of slight claustrophobia to everything. In the front showroom, everything was lit by the gentle glow of table lamps, but here, it was strictly overhead fluorescents. All the furniture was arranged by type, instead of completely put-together rooms.

"Ah," Veronica said. "I think we've arrived at my budget. Most important question. Do you deliver?"

"There's always free delivery at Coleman's furniture, yes."

"Great. You won't mind if I live in Eugene, then?"

Todd's face fell, but Veronica let him off the hook. "Just teasing, Todd. I live in the Rivercrest apartments, a couple of miles away."

Veronica sat down on a tan couch that looked staid and boring, compared to the brighter colors around it. *I think I like this one. It won't be out of fashion as quickly as the rest of these.* She looked at the price tag. $49. *A little more than I wanted to spend, but I can swing it.*

"That couch is a good choice. It looks even better with you sitting on it."

Veronica's head snapped up. Todd had melted away, and Danny Coleman was standing in his place.

Chapter Twenty-Nine

"Hello, Danny." Veronica shifted in her seat. "I thought you were still off at school." Veronica's words were calm, but her heart was beating a trip hammer rhythm in her chest.

Danny hadn't changed. He was still tall and lean, with his hair still neatly cut into a short crew cut. He looked a bit older because of the white, short-sleeved shirt and tie he wore while working in the store.

Danny shook his head. "Dad had a heart attack a few weeks ago, and he isn't able to work. It looks like he might not be able to come back at all. We're just glad we've still got him with us. But, it left us short-handed, so I came home to help out. If he's able to come back to work, I'll go back to Portland and finish up my last semester. If not, it's not that big a deal. I've learned everything I need to learn. I'm only missing the degree, and I don't really need that."

"So sorry to hear about your dad, Danny," Veronica said, trying to gracefully get up from the couch and failing to do so. "He's a nice man."

Danny nodded, thoughtfully, and reached out a hand to help her up. "I've been back for a few weeks. I meant to call you, but ..." he trailed off, unable to finish the sentence.

Veronica laid a gentle hand on his arm. "Hey, don't worry about it. No guilt, remember? That's why we did it this way. You're a good person, and I never wanted to be a source of bad feelings for you."

"I know, I know. You're right. And still, I feel it. It's not your fault. You were the absolute best about it, and that makes me feel worse still."

Veronica laughed a little. "There's no way around this Judeo-Christian guilt we feel, no matter how adult we try to be, is there?"

"I guess not. Are you seeing anyone?"

"A few people, but nothing serious. I've been keeping it light." *Not to mention, keeping it boring.*

"I was wondering if you would go out to dinner with me?"

Veronica tilted her head, considering. "You left your girlfriend back in Portland, then?"

"No. Didn't have a girlfriend. I mean, I did for a while, but that ended a few months ago." Danny sighed, a rueful smile playing across his face. "It didn't end well."

Knowing you, Danny Coleman, that likely means she cheated on you somehow. And now, the small-town girl back home, steady and dependable, looks pretty good.

Veronica stood toe to toe with Danny. His 6'2" towered over her 5'5. Somehow, he seemed the smaller of the two.

After another moment's consideration, Veronica said, "When?"

A broad smile broke out on Danny's face. "Is tonight too soon?"

"No, tonight is fine. I live over in the Rivercrest apartments. B-3. I'll go out to dinner with you if you'll throw free delivery in on this couch," she said, nudging it with her toe.

"We offer free delivery on everything we sell."

"I never said I was a tough negotiator."

DANNY PULLED INTO THE Rivercrest Apartments a little before six. He had long since traded in his parents' wagon for a sleek 1960 Corvette. The car growled as he rolled slowly past the building, looking for B-3. Veronica spotted him from the window and came out to meet him.

"So, where do you want to go? The world is our oyster. Well, at least, Western Oregon is our oyster. If you want Paris or London, you're probably with the wrong guy. Want to drive up to Portland? Eugene? Salem? You name it, and off we go."

"So many choices. Let's see. I'll take," she paused and looked out the window, letting suspense build, "Artie's."

Denny did a double-take. "No, not really?"

Veronica nodded emphatically.

"If you don't want to leave town, we could go to Verrazano's Ristorante, or Burl's Steakhouse."

"Oh, okay, I thought you meant it when you said it was my choice. That's fine then, you choose."

Danny held his hands up in surrender. "I know when I'm beat. All right, Artie's it is."

Ten minutes later, they turned into Artie's. It was a Saturday night, and the KMFR tower hadn't fallen yet. Scott Patrick was up high, broadcasting the greatest hits of the early sixties to the steady stream of cruising teenagers.

I wonder if I could change that bit of history. What if I spent my Halloween night standing guard over the tower. Would I prevent it from getting hit, or would I get smooshed in the process? Questions for another day. For this day, I have to figure out what to do with this sweet, earnest young man.

Danny ordered for both of them—exceptionally easy to do when there are so few choices on the menu. He splurged and got both of them a chocolate shake to go with their burgers and fries.

They sat in companionable silence, listening to the Everly Brothers playing on both the car radio and from the loudspeakers outside. Once they had finished their dinner, Danny said, "How about a drive before I take you home? That's the real reason I wanted to drive somewhere else. I just wanted to spend more time with you."

Veronica giggled. "The easiest thing to do is to just tell me that. Of course we can go for a drive. I'm at your mercy." *Another man might take that the wrong way, but not Danny.*

He sat at the edge of the parking lot, waiting to merge into the steady stream of teenagers cruising the loop, laughing and honking. "I feel like I'm so much older than these kids."

"You are a premature old man, Danny Coleman."

Eventually, they merged and quickly got off the loop, onto other surface streets. Veronica didn't pay any attention to where they were driving. She laid back and closed her eyes, enjoying the feel of the powerful engine and letting Danny drive. After a few minutes, she looked around and realized Danny had brought them back to the same small country church where Veronica had set him free.

Danny turned the engine off. He shifted his lanky frame around in the seat so he could look directly at Veronica. "I've been coming back out here every time I came home. I think this is where things went south for me. Ronnie, you're the sweetest, nicest girl I've ever met. I know we've barely talked for the last few years, but I could never forget about you."

He glanced away, nervously, then focused on her.

"I always get a little flustered when I look at you. But, here's what I wanted to say. Veronica McAllister, I think I love you."

Chapter Thirty

Danny did not rush into a marriage proposal like Christopher had. He preferred to take things slower, consider them from all angles. Still, from that first dinner date at Artie's, neither of them saw anyone else, and they spent more and more time together. They never spoke again about the time they were apart.

They dated steadily for a year and a half, and Danny decided he would pop the question on Christmas Day, 1963. Then, Kennedy was assassinated in Dallas that November, and the whole country went into a funk. He decided to wait, as he didn't want that pall hanging over the beginning of their new life.

Instead, he waited for her birthday in March. Her birthday was on a Wednesday that year, so they didn't have any big plans. Danny had asked her to go to Artie's for a burger basket—their special place.

When he came to pick her up, he couldn't wait any more. He got down on one knee in her living room, opened the small black box, and said, "Ronnie, will you? Will you make me the happiest man in America and marry me?"

Veronica did not immediately jump and squeal, and say, "Yes, yes, yes!" Instead, she smiled sweetly at Danny, sat down on the couch, and patted the cushion beside her. "Let's talk a little first."

Danny's face fell. A talk was not what he had expected.

"What, Ronnie? Have I done something wrong?"

"No, you absolutely have not. I want to marry you. I do. But, I want us to have an understanding first."

"Okay. Sure. Anything!"

"I've been at the tire shop for a few years now, and I like working there. But, even if I should choose to leave that job someday, I'm going to want to keep working somewhere else. I need to know if you're going to be okay with having a wife that works."

That sat Danny back a bit, and he didn't answer immediately. "I didn't know you would want to keep working."

"That's why we're having this conversation now."

"So, you *want* to keep working? I figured you worked to pay the rent. After we got married, you'd stay home and take care of the house." He blushed a little. "And the kids, when they arrive. I'd work to pay our bills."

The mention of kids was a small stab in Veronica's heart.

"I know it will keep me busy, trying to work and keep up a house and dinner on the table. I like to be busy, though, and knitting circles and bridge groups aren't for me. When we have kids to worry about, I'll reconsider then."

Danny shifted on the couch, clearly uncomfortable that his big moment had come to this. "I thought I'd be borrowing your phone to call Mom and Dad and tell them you said 'yes' right about now."

"You still can, but don't you think it's better that we work this out in advance, instead of having it be a problem after we're married?"

Danny nodded, slowly. "But, you do want to marry me?"

"Yes, honey, I do."

His face brightened with a sudden idea. "Hey! How about this? Instead of working for the tire store, why don't you come handle the books at the store? Then we could see each other all the time, and have lunch together, and that would be great, wouldn't it?"

Veronica hesitated. *This is hard for him. I guess it was hard for any young man in this era. Their mothers hadn't worked, and they feel like it's a mark against them if their wives do. But, if I work for the family business, he can justify that somehow. But, I remember how things changed for Christopher and I. Good at first, then worse and worse. If it gets like that for Danny and I, will seeing each other all the time really be great? I can't go into something thinking it's going to fail, though, or I should say 'no' to the whole thing right now.*

Veronica reached out and took Danny's hand. "Yes, that would be great. Thank you for thinking of it. I love you. I'd love to be your wife."

THE BEATLES HAD INVADED America and youth culture took another giant step forward. The country would never be the same. Danny Coleman, a man built for the 1950s, maintained his steady approach, and his crew cut. He was the last person under the age of forty in Middle Falls to give up that particular haircut.

Veronica and Danny's wedding was bigger and more formal than either of her weddings to Christopher had been. As the owner of one of the biggest businesses in Middle Falls, when a Coleman son got married, it was a social occasion.

By the time of the wedding, Danny's father, Stan, had recovered from his heart attack enough to go back to work. It was hard to tell who was more excited about him getting out of the house—Stan himself, or Danny's mother, Thelma. The smart money was on Thelma, who was thrilled to have her house to herself again during the day.

When the last handful of rice was thrown on their wedding day, Veronica and Danny left on a honeymoon trip to New York. Neither of them had ever been to the east coast, or seen a city the size of New York. They took a horse-drawn carriage trip through Central Park, rode an elevator to the top of the Empire State Building, ate hot dogs in Washington Square Park, and climbed the dizzying spiral staircase to the top of the Statue of Liberty.

When they had arrived in New York, they thought they would never be able to fit everything they wanted to do in seven days. On the evening of the sixth, as they walked in a drizzling rain, back to their hotel, Veronica said, "It was a wonderful time."

"What? Seeing Fiddler on the Roof?" Danny shifted his umbrella to make sure no rain hit Veronica.

"Well, yes, it was a dream come true, seeing that on Broadway." *Can't tell him I owned first the VHS tape, then the DVD of the movie starring Topol. It was a thrill to see Zero Mostel do it. I think I could move to Greenwich Village, and take a bus up to the theater district and see a different play every night, and I'd be happy.* Then, a vision of buttoned-down Danny, living in the Village and rubbing elbows with the beatniks popped into her mind and she couldn't help but giggle a little.

"What? What's funny?"

"Oh, nothing. Just the thought that no matter how wonderful a trip is, it will be even better to get home and get moved in to our new house."

They had closed on a nice house in his parents' neighborhood a few days before the wedding,. They had decided to wait until they got back from the honeymoon to spend their first night there.

"I asked Dad to have someone drive over and turn the heat on, so it's not freezing cold when we get home tomorrow night."

"You are a thoughtful man, husband of mine." *And this can truly be our house, unlike when I moved into Christopher's and always felt like I was an intruder.* "I can't wait to get home and make our house a home."

Chapter Thirty-One

Veronica had given her notice at the tire shop a month before the wedding. She started as a bookkeeper at Coleman furniture the Monday after they got back from their honeymoon.

Her marriage to Danny Coleman was much better than either of her marriages to Christopher Belkins. But then, any cross-Atlantic ship that doesn't sink is better than the maiden voyage of the Titanic. The old saying is that a man marries a woman, hoping she won't change, while a woman marries a man, hoping he will. Veronica didn't want Danny to change, but she hoped that over time, they would develop more mutual interests—a hobby, books they both read, travel, *something*.

Instead, as the years passed, they drifted apart. Danny's father passed away from another heart attack in 1972, and Danny worked even more tirelessly to grow the business. He had dreams of expanding and turning Coleman's Furniture into Coleman's Department Store. Veronica continued to handle the books for almost ten years. Eventually, she came to believe that all she was doing was putting someone who needed work out of a job. That's when she decided to quit and stay home.

Over the years, there were never any harsh words between them, or fights, or even many arguments, but all the blood drained out of the marriage. Their life fell into habit. Routine. A day dissolved into a week, a month, a year, and soon the sixties were a thing of the past. Middle Falls stayed true to its small-town roots. Artie's remained the anchor of the Friday and Saturday night cruise in Middle Falls. The only thing that changed was that the cars were a little newer, and the music a little heavier.

Veronica felt lost, floating in a sea of indifference, holding neither a map nor a compass. She returned to Middle Falls City College and took some classes on "Women in Business" and "Understanding Poetry," but gave that up as a bad bit of business, too. She retreated to decorating the house and having coffee with Doris, Ruthie, or anyone else she could lasso. She thought of going back to Artie's and asking Zimm if she could get a job carhopping again. Again, though, she would only be taking a job away from some teenager who needed it.

Danny sat down on their beautifully-appointed living room furniture one Saturday evening in January, 1979. He said, "We need to talk,"

Veronica felt a sense of relief more than anything. *I don't know what's up, good or bad, but even something bad would almost be a welcome change of pace.*

"Ronnie, when I asked you to be my wife, I told you that you were the sweetest, best person I knew. That's still true."

Oh, it's this talk. I can't be too surprised. We haven't had a conversation about anything other than scheduling business trips, how dinner is, or what's on TV tonight, for years. This is where that leads.

"But," Danny continued, "it feels like we've both been growing in different directions for a long time. You have your Mom, and Ruthie, and your book club at the library. Meanwhile, I've poured myself into the business, traveling on buying trips, spending what feels like every waking minute at the store when I'm in town."

"You've been a good provider for us, and I appreciate that."

That stopped Danny cold. He sat with his hands between his knees, his head hanging down. "That's not enough, is it?"

"For a real marriage? No. That's a start. Not being mean to each other is a start. But, neither of those things is enough to make a happy marriage. I think a happy marriage should involve shared interests, and in the end, what do we really have in common? We've always liked each other, and I think we still do, but what else? These past few years have been more like living with a roommate than a husband. I'm sure it's the same for you."

"Children would have made a difference."

There's the rub. Why didn't we ever have kids? I had children before. Danny did too, in my first life. It should be possible for us to do it again this life, but it's never happened, no matter how hard we tried early on. Without that to build a life around together, we each built a separate life, instead.

Veronica's face softened. "Kids would have probably distracted us from having this conversation for another ten years, but we would have gotten here eventually."

She scooted across the couch and laid her head on his shoulder. "I'm so sorry, Danny."

That jarred him a little. "What do you have to be sorry about?"

Ah. So, it's like that then, is it? You have something to be sorry about.

"Just that I feel like I could have found a way for us to stay connected, and I didn't. So, there's someone else, then?"

"No, not really." He glanced quickly at Veronica. "Well ... "

Veronica held her hand up. A stop sign to that particular dark alley. "You don't need to finish that sentence. I do still know you. You aren't capable of doing something awful, like having an affair. But, the heart wants what the heart wants, and if you found somebody else, what's the first thing you would do? Pray about it, maybe talk about it with your mom. And what's the second thing? You would come to me to talk about it, because that's who you are." Unexpectedly, tears formed and fell. In a thick voice, she said, "And here you are."

Danny didn't speak, but his tears welled, too. He seemed truly torn, but eventually he nodded and looked at Veronica with guilty eyes. "Is this it, then?"

"This was the hard part. The divorce will be easy."

AND SO IT WAS. THEIR marriage had been as quiet as a museum at midnight for the previous decade, and their divorce was the same. Danny felt guilty, and offered to let Veronica have the house. As much as she loved it, she didn't need a three thousand square foot, four bedroom house. So, she suggested they sell it and share the proceeds, which they did. Between that, their shared savings, and her share of the portion of Coleman furniture that was Danny's, Veronica started the next phase of her third life with a nice little nest egg.

She didn't have to work for quite some time, if she didn't want, but that was just the problem. She didn't know what she wanted to do.

Chapter Thirty-Two

A number of things happened in October of 1979. Mother Teresa won the Nobel Peace Prize. The deposed Shah of Iran, Reeza Pahlavi, arrived in New York, an event that would have long-lasting consequences for both Iran and the United States. Charlie Smith, the world's oldest man, died at a reported age of one hundred and thirty-seven years old.

A week later, Vera Miller, fifty-nine, the widow of Mr. William Miller and the mother of Ruthie Miller, likewise passed away. Unlike the death of Mr. Smith, Mrs. Miller's death was premature and unexpected. She left for work on the morning of October 8th. She stopped at a red light at the intersection of Mayflower and Main, when an aneurysm in her brain burst. She died instantly.

Veronica spent the following weeks doing her best to put Ruthie back together again. She helped her arrange for the funeral and memorial service. She even stayed with her, so she didn't have the shock of living in a too-quiet house so suddenly.

By then, Veronica's divorce was final. The house she had shared with Danny was sold, and she, too, was at loose ends. Her bank account was fat, but her life was flat.

On Halloween night, she and Ruthie sat in the tiny living room in what was now Ruthie's house. They handed out candy to the ghosts, witches, and various ghouls who haunted the streets of Middle Falls.

"It's been a pretty lousy year so far," Veronica noted.

Ruthie nodded. "First your marriage, now Mom. I don't want to know what comes next."

"I'll tell you what's next. We're going to take charge of our own lives, that's what."

"We are?" Ruthie seemed doubtful.

Veronica took Ruthie's hand. "Yes. We are. That's it. And I think we should start changing our lives by you quitting your job as Lunch Lady Ruthie."

"What? Oh, no. I don't think I could ever do that. I've got bills to pay."

"Oh, right. A mortgage on this house?"

"Well, no. Mom had just managed to pay it off." The thought washed over Ruthie's face and she looked away.

"I know. I was here when we burned the mortgage paperwork in the barbecue. I'm asking the question to make a point."

Ruthie nodded, still looking away.

"Do you have a big car payment, then?"

"Come on, Ronnie. You know I don't. My car's been paid off for more than a year."

"Right. You're making my point for me. So, what are all these big bills you've got, then?"

"Well, I've still got insurance on the car and the house, the light bill, and I still have to eat."

"So," Veronica said, her excitement building, "if we were to sell your house and car, what would we have?"

"A homeless, unemployed bum?"

The doorbell rang and Veronica said, "Hold that thought." She jumped up, grabbed the bowl of candy and opened the door to a young boy dressed as a hippy. He was wearing striped bell bottoms, a leather vest, and what looked like his mother's wig. He flashed Veronica a peace sign and said, "Trick or treat, man."

Veronica chuckled and dropped a Tootsie Roll into his bag.

"I don't want to hold onto the thought of being a broke, unemployed, homeless person, you know."

Veronica sat down on the couch again and spread her hands in front of her as though she was sharing a magical vision of the future. "Think about this. You quit your job and sell your house, so you've got a little change in your pocket. My divorce is final and my house is sold, too, so I'm in the same boat."

"Homeless and unemployed?"

"Hush. No, footloose and fancy free. I think what we need is a break. You don't have to sell your house, of course. We could shut it up tight for a while. The grass doesn't grow in the wintertime, so you wouldn't have to worry about that. You could park your car in the garage, and everything would be good. This isn't some crazy, spur of the moment adventure." Veronica stopped, considered, then said, "Okay, maybe it is, but hear me out."

Another knock at the door, another candy delivery, this time to a tiny girl dressed like a fairy.

"I'm lucky to have more money than I need right at the moment. Not enough to never have to work again, but enough to not worry about it for a good long while. I want to get away. No. Wait. I *need* to get away. But, it will be absolutely zero fun to do that all by myself. So, I want you to come with me. The whole trip will be on me. I'll pay for our airplane tickets, our hotel, and as much booze as you want."

"Which would be zero. I haven't drunk alcohol since I threw up after drinking too much Boone's Farm in eighth grade." She shuddered at the thought of it.

"And that's fine, too. But think about it." She once again waved her hands like a magician conjuring a magic image. "Sun, sand, a cold, perfectly non-alcoholic drink sitting on the table beside us. We're slathered in suntan lotion and every good-looking guy in the area is checking us out."

The look on Ruthie's face said, *Well, maybe checking* you *out, but not me.*

"C'mon, Ruthie. Don't make me beg. Yes, we could do the sensible thing and wait until school is out. But, wouldn't it be fun to blow back into Middle Falls in the middle of winter and show off our tans?"

"I don't think I could sell the house—" Ruthie started to say, but was drowned out by Veronica's happy squeal.

"Yes! I knew I could be a good saleswoman if I put my mind to it!" She hugged Ruthie happily, and said, "Well, what are you waiting for? Go pack your bags!"

THINGS ARE NEVER QUITE that easy. Ruthie, who had been one of the lunch cooks in the Middle Falls Elementary kitchen for twenty years, didn't want to leave them in the lurch. When she told them she wanted to quit, they asked if she would give them until the Christmas break to find someone else, which she did.

In any case, as easy as Veronica made it sound to "shut the house up tight," the reality was it took a little planning. Ruthie made sure she had all her winterizing done. She didn't want to come home to burst pipes and soggy carpets.

Also, Veronica couldn't imagine telling her mother she was going to be gone over Thanksgiving and Christmas. Barb had been married for more than a decade, and she and her husband had two children. Johnny had been out of the service and living back in Middle Falls for longer than that. The holidays were a festive, fun time at the McAllister home, and Veronica didn't want to miss that. She made sure Ruthie was invited to every family meal and gathering. She knew there was nothing sadder than eating a can of cold pork 'n beans and watching the Macy's Thanksgiving Day Parade all alone.

By December 26th, though, all the loose ends had been tied up into bows, the tickets had been bought, and reservations made. Veronica and Ruthie hitched a ride to Portland with Doris. She always looked for an excuse to hit all the after-Christmas fifty percent off sales at Lloyd Center Mall anyway.

The three of them spent the day after Christmas hunting down bargains. Few things in life made Doris happier than finding Christmas decorations at half price, even if she wouldn't be able to use them for almost a year. They spent the night at a noisy hotel near the Portland International Airport. While being close to the airport made catching their plane the next day easy, it wasn't conducive to getting a restful night's sleep, thanks to the planes constantly overhead and the amorous couple in the room next door. The next morning, Doris dressed up in a warm sweater, coat, and gloves. Veronica and Ruthie put on bright sundresses, wide-brimmed hats, and sunglasses in anticipation of their flight to Acapulco, Mexico.

At the airport, Doris walked them to the gate, which a person could still do in 1979, an era unaffected by shoe bombs and planes flying into buildings. At the gate, Doris hugged both women and watched them walk toward the ramp to the plane. Just before they disappeared, Doris called out, "Ronnie! Ronnie!"

Veronica had to fight her way back upstream to her mother who stood, embarrassed and clutching her purse. "What, Mom?"

"Nothing. I'm being silly. For a minute, I wanted to get on that plane and come with you."

Why didn't I think of that? You definitely deserves a getaway. "That's not silly at all. I'd love that. We'll plan that trip as soon as we get back from this one."

"That would be wonderful. Okay, foolishness over." Doris smiled, made a shooing gesture at Veronica. "Go on now, Ruthie is waiting for you."

Chapter Thirty-Three

Acapulco was the trendy destination for jet setters from JFK to Elizabeth Taylor from the mid-fifties through the late sixties. By the week before New Year's Eve, 1979, the bloom was off that rose for most of the world. But, word of kidnappings, murder and a soaring crime rate had not reached small towns in western Oregon, yet.

Veronica and Ruthie didn't have a care in the world about being in the right place to see and be seen. They just wanted to find warm sandy beaches, work on their tans, and maybe dance at a discotheque. They craved a carefree, responsibility-free life for a few weeks. Then, they could head home to winter and the blank slate staring them both in the face.

They didn't touch down in Acapulco until after dark. That meant they couldn't see the promised ocean view from their balcony, but the sound of the surf softly crashing on the shore promised it was there.

Veronica twirled around in the middle of their room. "I swear, I could get used to living like this."

Ruthie opened the cupboards of the small kitchen attached to the living room, and said, "Hey, looks like we've got everything we need here."

"Ruthie, Ruthie, Ruthie, if you are thinking we are going to be cooking while we're here, you are out of your ever-lovin' mind. This is a vacation! We can pick up some fruits down at the Farmer's Market, but we are here to indulge. If I don't gain at least ten pounds while I'm here, I'll know I've done something wrong."

"I feel like I'm sponging off you," Ruthie said, walking into the living room.

"Let's reverse this. Let's say you had a bunch of extra money piled up in your savings account, and I was broke. What would you do? Go off to sunny Acapulco all by yourself?"

"No, you know I wouldn't."

Veronica took three quick steps toward Ruthie, threw her arms around her, and said, "Relax, my young friend."

"Stop it. You're three weeks older than me."

"As I was saying, my young friend, this is the time for us to live! So, what do you want to do first tomorrow? And, if you say, 'Go to the market,' I'm gonna haul you down to the beach in the pitch black and throw you in the Pacific Ocean."

"Lay out?"

"Yes! Lay out. Then, find someplace for a decadent lunch, order a drink with a silly umbrella in it for me, and look for cute men to ogle. Deal?"

"I love you, Ronnie," she said, laying her head against Veronica's shoulder. "I don't know how I would have gotten through this without you."

"You are much stronger than you give yourself credit for," Veronica said, kissing the top of her head. "Now, I'm off to get my beauty sleep, because that flight did me in."

VERONICA AND RUTHIE both slept in much later than they had intended, and woke only when the sun rose high enough to slant through both their bedroom windows.

"No way am I sleeping my whole vacation away," Veronica said. "Or, at least if I do, I want it to be while water is lapping at my toes.

Come on, I'll buy you a virgin Bloody Mary, and we can count the celery as breakfast."

Fifteen minutes later, they were in chaise lounges in front of their hotel. The promised Bloody Marys sat chilling on the small table between them.

Ruthie had a natural olive complexion, so she slathered herself in baby oil. Veronica, with her red hair and pale complexion, opted for the SPF 36. Still, after only an hour in the sun, Veronica was the first to feel the tingle of sunburn.

She lazily turned her head to Ruthie and said, "This trip will turn me into one giant freckle. I am perfectly fine with that. Freckles are cute, right?" She dropped her oversized sunglasses down the bridge of her nose and looked Ruthie over from head to toe. "I think I hate you. You're already tan."

"It's the luck of the genetic draw, Ms. McAllister," she said, putting the emphasis on the 'mac' in her name.

Not used to that, yet. I'd been a Coleman for so long, but it didn't seem right to keep it after the divorce. Not in Middle Falls, where that's like being named Kennedy.

"Hey, what are you saying, that we Scottish girls can't tan?"

"That's exactly what I'm saying," Ruthie said, undoing the strap on her top and rolling over onto her stomach with an "oof."

"I'm going to take a dip and cool off, then maybe we can hike up to where the cliff divers are?"

"Muscular guys in swimsuits performing feats of derring-do? Yes, please."

Veronica waded out into the blue water of the small lagoon in front of them, then shouted over her shoulder. "Oh, my God, Ruthie! Come in with me. It's like bath water!" She turned onto her back and kicked out from the shore. "I don't think two weeks is going to be enough," she yelled and turned to swim back. She picked up a towel back at her chaise and rubbed her hair. Ruthie seemed lost in her sun worship.

Veronica nudged her. "Come on, Miss-I-tan-don't-burn. Let's go slip a sundress or shorts on and walk over to the cliff divers. Miguel at the front desk said they'll be diving this afternoon."

"Okay, okay. Whatever happened to laying around all day and doing nothing?"

"That's on the agenda for tomorrow, I promise. I've just got all this energy today!"

Ruthie reluctantly rolled off the chaise lounge, took one last sip of her Bloody Mary, and followed Veronica back up the path to the hotel entrance.

They walked into the dim interior and were crossing the lobby toward the elevator, when they heard the man at the front desk say, "Miss McAllister. Miss McAllister!"

"I don't think *Ms.* has caught on in southern Mexico yet," Veronica whispered to Ruthie. "Yes?" she said, walking toward the front desk.

"There's a message for you. The man said it was urgent, but I didn't know where you had gone."

About 100 feet outside the front door. Thank God our lives didn't depend on your tracking ability.

Veronica reached for the note, which only had two words on it: *Call home.*

She hurried back to Ruthie, standing at the elevator, just as the doors opened. They stepped inside and pushed their floor number. Veronica unfolded the paper and, grim-faced, showed it to Ruthie.

"It's probably nothing," Ruthie said, but Veronica could tell she didn't believe that. It was just something empty you say when you have no idea what else to say.

They hurried to their room and were flummoxed by how to make an international call. Eventually, Veronica called the front desk and asked him to connect the call and charge it to her room. Each second of delay in making the call stretched out, until Veronica's nerves were stretched taut with worry.

Is there any reason Mom or Dad would call me here that isn't horrible? Why can't I think of one?

Finally, she heard a far-distant ringing. After three rings, her brother Johnny's voice answered.

"Johnny? Why are you at the house?"

"You need to come home, Ronnie. Mom and Dad are gone."

Chapter Thirty-Four

Flying on the red-eye flight to Portland that night, Veronica and Ruthie didn't speak. Ruthie held Veronica's hand and squeezed it from time to time, but there was nothing else she could do.

Other information, unimportant details in the grand scheme of things, had followed those initial two sentences that changed this life for Veronica.

You need to come home, Ronnie. Mom and Dad are gone.

Johnny hadn't told her many other details, just enough. A surprise weekend getaway. Slick roads. A horrible accident.

Mom and Dad are gone.

This isn't the way this life was supposed to turn out. I know things are different in each life, but no one has died when they're not supposed to.

Her mind pulled her inevitably to a mental image of her father's Cadillac, spinning out of control, going through a guardrail and plunging down an embankment, then slamming into a tree with incredible violence. Veronica did her best to push the image from her mind, but like a tongue seeking out a sore tooth, she kept returning to it again and again.

WITH RUTHIE, BARBARA, and Johnny to lean on, Veronica made it through the next few weeks. Barbara had inherited her mother's knack for organization, and took the lead on handling the near-endless arrangements.

The funeral was almost more than Veronica could bear. The church was filled, and the sight of the two white coffins, lined up side by side, tore at her heart. Time and again, she thought of Doris running up to her, calling her name as she boarded the plane to Mexico. *Had she known, somehow?* She couldn't reconcile how her parents, so alive and vibrant in her mind, were in those two boxes.

But of course, they aren't. They're gone on somewhere, too. Are they back in their youth somewhere, trying to figure out how to make Johnny, Barbara, and me happen again?

Once they got through the ceremonies that accompany death in America, the three siblings agreed that since Veronica was effectively homeless at the moment, she should stay in the family house while they prepared it for sale. As dear as it was to all of them, Barbara and her husband already had a home they loved. Johnny couldn't imagine living in such a large house as a perpetual bachelor, and Veronica couldn't stand the thought of living with so many memories, but none of the people who made them.

Veronica had a few arrangements of her own to make, then she had decided to spin the wheel again. *How many lives does it take to get something right? I thought Danny and I together would be the answer. The only answer was, it was a little better than my life with Christopher. But, there's got to be something more than that. I wanted to get away and think, and plan. Did that cause both Mom and Dad to die somehow? Did Dad know that Mom wanted to get away, and that's what made them take that unplanned trip? They weren't supposed to die for a long time. I thought I had more time with them. And, I guess I do, if I just start over again. I've got things to do, first, though. I have no idea what happens to these worlds I leave behind, but I want to do what I can.*

A week after the funeral, when everyone had gone back to their own homes, their own lives, Veronica kept an appointment with an attorney who specialized in family planning. It was a fast and simple meeting—she wanted him to draw up a will that would leave everything to Ruthie in the event of her death. It wasn't a fortune, but as frugal as Ruthie was, Veronica knew it would make a long and lasting difference in her life.

Her meeting with the attorney lasted fifteen minutes. He told Veronica it would take him a few days to draw the paperwork up for her to sign. That gave her those days to wander around Middle Falls and plan out what she would do if it all happened to her again.

In the course of this wandering, she stopped by the Middle Falls Library. If she had a few days to kill, she knew she would need a few more books to get her through.

This is one of the problems with living the same years over and over. I'll never see any new books published—only ones I missed the lives before. I'm going to have to expand my horizons, pick up some new genres.

She walked through the wide double doors of the library and inhaled that unmistakable smell of a building filled with books. Libraries of the era were still depositories for books—they hadn't evolved into row after row of computers, with people making travel plans, checking their Facebook, or looking for jobs. It was just books, magazines, and newspapers, and Veronica loved it.

There was a series of meeting rooms off the main hallway where book clubs or civic groups could meet. Outside one open door was a handmade sign. Across the top of the sign, it read: *Do you remember these?*

Below that were hand-rendered ink drawings of some unmistakable corporate logos—Google, Starbucks, Amazon, and Apple.

Veronica actually took two steps past the sign, not thinking anything of it, then stopped cold. The incongruity of the images cut through the fog of grief and snapped her to attention.

Wait. Hold on. None of those things will exist for decades yet. How am I seeing this?

Slowly, she approached the empty door. Inside the meeting room, a young man of maybe twenty, with longish, shaggy hair sat behind a table, reading a book. He was alone in the room. He was turned sideways, so she could only see the right side of his face.

"Hello," he said, turning to face her. "I'm Joe. Joe Hart."

Oh! Oh, you poor boy.

The entire left side of Joe's face was covered in a reddish-purple birthmark that extended from his forehead, across his nose, and all the way down to his chin.

His eyes acknowledged that it was normal for her to have a reaction to seeing him, but he didn't mention it beyond that.

"Nice to meet you. I'm Veronica McAllister."

"Do you have a group meeting here next? I know my time is almost up. What are you guys? Book club?"

Veronica shook her head, feeling like she was in a dream.

"Ma'am? Are you all right?"

"I think I need to sit down."

Joe jumped up and hurried around the table with another straight-back library chair. "Here, here. Sit down."

When Veronica was settled, Joe returned to his side of the table and began to pack up his few belongings to leave. When he had everything neatly stacked, he looked up at Veronica and said, "Wait. I assumed you were here for another meeting, because I've been sitting her once a week for months, and no one else has ever shown up. You don't remember any of those things on the sign out there, do you?"

Veronica nodded, but had difficulty gathering her thoughts. Finally, she said, "Google. Search engine. Amazon. The everything store. Apple computers, and Starbucks coffee. But, how?"

Joe's eyes lit up, and he jumped out of his chair so fast that it tipped over behind him. He pumped his fist like he hit a game-winning home run, then leaned across the table. He stared intently into Veronica's eyes.

"Hello, fellow time traveler."

Chapter Thirty-Five

"Sorry. That sounded cheesy, didn't it?" Joe said. "Like a line out of an old B movie or something. I should have had a smoke machine, or lasers, or something. I've been sitting her so long, I'd kind of given up on anyone like you coming in."

"So, you're like me, then? You..." Veronica paused, looking for a polite way to say "died," then went on, "passed away, then woke up back in your younger self?"

"I can tell you're the real deal, because that's exactly what happened. I died," he said, without elaborating, "then woke up when I was nineteen years old again." He looked Veronica over. "How old were you when you died and then woke up?"

"I was seventy-eight years old when I died, eighteen when I woke up. As you can see, I'm not that young anymore. I've been living this life for twenty years now, not that I'm doing a great job of it. But, how many lives is this for you?"

"How many lives?" Joe asked. "What do you mean?" He snapped his fingers. "You mean, if you die again in this life, you just start over somewhere again?"

"Apparently. At least, I did. Not *somewhere*, though. The exact same place."

"Holy Toledo. Like a save point in a video game. So, if I ran into traffic and got hit by a bus, I'd wake up where I did this time?"

"As far as I know, but I took that route once, and I don't recommend it. Those few minutes between being run over and starting over are extremely painful."

"How many times have you, umm, started over?"

"Twice. I'm about to make it three, though. See if my luck holds."

"Why?"

Veronica shook her head. "We obviously have a lot in common, but there are things I don't feel like talking about."

"I can respect that."

"My best advice is, don't count on things staying the same. Just because someone died in one time frame, doesn't mean they'll do the same this life. Everything changes."

Joe nodded. "I haven't been back here that long, but I've already noticed that things change. In fact, that's what I'm trying to do—change things. There are a lot of things I saw in my lifetime that I would have liked to change, and now, maybe I can."

"You mean things in your own life, or ... "

"Both. I mean, I've already changed some things in my own life, but there are other things that I'd like to fix, too."

Well, that's interesting. Am I too self-centered? Here I've been worried about myself, instead of what's going on in the world. But, then. But. Then. Veronica pictured huge happenings like JFK's assassination, or Martin Luther King's. *What could I do, one single woman, to change a situation like that. I admit, that would scare me to death. I can't even get my own life together, let alone try and change history.*

"I wish you luck with that, Joe. I mean it."

"It would be interesting to have someone else with me, helping me. Right now, there's no one else I can talk to. I literally don't have a friend in the world."

Veronica shook her head. "I don't have the strength. But, if I wandered by and saw your sign, maybe someone else will, too. For all I know, Middle Falls is crawling with time travelers."

Joe cleared his throat. "Have you, umm, you know, made yourself rich? It's not as easy as everyone would think, is it?"

"No, I haven't. And you're right, it's not all that easy."

"I suppose, though, if you are able to go back again and again, you could figure it out. My problem is, I never paid any attention to the stock market, so I don't know what to buy. I suppose I could buy land where Microsoft will eventually build their campus in Redmond, but that takes a lot of money to get started. But, if what you say is true and we start over again, a little bit of research now could go a long way when we were back there again."

That's true. A little study these next few days could do wonders when I get back to 1958.

"It could," Veronica said, smiling. "You've given me an idea. Thank you. I hadn't figured it out. Just because I know Apple is going to build the iPhone, or that Blu-Rays are coming, doesn't mean I have any idea how to build them. I'm not a technical person."

Something about Veronica's mention of Blu Ray players brought Joe up short. "You don't have to answer, but how far did you make it in your first life? What year was it?"

"2018."

"Oh, wow. 2018. That seems like an undiscovered future to me."

These conversations feel so delicate. He doesn't seem like the type to be offended, but still.

"How far did you make it, Joe?"

"Only to 2004. I'm guessing we probably didn't get the long-promised flying cars by 2018, then?"

Veronica smiled and shook her head. "No. I'm sure there were lots of interesting developments those last fifteen years or so, but I was tuned out. I had retired, and was barely eking out my day to day survival. Not much fun."

"You know, it's hard to stand here, looking at you, still young and beautiful, and think of you as an old retiree, getting by on social security."

Veronica's cheeks reddened a touch. *Young and beautiful? I'm old enough to be your mother.*

"I'd say that none of us that are walking this particular path are what we seem at first glance."

Joe nodded to himself. "You haven't met anyone else like us, then?"

"No. Honestly, I'd never even considered it. I thought this was just my own personal heaven or hell, whichever I manage to make of it."

Joe stared at Veronica intently. "I wish you'd change your mind. It's been lonely."

An image of her childhood home, standing empty and cold, popped into her mind. It was followed by the picture of that same home in 1958, smelling like her father's pipe, her mother's cooking, and the sense of life that had always filled the house.

"Thank you, Joe. You are very sweet. But I've got to go."

Veronica stood and hurried out of the room, the library, the parking lot.

Chapter Thirty-Six

The next few days, which had stretched out in front of Veronica like a jail sentence, became busy. On her way home from the library, she pulled into the local branch of a national investment firm. She walked into their office, filled with glass, brass, and thick carpeting, and was greeted by a pretty young woman sitting behind a reception desk.

"Hello," Veronica said. "Can I ask who is the most junior investment person here?"

The young woman opened her mouth to reply, then closed it. "Did you say most *junior* person? People usually ask for Charles Schwab himself."

"Yes. Well, that's not what I'm looking for. I would like to find someone who is just getting established, and I would like to pay him to do some research for me."

"Oh, you wouldn't need to pay him. We provide free research and advice to all our clients." She glanced down at an office roster and ran her finger down it, all the way to the bottom. "I think you're looking for Todd. Todd Bellamy."

"Yes. Todd will be perfect. Is he tied up at the moment?"

The young woman smiled. "No, he's not. He's available. Can I tell him who would like to see him?"

"Of course. Veronica McAllister."

The woman picked her phone up, punched a button, and said, "Todd? Ms. McAllister is here to see you."

Ten seconds later, a young man came bustling down the hall, full of curiosity and nervous energy.

I'm going to guess he doesn't get summoned to the front desk too often.

"Hello, I'm Todd Bellamy. Would you like to come back to my office?" He led Veronica partway down the hall and into a small office that was one step above a cubicle.

Todd squeezed in behind a junior executive's desk and indicated the chair on the other side.

Veronica slid in, and said, "I need you to do some research for me."

"Of course," Todd said, "Research and investment advice is what we—"

Veronica held her hand up. "I'm sorry, I don't have much time. Please allow me to tell you what I need."

"Of course, of course!" Todd said, pulling a legal tablet out of a drawer and uncapping a pen. "How can I help you?"

"I want you to pick one single stock that is the best possible investment for each year between 1958 and 1975."

Todd sat back in his chair, non-plussed. "I'm sorry?"

"Here's the scenario. If you had one thousand dollars to invest in each year between 1958 and 1975, knowing everything you know now, what would you invest in each year. One single stock only."

Todd pushed his hand through his already-thinning blond hair. "I don't understand."

"I don't expect you to. I know this is an unusual request, and it will take up some of your valuable time." Veronica reached into her purse, pulled out an envelope, and laid it on the desk. "I'm sure you normally work on a commission of some sort. I won't be investing at this time, so I'd like to give you this to do the research for me."

Todd tentatively reached across the desk, opened the envelope and gaped. He riffled through the bills, and said, in a quiet voice. "There's a thousand dollars here."

"Yes. I'd like to be able to stop back by and get that list tomorrow, which I know is a bit of a rush. Could you manage that?"

"Of—of course. Yes." He wrote *1958-1975. One stock per year.* On his pad. "Just to verify. You want to know the stock that would have performed the best within that single year. Not what would have necessarily performed the best beyond that."

"Excellent question. If you could add a date when each date could have been optimally sold off, that would be very helpful."

"I'll have this ready for you by close of business tomorrow."

VERONICA RETURNED HOME, and immediately couldn't stand the way her footsteps echoed in the empty house. She called Ruthie. "What are you doing?"

"What I'm always doing when I'm not hanging out with you—nothing."

"Good. I'll be there in five minutes. Get your shoes and bra on."

"I'll have my shoes on. No promises beyond that."

Veronica pulled up in front of Ruthie's house to find her sitting on her front porch. She ran out to Veronica's car and climbed in. "Heya, chickie. What's up?"

"I had this insane craving to go to Artie's, but it's been closed for years now, so we'll have to hit somewhere else. Have you eaten yet?"

Ruthie shook her head.

"Then off we go."

Just for nostalgia's sake, she drove the strip and by Artie's, even though she knew it was closed. *Zimm died of a heart attack, standing right behind the counter, like he always said he would. Now, it looks so sad and deserted. But, for me, very soon, it will be the same as it always was—fun, vibrant, and delicious. And, Zimm will be there, too. I can see where this restarting could get addictive.*

She turned around in Artie's parking lot and said, "Let's hit that new Italian place over by the freeway."

She reached out, grabbed Ruthie's hand and held it tight. *I'd say I'm going to miss you, but I'll be seeing you again soon, too.*

The new Italian place turned out to be just that—new. That was about all it had to recommend it, and they both wished they had gone to Verrazano's instead. *Newer isn't always better. In fact, it's usually not.*

The food was a little bland, but the company was good, and she and Ruthie chatted about everything and nothing, just like they always did.

The waitress laid a bill for $12.65 on the table.

Ruthie turned it toward her and her eyebrows shot up. "Holy heck! Twelve bucks for a couple plates of spaghetti and two Cokes? Inflation is crazy these days. Did I tell you I had to pay ninety cents a gallon to fill up yesterday? That's insane."

Veronica nodded, laid a twenty dollar bill on the table, and said, "Let's go."

"Did you tip that girl eight dollars?"

"Not quite, but close. That'll make her whole shift. What else can I do with that money that will make someone so happy?"

"Good point."

As soon as they got back in Veronica's car, she said, "I want to talk with you."

"Am I in trouble, Mom?"

Veronica smiled, shook her head, and said, "I know this life hasn't been great."

But let's be honest. You don't have the options I do. Or, at least I don't think you do. After meeting Joe at the library, I can't be so sure.

"But, you've got to get out there a little more. You're still young. You're beautiful. I want you to promise me you're not going to disappear into your mom's house and pull the sidewalk in after you."

"How can I, when you're always asking me to go somewhere?"

"Even if I wasn't here, you should go and do it on your own. Right?"

Ruthie nodded, but not vigorously.

"I haven't asked you for too much, have I?"

"You asked me to forgive you for ignoring me all those years in high school."

"You've got a memory like an elephant. You're right. I did. I think I should get a new request every twenty years, though. And here's what I want. I want you to promise me you're going to get up and at 'em."

"I swear, you are my mother today."

"It's what she would want for you too, and you know it."

Ruthie looked at her feet for a long moment. Finally, she raised her chin, took a deep breath, and said, "You're right. I feel like I never got my legs under me after Dad died, and then when Mom died, too, I kind of lost any motivation."

And now, you're going to miss me, too. I'm sorry, Ruthie. I love you.

"But, I know you're right. I need to quit making excuses and figure out what I want to do." She turned to look at Veronica. "Is it crazy that I kind of want to go back to school? I think I can swing it, if I can find a part-time job."

"No, that's not crazy. That's wonderful. That's a great idea. What do you want to study?"

"I've always wanted to study nursing. I like helping people."

"I think that's perfect for you. You are such a gentle, caring person. I'm so glad you came out with me tonight. I love you, Ruthie."

So glad I had a chance to say good-bye.

THE WEEK AFTER WALLACE and Doris McAllister had died, Veronica had gone to Dr. Graham and told him she was having a hard time sleeping.

"Perfectly understandable," he had said, writing her a prescription for Seconal. "That's got two refills on it. If you're still having a hard time sleeping then, come see me."

Veronica had waited the minimal amount of time she could, then gone in for the second refill.

Now, two days after that dinner with Ruthie, she sat on the twin bed in her old childhood room, with sixty Seconals spread out in front of her.

She had spent the previous two days memorizing the list that Todd had given her. She felt sure she would remember them long enough to write them down when she woke up. She had collected the will from her attorney, signed it, and brought a copy of it home with her. It sat next to the small mountain of pills.

Damn it. I hate swallowing pills.

She considered writing a note to Ruthie, but decided to leave things where they were.

That's as good an ending with her as I can hope for.

She looked at the small mountain of pills in front of her.

That's it, then. I've done everything I can to make sure I have a good life next time around.

One by one, she swallowed the pills.

Chapter Thirty-Seven

Veronica McAllister opened her eyes. A paperback book slipped off her lap, and she caught it before it hit the floor.

Here I am again. Another chance. This time, I think I'm ready.

She stood up from the low-slung orange couch, smoothed out her skirt, and walked into the kitchen. She opened drawers until she found a notepad and pen. She tore a sheet off, laid it on the counter, and began to write. She wrote down every stock Todd had found for her in 1979. She jotted a date afterward –the optimal sell date for each stock. Five minutes later, she was done, relieved she could let the information slip out of her mind.

She folded the paper and walked to the closet. She retrieved her jacket and slipped the paper and her book into the pocket. She folded it over her arm and turned to the front door just as it opened, and James and Anne Weaver walked in. They seemed slightly surprised to see Veronica standing near the door, waiting for them.

Veronica smiled at them. "I saw you pull in, so I grabbed my coat."

"Of course," James replied. "So was Zack a little monster, like usual?"

If I ever come back to this moment again, I've got to go up and check on that little guy, so I can see for myself.

"Oh, James," Anne said. She turned to glance at Veronica. "Don't pay any attention to him. Zack is just spirited, that's all." Turning back to James, she said, "Will you pay Veronica and give her a ride home, while I go up and check on our sweet boy?"

"Yes, dear," James said, completing a quick inspection of the house by glancing into the refrigerator. He came back into the living room reaching for his wallet.

"Twenty-five cents an hour, plus fifty cents after midnight, so it'll be a $1.75."

James looked at her with amusement in his eyes. "I like a girl that's all business." He opened his wallet, handed her two one dollar bills, and said, "Here's two. Keep the change. Good babysitters are hard to find."

I'll put that quarter to good use, Mr. Weaver. This life, I'm all about the business, then the pleasure. If I foul it all up again, I guess I can always start over again, God forbid.

Ten minutes later, after making small talk with James Weaver on the car ride home, she stood once again on the sidewalk leading up to her house.

I saw this house a few hours ago, and it didn't look all that different than it does right now, even though it's twenty years earlier. But, it sure felt different without Mom and Dad in it.

Veronica hurried up the walk, opened the door and shut it with a little more force than was necessary. She wanted to make sure her mother heard her come in. She slipped her shoes off—*don't want to get off on the wrong foot this lifetime*—and retrieved the paper she had written the stocks on from her jacket pocket.

She inhaled deeply, stood still and felt the sense of life that was back in the house. Her father and Barbara were asleep upstairs, her mother no doubt about to come down and check on her.

I'll have things to set right. Make things good with Mom and Ruthie. I think I'm going to need to recruit Dad into my scheme too, if it's going to work early. If not, I'll have to let a little time pass.

She slipped into the kitchen, poured herself a half-glass of milk and drank it, then realized Doris hadn't come down the stairs. A knot tied in her stomach. *It's not possible that because she died in my last life, that she'll still be dead here in 1958 too, is it? Surely not. But why haven't I seen her?*

Veronica set the glass in the sink and hurried down the hall to the stairs. Just as she turned to run up them, she saw Doris coming down. *Oh, thank God.*

Doris McAllister, dressed in her blue bathrobe over her night-clothes, her hair up in curlers, came silently to the bottom of the stairs. She looked Veronica up and down and fixed her with a stern look.

Veronica didn't care how stern she looked. *She's alive.*

Veronica threw her arms around Doris with enough force to make her take a half step back.

"Ronnie!" she said in a hoarse whisper. "Are you all right?"

I am now.

Veronica buried her head against Doris's neck and nodded. "I'm fine, Mom. Just glad to see you."

"First time for everything, I guess," she said, but there was the hint of a smile on her lips. "Don't forget—"

"I know, I'm scheduled at Artie's tomorrow. I'll be up and ready." She squeezed Doris happily and ran lightly up the stairs. Inside her room, she sat on her bed and grabbed one of the notebooks from underneath her bedside table. She slipped the paper inside it, then replaced the notebook.

So many things to remember. So many things to do. I can't wait to get started.

Chapter Thirty-Eight

Veronica's alarm went off at 8:00 a.m. and pulled her from the depths of the slumber she always fell into on her first night back in 1958. She got dressed in her Artie's uniform and spent a little extra care in the bathroom. She fixed her hair and put on as much makeup as she knew Doris would let pass without an argument. She had only been thirty-eight the day before, but still, she could see the difference in her face.

Losing both parents in one day ages you. Plus, there is no substitute for being eighteen. Youth is wasted on the young, unless you're living the same life over and over, then we learn to enjoy it.

She hurried down the stairs and found Wallace McAllister sitting in his easy chair, sipping a cup of coffee and reading the morning paper.

Oh, Daddy, it's so good to see you alive. I won't embarrass you by running over and jumping in your lap, but I'd sure like to. You're such a good man.

"Morning, Daddy," Veronica said, walking into the kitchen to make her breakfast.

Wallace made a show of looking at his watch, then looking at Veronica. "As I live and breathe, my little girl, up and chipper as can be this early on a Saturday morning. Are you feeling all right?"

Veronica stuck her tongue out at him, and settled on a bowl of Cheerios. *Is this the same box of Cheerios I've already eaten at least twice before, maybe three times?*

She took it to the kitchen table and sat down so she could still see into the family room. "Golfing today, Daddy?"

"Mmm-hmm," Wallace said, without dropping his newspaper down.

Before she poured the milk on her cereal, she said, "Can I talk to you about something?"

These are not words that any father of a teenage girl typically wants to hear, so that caused him to put his paper down and say, "Of course, Ronnie. Come in here and sit down."

This is my best shot. Mom's not down yet. Dad's always in a good mood in the morning.

"I know this is going to sound a little weird, but I've started to follow along with the stock market."

"A *little* weird? Honey, if you had come in here and told me you want to fly jet planes, I wouldn't be more surprised."

Hey, women can fly jet planes too, you know. Now is not the time to argue that point, though.

"Well, we were studying it in class, and I started looking into it, and it's pretty interesting. Do you own any stock, Daddy?"

"Well, I'm not sure I completely trust the stock market. It's crashed before, you know, and it took a lot of people down with it."

Right. It crashed less than thirty years ago. You would have been old enough to remember that, and you lived through the Depression that came after.

"I know it did. We studied that, too. Still, I've been following along with some of the stocks in your newspaper, and I've gotten pretty interested in it."

"Well, there's nothing wrong with being interested in things, but it doesn't make much sense to think about it too much, does it?"

I know. To you, a career as a stock broker for your daughter is unimaginable.

"I've been doing some research, and I think there's an opportunity in the market right now that everyone's missing."

"An opportunity in the—Veronica, what the heck has gotten into you?"

Too much. To him, yesterday, I was worrying about who was going to ask me to Prom. Now, I'm up early on a Saturday, babbling about the stock market. Time for Plan B.

"Nothing, Dad. I'm probably going overboard, like I usually do."

Wallace narrowed his eyes at her. "Usually, when you go overboard, it's because some cute boy looked at you in Geometry, not something that's over my head, like this."

"I'll forget about it, but let's play a game, shall we?"

"Sure," Wallace said, laying the paper down and standing up with a slight grimace. "Gotta get loosened up for my golf game, but what do you want to play? I'm not good at charades."

Veronica picked up the newspaper and leafed through it, looking for the financial section. "You go get ready for your golf game, and I'll have something to show you before you leave."

"Sure, kitten. I have to go upstairs, but I'll be down in a minute."

Veronica knew what it meant when her father *had to go upstairs* after drinking his morning coffee. *You don't actually buy coffee, Dad, you just rent it for a few minutes.*

She sat down in the vacated easy chair and located the financial section of the paper. The headline on the front page read "Detroit unemployment reaches twenty percent in recession." *Guess we didn't invent recessions. I always thought the economy was booming during this time. I guess Dad did a good job to keep us insulated from it all.*

The last two pages had lists of stocks in agate type. *Thank goodness for young eyes.* She peered closely at the page until she found what she was looking for, then carried it over to her mother's kitchen desk. She sat down, circled the stock price of Amalgamated Plastic. She reached in the center drawer and drew out a pair of scissors. She neatly cut out the section that showed the price, along with the date and the banner of The Oregonian.

She sat back at the kitchen table, poured the milk on her cereal and happily munched away.

Each life, this is the happiest time. Everything seems to dissolve into tears and unhappiness when I leave home. She thought back to a poster she had seen hanging in the hallway of Middle Falls City College when she had attended classes there in the seventies. It had shown a harbor, with a breakwater protecting all the ships anchored within it. The caption had read, "A ship in harbor is safe, but that's not what ships are for." *And I guess that's not what human lives are for either. We're supposed to go out into the storm, but every time I do, I get sunk.*

Wallace padded down the stairs, disappeared into the garage, and reappeared a moment later with his golf clubs over his shoulder, golf shoes in hand. He set the clubs and shoes next to the front door and walked back into the kitchen.

"I've got to leave in just a minute for my tee time, but what's this game you want to play?"

"It's simple, Dad. "Veronica held up the newspaper clipping. "I just want to show this to you. Then, I'll show it to you again at the end of the year. I've circled the stock I have a hunch about, and now I'm going to fold it and put it in an envelope. I want us to look at it around the end of the year. I think it's going to really take off."

Wallace smiled, and said, "I think we'll both have forgotten about it by the end of the year, but sure, honey, we can do that. But now, I'm going to be late if I don't get going."

Okay. That's all I can do for right now. No one's going to take a barely-eighteen year old girl seriously about this. But when I show Dad what he missed out on, that will plant the seed with him, and he might listen to me next year. That means I've got to go to work, save up as much as I can, and talk Mom into giving me the rest of my savings account. No problem. In the meantime, I get to work at Artie's, stay here with Mom, Dad, and Barb, and live my life. I'm ready.

Chapter Thirty-Nine

It had been twenty years since Veronica had been a high school student. This was her fourth time through the last two months of her senior year, though, so she was prepared. She had memorized her locker number and combination. She immediately went about rebuilding her bridges with Ruthie, and let go of her connection to the more popular girls she had been spending time with.

At work at Artie's again, Veronica settled into her routine easily. She had missed Perry Zimmerman, DJ, and everyone she worked with. She had even missed the non-stop hit parade of Elvis Presley, The Fleetwoods, and Buddy Holly.

Her first shift back at Artie's, Danny Coleman had pulled in with Lisa Berry in the passenger seat. He had come back again the following Tuesday. This time Veronica was prepared, so when she brought the food to Danny, she knew Christopher Belkins would be along shortly.

I'm oh-for-two on romance, so I'm taking this life off from it. I'll bet I'm happier in the long run.

As she took the tray to Danny, the silvery-blue Thunderbird pulled in on the other side of him. She hooked the tray to Danny's window, and said lightly, "No Lisa today?"

"Umm, no. Uhh ... We kind of broke up."

"Well, those things happen. Gotta run, we're getting busy."

"Hey, Ronnie? Can you come back out in a few? There's something I'd like to ask you."

"Sure, as long as it's not about Prom."

"Oh, right. Wait. What?"

"I've decided I'm not going to go to Prom. I've got other things I'd rather do."

Shock played in a wave across Danny's face. The scion of local merchant royalty was not accustomed to being shot from the sky before fully engaging the enemy.

"Uh, okay. Yeah, then, never mind. I just remembered I'm supposed to be back at the store." Turning red, he scooped his food off the tray. "You can go ahead and take the tray."

"Sure, Danny. Maybe you should unbreak up with Lisa. She's a sweet girl."

Danny raised his hand in acknowledgement, backing out of the parking spot as fast as he could. When he did, Veronica saw Christopher sitting in his car, tapping his hand on the steering wheel. The sight of him did not arouse the strong feelings she'd had the last time she'd seen him. She found that she didn't feel anything for him.

A few minutes later, when she took the tray out to him, she didn't even bother to try and put the tray on the window. Instead, she pushed the tray against her hip and handed the food in the window. She said, "Forty cents, please."

Christopher handed her a dollar, then said, "I'll just take two quarters back, please."

Veronica made the change and handed him his two quarters. When she did, Christopher did a double take and said, "Has anyone ever told you that you have the most amazing green eyes?"

She batted those amazing eyes at him and said. "Why, yes. Almost every day. Thanks for the tip." She flipped the dime in the air, caught it neatly, and turned and walked back into Artie's, whistling along with Eddie Cochran's *C'mon Everybody.*

SITTING IN HISTORY class listening to Mr. Burns lecture about the fall of the Roman Empire, Veronica mulled over whether to go to college this life. *I like going to school and learning new things, but all my money went to paying for school, and books. I wasn't able to save anything. Plus, my grades are too mediocre when I start over each time, so I can't get into a great school.*

Veronica leaned back in her desk chair, twirling her hair around her finger. *If Dad decides to help me with my investing next year, I'll need money to put in to show I'm serious. Besides, I've already got my Associates in accounting, even if I can't prove it to anyone in this life. Sit me down with a ledger and I can prove it, though. I think that's it, then. Work hard at Artie's, save my wages and tips as much as I can, and keep my head down. Maybe I can pick up a second job after school ends. I could help out with the books at Coleman's. Danny will be gone to school, so that won't get complicated. That won't be so bad.*

Chapter Forty

In the end, that's exactly how it played out. Veronica worked as many shifts as Perry would give her. She applied for, and got, an entry-level job doing daily cash counts for Coleman's Furniture. Mrs. Beeman, the head bookkeeper who Veronica had worked with for more than a decade in her previous life, trained her.

"You give me hope for the younger generation," Mrs. Beeman said. "So many of the girls who come in here are flibbertigibbets who can't do a lick of work. You catch on so fast, though."

Veronica had smiled and nodded her thanks. *Every generation thinks the one coming behind it is going to be the end of the world.*

She felt guilty about living rent-free at home, so she started paying Wallace and Doris twenty-five dollars per month, and pitching in on groceries. Even doing that, she was able to save almost two hundred dollars per month.

By December, between what she had saved and what was already in her savings account from before, she had slightly over one thousand dollars.

Veronica dipped into her savings to buy everyone something nice for Christmas. She bought Doris a bottle of Chanel #5, because she knew how she loved it, but would never buy it for herself. For Wallace, she sent away to New York for a tin of Erinmore Flake pipe tobacco she had heard him yearn for. Barbara was easy—an entire collection of hair clips, barrettes, and her first adult makeup.

She even bought gifts for Ruthie and her mom. It was the happiest Christmas she could remember, because she was content with where she was and what she was doing. She wasn't waiting for anything to start her life.

A few days after Christmas, Doris was in the kitchen, getting a ham ready to go in the oven. Barbara was at a friend's house, and Wallace was once again reading the newspaper in the den.

Veronica sat down in her mother's chair, and said, "Daddy?"

"Mmm-hmm?"

Veronica waited patiently, silently. Eventually, Wallace remembered that she had spoken. He folded the paper up and laid it across his lap. "Do you need something?"

"Do you remember last spring, when I told you about that stock I was interested in? Amalgamated Plastic?"

Wallace tilted his head, searching his memory, then it snapped into place. "Oh, sure, honey. Why?"

"Have you looked it up lately?"

"No, I told you, I don't trust the stock market. My father always gave me this advice—the quickest way to have a million dollars is to put two million into the stock market and wait."

"Can you check it in the paper for me?" *I already did, but it will be better if you do it for yourself.*

Wallace opened the financial section to the back pages, then searched the rows of tiny print. "Hmph. $27.52. That's more than it was back then, isn't it?"

Veronica walked into the kitchen, pulled an envelope and a pad of paper out of her mother's desk and wrote out some calculations. She walked back into the den and handed the envelope to Wallace.

He opened it and muttered, "$7.62 a share." A small cloud of regret passed over him.

"They got some pretty lucrative defense contracts." Veronica turned the paper with her calculations on it to Wallace. *If we had put*

$1,000 into it in April, we would have been able to buy one hundred and thirty-one shares. Right now, those same shares would be worth a little over $3,600. Not enough to retire on, but we'd sure be ahead of the game."

"How did you know about this? What made you pick this stock?"

"I think I've got a knack for it. I'm not saying I can pick a winner every time. No one can do that, but if even half my hunches turn out like this, it would be good."

"I'd say so, yes."

"I'd like to invest my own money into another stock I have my eye on. But, no one wants to deal with a young girl on something like this. I need someone to help me. You and Mom are the only ones I trust enough to do it."

"To do what?" Doris said, wiping her hands on a dish towel as she came into the den.

Wallace looked at Doris. "Ronnie's been wanting to invest some of her money in the stock market."

"What? Oh no, that's foolishness. It's perfectly safe in the bank, and it's earning compound interest."

"Right, but it's not earning me three hundred percent per year," Veronica said.

Wallace held up his hand, warning her off, then turned his attention to Doris. He looked a little guilty. "Ronnie's been interested in this for quite a while. She told me about it before she graduated. I told her she could pick one stock then, and if it did well, we could talk about it more." He handed the envelope with the clipping in it to Doris. "This is the stock she picked."

Doris took it, put her reading glasses on, and said, "All right. So?"

He gestured her over with the newspaper. "Look here." He pointed to a line of agate type. "Same stock, eight months later."

"So what does that mean?"

"It means that if I had let her invest in the stock when she wanted to, she would have made more than triple her money back. Oh, there would have been some commissions paid, and taxes, but she still would have done very well."

"I see."

Veronica stood a few feet away, watching the conversation like it was a tennis match.

"I told her in April that if that stock did well by the end of the year, I would help her invest some of her savings."

Wallace turned to Veronica with an innocent look on his face.

Why, Dad, you old liar. Good for you.

Doris looked from Wallace to Veronica, narrowing her eyes.

She can tell something's going on here, but she can't quite put her finger on it. She's never seen Dad and I team up like this before, and she doesn't like it.

After a moment's thought, Doris nodded. "I don't want to see you risking all your money on some foolish scheme. I know you are working and earning your own money, but I'm still your mother, and it's my job to look out for you. How much money do you have in your savings account?"

"One thousand, twenty-two dollars and fifty-one cents." *I know you like precision. Mom, and I love you for it.*

Doris fixed Wallace with something between a stare and a glare—leaning more toward the glare. "I don't know why you agree to foolishness like this. All right, I'll agree that you can take half your savings out and risk it, but no more." The glare intensified. "But Wallace, if you take one dollar out of our own savings, we'll have a talk."

"Sure, honey. I agree."

Better than nothing. It's a start.

Chapter Forty-One

T he next four years were happy ones for Veronica and her family. There were no crises, no bad marriages, and no car accidents. The greatest tragedy was that Barbara got the measles in May of 1963, which meant she wasn't able to walk with her class to get her diploma. Measles were still a dangerous disease during this era. More than twice as many children and young adults died from measles than polio, but the worst Barbara got was some minor scarring that was soon forgotten.

Veronica's stock pick of 1959—Generra Oil—outperformed Amalgamated Plastic by a factor of three. Her initial $500 investment had turned into $4500 by the end of that year. Her two year winning streak was enough to finally convince Doris that she and Wallace could invest some of their savings into Veronica's next pick. She chose a small company that had created light-emitting diodes, or LED lights, the year before.

By the end of 1964, Veronica had more than $200,000 in the bank and another fifteen years of sure bets still in that same notebook.

By then, she had moved out on her own and bought a lovely Craftsman-style home in Falling Waters, the nicest neighborhood in Middle Falls. Veronica's neighbors—doctors, lawyers, captains of local industry—weren't at all sure what to make of "that single gal" who owned one of the prettiest homes in town. Especially since her parents weren't wealthy, and she never seemed to go to work.

In July, 1965, Veronica invited Ruthie and her mom to come over for coffee. While Veronica's financial situation had soared, Ruthie and Mrs. Miller's had remained sadly constant—fighting for each month's bills.

They had their tea on Veronica's back deck, which looked over a man-made lake with a small waterfall built in. This was the falling waters that gave the community its name.

"Veronica, you've done so well for yourself, and I am so pleased. You've always been such a lovely girl."

Veronica nodded to the house next door. "What do you think of that house?"

"Oh, goodness," Vera Miller answered. "It's a dream house, isn't it? All the houses in this neighborhood are."

"The people who lived there moved out a few months ago, but they left me a key. Do you two want to sneak over and see it?"

"Can we? It would be fun to see how the other half lives," Vera said.

Ruthie didn't say anything, but furrowed her brow, looking a question at Veronica, who pointedly did not notice it.

They went in the front door, into a lovely entryway with a high ceiling. There was a formal living room to the right, a music room, still furnished with a grand piano, to the left.

"They left the piano behind when they moved, because they didn't want to move it all the way to Wisconsin with them."

"I can't imagine having so much money that you would leave a beautiful instrument like that behind," Ruthie said.

"Do you still play?" Veronica asked.

Ruthie shook her head. "I haven't played in years."

"It comes back quick, though. Why don't you sit down and play something?"

Ruthie took a little more persuading, but finally sat down at the sleek piano, raised the keyboard cover, and played Beethoven's *Fur*

Elise. The acoustics were perfect, and although she stumbled once or twice in the early passages, by the end, she was playing beautifully.

With happy tears in her eyes, Veronica quietly laid a legal-sized envelope on the polished surface of the piano. "I've done something for you both, and I don't want to hear any objections. It's already done." She looked from Ruthie to Vera and back. "Please."

Ruthie and Vera exchanged puzzled glances.

"What's all this, then?" Vera asked.

"I bought this house a few weeks ago. I thought it would be a good investment. But, more than that, I wanted to do something for you two. That," she said, pointing to the envelope, "is a copy of the deed. There's a rider attached to it that gives the two of you a Life Estate. That means that for as long as you want, this house is yours to live in. No matter who owns it, even if I were to sell it tomorrow, you will never have to pay any rent, any taxes, *anything*. It's yours to live in."

Ruthie and Vera stood looking at her in stunned, uncomprehending silence.

Ruthie managed the first syllable. "What?"

"This house is yours. Let's go down to Coleman's and furnish it this afternoon. Of course, you can bring any of the furniture you want from your house, but I thought it would be nice to pick up some new things too."

"I can't imagine bringing our ratty old couch or kitchen table into this house," Vera said quietly. "Why, Veronica? Why would you do this for us?"

"Because I wanted good neighbors. But, mostly," Veronica said, enveloping them both in a hug, "because I love you."

THREE MONTHS LATER, Doris and Wallace sold their home—*the nicest home on the block*—and also moved into Falling Waters, half a block down from Veronica and the Millers.

Veronica loved having everyone she cared the most about within walking distance. She had to admit to mixed emotions when she saw the For Sale sign go up in the front yard of her childhood home, though. She considered buying it as well, but that seemed too complicated, so she watched as another family bought it and moved in. In all her other lives, her parents had lived in that house until they died.

Still, it made her happy that her father was able to retire early, could golf all he wanted, and that they never had to worry about money again.

In January, 1966, Veronica made her annual stock pick, and discovered that although things were going along smoothly, she had never bothered to plan beyond this point. She sat in her huge open kitchen, drinking tea and watching the sparrows and Steller's jays eating the seed she had spread around on the back deck for them.

All my plans were to get here. Young, healthy, wealthy, unencumbered. And now that I am, so what? I can afford to buy anything I want, and find there's nothing I care about. I can make more and more money, but what does it matter, when I don't care about what I have already? I guess I'll keep buying the stocks. There's no reason not to, but now I've got to figure out what I want to do. Maybe live a little.

With that in mind, and with a healthy budget at her fingertips, Veronica began planning a dream vacation for everyone to Hawaii. Wallace was reluctant to go, until Veronica told him about the eighteen hole golf course that would be right outside his front door at the Royal Lahaina in Kaanapali, Maui. Veronica tried to talk Barbara into coming along, as well, but she was engaged to Steve, who would become her husband for the fourth time in Veronica's memory. Steve had a good job at the local power plant. He couldn't get away for that long. Barbara didn't want to leave him for a month, so she stayed behind.

In mid-March, Veronica, her parents, and Ruthie and Vera flew to Maui. It wasn't as easy to fly to Maui in 1965 as it would be eventually. First they had to fly to San Francisco, change planes, and then fly to Honolulu. They changed planes again and got on a small island-hopper that finally landed in Kaanapali. It was fourteen hours after they had boarded the first plane of the day in Portland.

Stepping down from the commuter plane, Wallace put his hands in the small of his back, drew a deep breath of island air, and said, "You can bury me right here, because I am never going through an ordeal like that again."

"You just want to stay here because of the golf course," Doris said, holding his hand and leaning into him. Wallace did not disagree with her. After seeing pictures of the course a few weeks earlier, it had been all he had talked about.

Veronica looked at her mother, dressed in white shorts, a sleeveless top, and deck shoes, her hair, now showing the first signs of gray, falling loosely around her shoulders, and could hardly believe that this was the same buttoned-down woman she had known in every other life. *She takes to island life well. It would be nice if we could live here, but she'll never want to leave Barb and the grandbabies that will be soon to arrive.*

Below the small airstrip, the Pacific rolled into shore in endless, gentle waves. A delicate breeze wafted over them, bringing with it the sweet smell of sugar cane growing in the fields behind them. *I think I could stay here, too. Is that a good way to spend a life? Laying on a beach, watching the waves and the tourists go by, until it's time to die and start all over again? There are certainly worse ways to spend a lifetime.*

She turned and looked at her family, lugging their suitcases toward the wiki wiki that would carry them to the Royal Lahaina. Exhausted as they were, they were still smiling, laughing, and joking.

She noticed that Wallace was carrying both his and Doris's suitcases, leaving his golf clubs for a second trip. *But there are better ways to spend that life, too. It would be nice to have someone to share everything with, but that's never turned out well for me.*

The smiling Hawaiian driver was waiting by the wiki wiki and hurried forward to carry as many suitcases as he could. "Welcome, weary travelers. You have spent many hours cooped up in a flying tin can. But now, leave all your worries behind. Come in, sit down and enjoy the natural island air conditioning as I drive you to the Royal Lahaina."

A few minutes later, when they pulled up to the front lobby of the resort, the driver stood up and said, "Go get checked in. I'll take care of your bags, and they'll be delivered straight to your room. You are our honored guests now. My name is Mike. If you need anything while you are here, ask anyone for me. They all know I am the one who can find anything."

The check-in at the front desk was smooth and within minutes, they were all gathered on Veronica's lanai on the second floor. The resort had put chilled champagne and fresh fruit out for them to enjoy while they reveled in their first Hawaiian sunset.

As the sun first touched the horizon behind the island of Lanai, Wallace lifted his glass and said, "A toast, to Ronnie. None of us would be here, none of us would ever have seen this, if not for her."

Chapter Forty-Two

The next day, the younger generation—Veronica and Ruthie—rented snorkeling gear and asked for a lift to the nearest beach. The older ladies elected to explore what the Royal Lahaina Resort had to offer, which was quite a lot. Wallace quite happily snuck off for his first 18 holes of golf.

At the small hidden beach that the Royal Lahaina driver had dropped them off at, Veronica and Ruthie dropped their blankets and cover-ups. They carried their snorkeling equipment to the edge of the clear blue water.

"Any idea how to do this?" Veronica asked?

"Absolutely none. Fun, huh?" Ruthie sat down in the shallows to put her fins on. While she put the first fin on, her mask floated away on a wave. As she retrieved that, her second flipper floated out of reach. This comedy of errors went on for some time, but eventually, she had her mask, snorkel, and fins on the appropriate appendages.

Veronica took note of her struggle and sat on the hot sand to put her equipment on. Once outfitted, she stood up and attempted to walk into the water, but found that the long fins made that impossible. A few feet away, a suntanned young man with blue eyes and a brilliant smile said, "That works better if you walk backwards in your fins." He stood up in his own and demonstrated.

"Ah, right. You can tell we're professional snorkelers, can't you?"

"Never had any doubt," the man said, knifing into the water and swimming rapidly away.

Veronica turned to Ruthie and mouthed, "Oh, my, God."

Ruthie, eyes wide, nodded in agreement.

Veronica crab-walked into the water until it was up around her knees, then sat down, rather ungracefully. She laughed and looked around for Ruthie, but she was gone.

Neither of them had ever been athletic, but Ruthie had always been the most awkward and unsure of herself. Until, that is, she put on flippers, a mask, and a snorkel tube. Then, Ruthie the ugly duckling bloomed into a swan. She swam gracefully on top of the water, breathing through her tube, until she saw something interesting below her. She dove down, stayed under a long time and slowly resurfaced, instinctively blowing the water out of her tube. She swam on without ever taking her head out of the water.

Veronica sat in the shallow water for a few minutes, watching her, then attempted to do the same. The first time she dove down to look at a shell, she surfaced and blew just like she'd seen Ruthie do. She didn't clear all the water, though, so when she breathed in, she swallowed several ounces of the warm Pacific Ocean. She ripped her mask and snorkel tube off and began coughing and spitting. She tried it two more times, with similar results, then headed for the shore.

Guess a career as a professional snorkeler is not in the cards after all.

Veronica spread her towel out, and flung her snorkel equipment down beside it. *I think I'd rather sit here and work on my tan anyway.* She dug through her beach bag, looking for her suntan lotion and discovered she had left it back in the room. *Oh well, I'll keep turning over. It's kind of cloudy out, anyway.*

She slipped on her oversize sunglasses, laid back on the towel and promptly fell asleep.

She was awakened an undetermined time later by Ruthie, rubbing her hair and sprinkling water all over her. "Hey, lobster-girl, you better roll over. Or, put your cover up back on. Or, get to a hospital." Ruthie bent over and peered closely at Veronica. "Oh, my God, look at you!" Ruthie reached out to touch her arm, but Veronica pulled away.

"How long were you out there?"

"I don't know. I completely lost track of everything, but it was a long time. It was the most amazing experience of my life. I saw a stick lying on the bottom, and I wondered what a stick was doing down there, so I dove down to it. When I was reaching down to pick it up, it swam away." Ruthie shuddered a little at the memory. "It was an eel! But still. So, so cool."

"I haven't seen you this excited since Billy Hammonds kissed you in fourth grade," Veronica said as she looked at her arms and winced.

"Oh, this is way better than that. Billy Hammonds had a booger in his nose when he kissed me."

"I did not need to know that, but thanks for planting that image in my mind. I think I need to get inside, though."

"Mike said he'd come pick us up at two o'clock. What time is it?"

"I have no idea."

They hadn't noticed the young swimmer who had spoken to them before, but he stood a few feet behind them, fins in hand. He looked at a watch and said, "It's 11:45." He cast an appraising eye over Veronica's rapidly reddening skin.

"We need to get you inside. You burn faster on a cloudy day than you do on a sunny one."

"Now you tell me. Where were you when I needed you?" Veronica said, wincing.

"I was swimming," he said, holding out his own golden arms, "but as you can see, I didn't try to get a finished tan in one day. You haoles want a lifelong tan on your first day on the island." He reached a gentle hand out to Veronica, helping her up and examining her more closely. "We need to get you inside. If you can see a burn outside, it's going to look worse once we get you out of direct sunlight. If you don't mind hitching a ride with a complete stranger, I'll give you a lift. Where are you staying?"

"The Royal Lahaina," Ruthie quickly answered, then extended her hand. "I'm Ruth."

Ruth? Really? You've been Ruthie since I met you in kindergarten, but we meet one cute islander, and suddenly you're plain old Ruth?

"Guy," the young man said, "which I know sounds like a made up name, but I promise you that's what it is." He nodded at an early sixties Volkswagen van parked twenty yards away. "I can give you a lift back to the resort, if you want. If not, we should probably move you over under the trees to wait for the wiki wiki to pick you up."

Ruthie didn't even glance at Veronica. "Oh, that would be so nice of you. We would appreciate a ride."

Sure, Ruthie. No problem. Let's take a ride with a guy we've known for two minutes. I suppose if he kills us, I'll just start over in 1958 again. I've still got the stocks memorized. I can do this again, right?

Guy smiled at Ruthie, then glanced at Veronica with raised eyebrows. "Copacetic?"

"Sure," Veronica said. "That's very kind of you."

Veronica walked a little like the Mummy—arms out from her sides, legs wide, trying not to touch her sunburned parts to anything else. Guy hustled ahead of her and slid the door to the VW open. As they got closer, Veronica could see the edges of the van's body were rusting, and there was primer covering a few spots.

Guy cleared out a scuba tank that was lying across the seat, then swept some other debris onto the floor. "Sorry, maid's day off."

What am I going to do, leave you a bad Yelp review? "No, that's fine, thank you."

Ruthie climbed in the front, then, while Guy was walking to the driver's side, looked at Veronica and once again mouthed *Oh my God!*

"We need to make one quick stop that's right on the way, but I'll be in and out."

Guy turned the van around and headed back toward the Royal Lahaina. Halfway there, he pulled off the highway at a small grocery store. "Be right back," he said, and dashed inside.

Veronica looked at Ruthie. "I see stars in your eyes."

"Pssh," Ruthie said, but she didn't deny it any further.

A few minutes later, Guy emerged from the store with a grocery bag, which he set between the seats. "Next stop, the Royal."

He pulled off the highway and into the drive of the resort, circling around the parking lot and coming to a stop at the front door. Immediately, a valet stepped forward. Smiling, he said, "Are you a guest, sir?"

Guy jumped out and ran around to the passenger side, where he opened the middle door. "Just delivering one of your haoles that got a bit burned."

The valet peered inside the van and saw Veronica, struggling to get out. He extended his hand. "Allow me, ma'am."

Veronica took his hand and eased out of the van. "What's your room number, ma'am?"

"273."

"I can't leave my post, but let me help you inside. I have someone there who will assist you to your room."

"No need, I'm not crippled. I just got a little too much sun."

The valet looked her up and down, then said, "Allow me to get someone to help you." Gently, he took Veronica's elbow and helped her inside.

Ruthie turned to Guy and said, "Thank you so much. I don't know what we would have done if you hadn't been there."

Guy reached into the van and retrieved the grocery bag. He reached inside and brought out a large bottle of vinegar. "Old Hawaiian remedy. Make her a bath. Cool, but not cold. Pour the whole bottle of vinegar in and have her soak until she is thoroughly pickled. When she gets out of the bath, let her air dry. Then," he replaced the vinegar in the bag and pulled out a large bottle filled with a thick, green substance, "have her rub this gently over her burns. It won't fix her overnight, but it's the best thing for her."

"You are so kind, Guy. What can I ever do to repay you?"

"Well, it was about four bucks for the aloe and vinegar."

"Oh!" Ruthie said, embarrassed, then dug into her purse. "Here's a five. Thank you, again."

"Thank you," Guy said, pocketing the bill. "Also, how about going out for a sunset swim with me?"

Chapter Forty-Three

Veronica lay across the soft sheets of her bed, resting on her unburned backside. *I will never fall asleep in the sun again.*

Doris insisted on asking the resort doctor to come and look at Veronica's burn. When he walked into the room, he wrinkled his nose a bit and said, "Vinegar?"

Veronica nodded.

"You must have a local friend. That's the number one home remedy here."

"That's why we called you, doctor. You must have something better than that, yes?"

The doctor put his black medical bag on the table, opened it, and withdrew a bottle of vinegar. "I was going to recommend this," he said with a smile. "Did whoever told you about the vinegar also tell you about aloe vera, I suppose?"

Veronica pointed to the bottle of green goop on the bedside table.

The doctor replaced the vinegar in his bag, and said, "My work here is done. You won't feel too well for another few days, but you'll be up and enjoying our little paradise before you know it."

Veronica lay in bed for two more days. She watched as much television as she could stand and read whatever Doris brought her from the resort's lending library, including James Michener's epic, *Hawaii*.

Meanwhile, everyone around her had a wonderful time. Wallace spent every day chasing a small white ball around endless yards of beautiful grass. Doris and Vera rode a wiki wiki into Lahaina, where there were dozens of shops, restaurants, and bars with decks that looked over the Pacific.

And Ruthie? Ruthie had it best of all. She spent every day with Guy. Ruthie thought Guy was the best-looking man she had ever seen, and they bonded over their mutual love of swimming and snorkeling. Guy had been in the water since he was little more than a baby and Ruthie had a natural aptitude for it, albeit undiscovered until recently. He even promised her he would teach her how to scuba dive.

On the third morning of Veronica's imprisonment in her room, Ruthie brought her a breakfast of fresh fruit and her favorite tea. She sat the tray down at the end of Veronica's bed, cast a guilty look in her direction, and said, "I'm being a terrible friend. I've abandoned you."

"Yes, you have," Veronica agreed. "And for what? A washboard stomach, blue eyes to die for, and a sparkling smile straight out of a toothpaste commercial? How dare you?"

Relief settled over Ruthie. "So you're not mad at me then?"

"How could I be? If Cupid's arrow had struck me instead of you, you'd likely never seen me again."

"Oh, it's nothing like that. Just a little vacation fling, is all."

Veronica sat up in bed. "For you, or for him?"

"For both of us."

"I have known you too long, Ruthie." Veronica grinned. "I mean *Ruth*. What was that all about?"

Ruthie shrugged. "I don't know, I've always thought it was kind of a little girl name. When I saw Guy, I thought that might be the time to make the switch. You can still call me Ruthie, though."

Veronica patted the bed beside her. "Here, come sit down and watch the Today show with me. Dr. Mom says I have to stay inside one more day, but I think she just wants to spend more time alone with your mom. They've been inseparable since we got here."

"You know, what your dad said the first night is true. All of this—your dad getting to golf every day, your mom and my mom becoming friends like this, me meeting Guy—none of it would have happened if it wasn't for you. You're like Cinderella's fairy godmother, waving your wand and making magic happen. I hate to think what our life would be like without you."

"If it wouldn't kill me, I would give you a hug right now, Ruthie Miller."

The next night, Guy and Ruthie invited Veronica to come out with them. They drove into Lahaina and went to The Outrigger, an open-air bar that had live music. The drinks were strong, the music was loud, and, no matter the best efforts of Guy and Ruthie, Veronica felt like an unnecessary appendage. After an hour, Veronica asked Guy if he would mind dropping her off back in Kaanapali. He did, then he and Ruthie drove to his favorite beach for a midnight swim.

After that, Veronica spent more time with her mom, dad, and Vera. It was not as exciting as the nightlife of Front Street in Lahaina, but everyone soon learned that Veronica had another skill. She was a killer pinochle player.

After a week at the resort, they went to the luau that was held right on the grounds of the Royal Lahaina. They invited Guy to join them. Everyone had fun, watching the fire dancers, drinking fruity drinks, and eating too much food.

As they walked back toward their rooms, Guy said, "Thank you for inviting me. I have never seen a luau quite like that."

"Authentic then, eh?" Wallace said.

"Mmmm, how can I say this? That's more for tourists." He snapped his fingers. "Hey, do you want to come to a real luau? I have some friends who are having one this weekend. Real luaus are a celebration of something. My friends are celebrating the birth of a grandson. They always say I can bring whoever I want, so what do you say?"

"I say we'll be there!" Veronica said. "Is it all right if all of us come?"

"I'm sure it is. I'll let them know. You'll be the honored guests. I've never seen a real luau where there wasn't too much food."

THE FAMILY LUAU BORE almost no relationship to the show they had seen at the Royal Lahaina. There were no fire dancers. In fact there were no dancers, period, aside from three young girls who were showing off their hula skills. There was however, food. Lots and lots of food, although it was not food that the McAllisters or Millers had ever seen before.

Instead of being on the manicured grounds of the resort, this luau was held in the back yard of the Kalamas. Their backyard wasn't manicured. In fact, the grass was sparse and there were a few bare spots. It did slope right into the Pacific Ocean, though, which was tough to beat. An immensely long table had been built out of whatever materials were at hand, and it bowed slightly in the middle from all the food.

A large man sat on the back steps of the modest house, playing the guitar. He had long hair, pulled back into an immense puff of ponytail.

Ruthie and Veronica stopped in front of the guitar player and listened, mesmerized.

"Never heard a slack-key guitar player before, eh?" Guy asked.

"No," both women answered in harmony.

"I'll just leave you here, then," Guy said, moving down to the food.

The guest of honor, week-old Kai Kalama, was passed around from person to person, each one telling the truth—that he was a gorgeous, happy baby.

Each of the visitors tried poi, the Hawaiian delicacy, and although they loved everything else that night, none of them could manage a taste for it. They decided poi was something you needed to be born into. The rest of the food had names they weren't familiar with—poke, kalua pig, lomi lomi salmon—but it was a variety of flavors that would stay in their minds forever. Months later, sitting around the dinner table, looking at a roast with mashed potatoes, Wallace McAllister's eyes would grow distant, and Doris would say, "You're thinking of the Kalama luau again, aren't you?" He always was.

As the sun set on the luau, everyone grew quiet. Red fire mixed with golden rays reached up across the sky, lighting the scattered clouds on fire. When the last of the sun disappeared over the horizon, everyone returned to their previous conversation.

Long after dark, everyone piled into Guy's beat up VW van for the ride back to the Royal Lahaina. Doris spoke for everyone when she said, "That. That was something we'll never forget."

Chapter Forty-Four

They returned to Middle Falls at the end of the month, but for Ruthie it was a temporary stay. She did her best to put a brave face on during the flight home, but she was so miserable. That attitude didn't improve with the passage of time, and by the end of summer, she gave up and made arrangements to fly back to Maui.

As soon as she got off the plane, Guy dropped to one knee and asked her to marry him, so they would never have to be apart again. They planned a wedding for early 1966.

That left Veronica living next door to Vera Miller. She loved Vera like a second mom, but it wasn't the same as having a best friend to talk to about everything.

Veronica spent her days managing her stock portfolio. She had branched out from betting on just her magical stocks and used her knowledge of what was coming to make many more good investments. She grew richer and richer, but was no happier.

She did her best to get out and mingle, to meet new people, maybe even have a relationship, but nothing ever materialized. Now that she was a wealthy woman, Veronica found herself looking at each new man as a potential opportunist, and that did not lead to moments of shared intimacy.

Since a relationship couldn't be found, she decided to be a connoisseur of experiences. She visited Europe, where she rode the train as far in either direction as she could without running into unfriendly borders. She spent some nights in the finest hotels, others in hostels with teenage wanderers.

In Spain, she gave a pregnant girl a thousand dollars to get back to America in time for her parents to see her baby born.

She spent three months traveling through Africa, and another two months in Australia. She flew to Portugal just to watch a full solar eclipse. In the summer of 1967, she flew into New York, bought a ticket to a show at Max Yasgur's farm in upstate New York. She watched Jimi Hendrix, Janis Joplin, Jefferson Airplane, Country Joe and the Fish, and the other legends do their sets at Woodstock. She even took an acid trip, accepting a purple tab from a friendly woman who was squatting behind the same tree to pee that Veronica was.

She and the woman, whose name she never knew, sat well behind the crowd and let the music of Ritchie Havens wash over them. *My life is one long acid trip, so why not do it for real?*

When Woodstock was over, she flew home, grateful for the hot shower and clean towels after a few days of being a hippy.

The next day, she sat, once again, at her kitchen table, watching the squirrels eat. *No matter where I go, I end up here, and that's not bad. It's not fulfilling, though. There's always an emptiness.* For the first time in many years, a dam broke and memories of Sarah and Nellie washed through her. *I don't even have a picture of them. I'll never have a picture of them, because I will never see them again.* She gasped at the almost physical pain that thought brought.

What am I supposed to do? What am I supposed to learn? If I'm supposed to be advancing on some path I can't see, I don't think I am. She watched one squirrel chase another away from a peanut, even though there were dozens more scattered around the deck. *I am a nearly-blind woman, walking an invisible path, using a flashlight with a weak beam to light my way.*

Finally, she walked down the block and had lunch with Doris and Wallace. She regaled them with tales of the sights she had seen at Woodstock, but didn't tell them about the acid trip. They worried enough about her already.

Lying in her bed in her lovely quiet bedroom that night, she tossed and turned. Her bedroom window was open, and she could hear the faint sound of the man-made waterfall and the cacophony of frogs and crickets that went with it. Those were her favorite sounds in the world, but on this night, they brought her no succor.

Is it because I cheated? I used an unfair advantage to make myself and everyone around me rich. Is that why everything I buy, every trip I take, feels so empty? I suppose I could live this life forever, but I'm not sure why, or what I gain by doing so. I've experienced everything I ever thought I wanted, and still, it doesn't make me happy.

She didn't sleep at all that night. As soon as the first rays of sun peeked through her blinds, she slipped a sundress and sandals on, grabbed a few thousand dollars from her closet safe, and left the house.

Without talking to her parents or Vera, she drove to Portland and parked at the airport. She went inside and paid cash for a first class ticket on the next plane to Acapulco.

She found some sense of peace and fell asleep as soon as the wheels lifted off the ground and slept all the way to Acapulco.

Veronica stepped off the plane with only her purse. She hired a limo driver to take her to the same resort she had gone to with Ruthie a literal lifetime ago. She tipped her driver a hundred dollars, then turned and walked down to the beach, carrying her sandals and feeling the sand between her toes.

It was well after midnight, and the beach was deserted. She dropped her sandals, shucked her dress off over her head, then slipped out of her bra and panties. She stood, naked to the world, invisible to everyone in it.

She walked out and let the warm water wash over her. She dunked her head under, then pushed her hair back away from her face.

There were a few clouds in the sky and as she looked up, the moon moved out from behind them. She turned and floated on her back, kicking gently and watching the stars and moon. Finally, she took a deep breath, turned, and swam away from shore. She swam until her arms were lead, then pushed on more.

When she could push no more, she stopped trying.

Good enough.

She slipped below the waves.

Chapter Forty-Five

Veronica McAllister opened her eyes and gasped for air. Her body jerked, and the paperback on her lap flew onto the floor.

Who said drowning is a good way to die? I don't think I'd choose that again.

She looked around at the now-familiar Weaver living room. *I've gotta see this kid I'm supposed to be babysitting.*

She picked the book off the floor, then ran quietly up the stairs and pushed through a door that was cracked open. Inside was a white crib, a changing table, and, in one corner, a sturdy rocking chair. Veronica crept into the room. *Don't wake the little guy up, or Mr. & Mrs. Weaver will be unhappy, and he might not tip me that extra twenty-five cents.* Her eyes adjusted to the near darkness and she walked to the crib.

Inside was a perfectly cherubic baby. Dark curls framed his face. Chubby cheeks moved in and out with each deep breath. *Zack Weaver, you are one beautiful baby. Glad I finally got to see you.*

She closed the door as it had been and was coming down the stairs as the Weavers came in the front door.

"I was just checking on Zack. He's such a beautiful baby."

"Hope you didn't tell him that," James Weaver said. "Not even a year old, and he already has a pretty big head."

"Oh, James," Anne said. "Will you pay Veronica and give her a ride home?"

"Of course." He looked as though he wanted to walk the house and make sure Veronica hadn't gotten into anything, but instead he cast his eyes around the living room. He smiled at Veronica and said, "Shall we?"

Back home, Veronica slipped inside, took her shoes off and walked quietly up the stairs. She met Doris at the top of the stairs. *I've made up with you so often now, it's hard for me to remember that we hadn't been getting along. That's for another day, though. Right now, I'm tired.*

She didn't speak to Doris—just gave her a peck on the cheek and a wan smile, and went into her bedroom. Five minutes later, she was fast asleep.

VERONICA WENT THROUGH the items of her check-list—build bridges with Doris, reconnect with Ruthie—but she did so without as much enthusiasm. She had built what she had thought would be the perfect life, and found it hollow and unfulfilling.

She drifted through her first few months back in Middle Falls, not paying much attention to anything. It was hard to get too excited for her high school graduation, when she had already done it four times.

Throughout the summer of 1958, Veronica continued to work at Artie's. Through all her lives, it had been a touchstone for her, and she felt like she needed the comfort of it more than ever.

One unusually hot day in mid-July, she reported for the late shift a few minutes before noon. Western Oregon is typically moderate, even in the summer, but on this day the thermometer outside the front door, which was decorated with happy, chilly, snowmen, read 92 degrees. *You cute little snowmen should skedaddle if you have any sense. You'll melt in this heat.*

Inside, both the dining room, and the grill area, had moved past hot, were well into stultifying, and edging toward unbearable. Perry Zimmerman was already a bit wilted as he stood at the counter, taking orders. When he saw Veronica, he reached under the counter and pulled up a white bottle.

"Salt tablets. Take a couple. I don't want you passing out on me today. Drink lots of liquids with them."

Before sports drinks, we always had salt tablets.

Veronica accepted a small handful and slipped them into her pocket. She noticed DJ back by the grill and wandered over to him. He was whistling along to the Frank Sinatra song playing on the radio. He looked remarkably fresh for someone toiling over a grill. He gave Veronica his crooked grin and said, "It's Artie's answer to Piper Laurie. How's tricks?"

"What, are you superhuman or something? I'd be half-dead if I had to work around this grill all day."

"Why yes, I am a superman. Thank you for noticing, oh lovely one." He flipped a row of burgers and spun open another bag of buns and began buttering them. "Seriously, though, the heat never bothers me. No idea why. Lucky to be this cool, I guess. Boring, huh?"

"DJ, you are many things, but you are never boring."

"Truer words and all that," DJ said, flipping a top bun on a burger and nestling it in a basket with an order of golden fries. "Number sixteen for that one."

For the rest of the day, Veronica watched DJ work. He complimented every woman who worked there and told them they were beautiful, but he had the knack of doing it without being creepy or overbearing. In all her lifetimes, she had never seen him go out on a single date.

Could he be gay? That wasn't the kind of thing you trumpeted about in the fifties, especially in a small town like Middle Falls.

Finally, when she took her dinner break in the late afternoon, she decided to find out. *This isn't the kind of thing young ladies did in the late fifties, but I'm not really a fifties girl.*

As she stood by the grill waiting for DJ to make her a "Ronnie Special," she leaned in close to him and said, "DJ, will you go out with me?"

DJ's cool demeanor melted away like an ice cube dropped on his grill. His mouth fell open a crack and he stuttered out a few syllables that did not actually form words.

"You're gonna give a girl a complex, you know."

DJ spun his right hand around in a gesture that would normally be to tell someone to continue with their story. In this case, it was an effort to connect his mouth to his brain. He nodded his head several times, like a stuttering boy trying to spit out a word with too many syllables.

Finally, frustrated, he stopped. Took a deep breath, and said one word. "Yes."

"That's better. Now, what's the next evening we both have off?"

Chapter Forty-Six

They were both off the following Saturday, so they decided that would be the day. It would be more accurate to say that Veronica decided. It took a lot of effort to get a straight answer out of DJ. He had always been bathed in hipster cool, but for the rest of that shift, he was more bathed in flop sweat. His resistance to the heat had evaporated.

Veronica found that completely endearing. She noticed that DJ was looking at her every time she glanced his way, then he would immediately look away. *I think he's a complete flirt until someone calls him on it, then he doesn't know how to handle it.*

DJ picked Veronica up at her parent's house that Saturday afternoon at 5:00. When he knocked on the door, Barbara answered it, and with a giggle she said, "You look like Elvis, but not as cute. Mom! You can come look at him now!"

Some things never change. Veronica hustled to the front door to rescue DJ from Barbara. Doris emerged from the kitchen and said, "Hello, DJ, so nice to meet you. Ronnie has told me so much about you."

Veronica had never seen DJ out of his Artie's uniform, and she was glad to see that he did own other clothes. He was wearing a blue sports coat with a light blue shirt underneath it and charcoal gray, somewhat baggy slacks. The outfit was completed by a red bow tie.

"Thank you, Mrs. McAllister. It's nice to meet you. Veronica has never mentioned her parents. I thought perhaps she was orphaned."

Doris blinked once, then twice.

Veronica swatted DJ on the arm. *I see he's recovered his terrible sense of humor.* "Oh, DJ, it's better if you get to know my mom before you kid around with her." She shot him a sharp look, and he looked properly abashed.

"I apologize, Mrs. McAllister, I was only teasing Veronica, because she talks about you and Mr. McAllister all the time."

"Oh, I see," Doris said, but her expression revealed that she may not have seen at all. "May I ask how old you are, umm..." she left the question hanging in the air.

"DJ, ma'am. My parents named me Dimitri John, but I've been DJ since before I can remember. And, I'm nineteen, as of last month."

Doris nodded. "Veronica has only just turned eighteen, which means in some ways, she is an adult. But, as long as she lives under our roof, she lives with our rules. Those rules include a midnight curfew for her, even on weekends."

My God, how old am I actually? It took Veronica a few moments to do the math, and she came up with one hundred and nine years old. She reached up and touched her face. *I look pretty good for an old broad, if I do say so.*

"Of course," DJ said. "That won't be any problem."

"And where are you taking her?"

"Well, I was hoping it would be a surprise, but ..." DJ leaned forward, cupped his hand around Doris's ear, and whispered for several seconds.

Doris's face softened. "Oh, I see. Yes, that's very nice. Good for you, DJ."

I have no idea what you just told my mother, but you won her over. There might be hope for you after all.

"Well," Doris said, "you kids have fun."

When they got to the curb, DJ opened the passenger door to his '51 Dodge Coronet. It was a bulky, unattractive car, but it was clean inside. DJ hustled around to the driver's side, fished in his jacket pocket for the key, inserted it and gave it a twist. There was a slight, muffled sound from the engine, then silence.

Veronica glanced over at him, and the life seemed to have gone out of DJ. He slumped forward for a minute, then perked up, and said, "Be right back." He clambered out, opened the trunk, and she could hear the thud and rustling of metal. A moment later, he was in front of the car. He opened the hood, and she thought she heard him say, "Not now, ya old bitch," but couldn't be sure.

He slipped behind the wheel again, tossed a pair of locking pliers into the backseat, gave a hopeful smile to Veronica, and made a show of crossing his fingers. He gently turned the key again, and the engine rumbled to life.

"Couple of teeth missing from the flywheel. It starts almost every time, but at the worst times, like when it's pouring rain—"

—or you're out on a date," Veronica interjected.

"—or I'm out on a date," DJ agreed, "it seems to happen with alarming regularity. Not that I've dated a lot." He glanced to his right to see how this revelation was taken by Veronica, then he turned the wheel away from the curb and accelerated.

It is not a major surprise that you haven't dated a lot, DJ. I was pretty sure that was the case when you about died when I asked you out.

"So, what's the big secret you and Mom are keeping from me?"

DJ raised a hand, indicating he would not be answering any further questions on the subject. He turned KMFR up, and they listened to Bobby Darin, Fats Domino, and The Diamonds as they drove. They passed through downtown, then continued on. Finally he turned into the last neighborhood inside the city limits.

He made two quick rights and pulled up in front of a two story house. It was a boxy house, gray with white trim. It was well-maintained, but not ostentatious. There were three other cars already parked in the driveway, so he parked in the loose gravel in front.

Veronica looked at the house, then looked at DJ. "So, where are we, exactly?"

"Oh, this is my grandmother's house."

"You're bringing me to meet your family? On our first date?"

DJ looked slightly nervous, but stood his ground. "It's not that big a deal."

"Why, do you bring girls here all the time? Is that why it's not a big deal?"

"In this lifetime, you are the first girl I have ever brought to my grandmother's."

Veronica sighed. "You are impossible. But, charming, in your own way."

"Halleluiah. That's exactly what I was going for—charming." DJ slid out of the car and hurried around to open Veronica's door. He crooked his arm and offered it to her. He didn't knock on the door, but pushed through. They walked into a maelstrom of laughing, conversation, the slamming of cupboard doors and scraping of floors. The kitchen and dining room was overflowing with both people and noise.

I swear, if everyone stops dead and looks at us, I am turning heel and running.

No one seemed to even notice they had arrived. DJ winked at her and led her by the elbow into the kitchen. A small gray-haired lady stood at the stove, an oasis of calm among all the hubbub. "Bunica? This is Ronnie, the girl I told you about. Veronica, this is my Bunica—my grandmother."

The old woman, who stood no taller than 4'10", turned and looked up at Veronica with sharp dark eyes. She inspected her from her red hair to her saddle shoes.

I've had MRIs that felt less invasive than her stare.

Finally, she nodded and said, one word. "Good." Then she opened the oven door and a heavenly smell emerged that made Veronica's stomach growl.

"You made sarmale! Mmmm." He turned to Veronica. "Cabbage rolls. Everything I know about cooking, I learned from my Bunica."

The old woman didn't look at DJ, but in a heavy accent, said, "You know nothing. Not yet. In time."

"Come on, let's run the gauntlet. I mean, let me introduce you to my family."

"I owe you, DJ."

"Yes, but you can take your time paying me back. Besides, this is only part of the family. If everyone showed up, it would be really loud in here." DJ took Veronica's hand and led her into the huge dining room next to the kitchen. He introduced her to his mother and father, three brothers, a sister, two aunts, an uncle, and a bevy of cousins, nieces, and nephews.

"I hope there won't be a test at the end of the night, because I won't remember half these names," Veronica whispered into DJ's ear.

He grinned. "No hurry. You've got plenty of time."

The noise level in the house never dipped below a dull roar, except for sixty seconds of quiet prayer before the meal.

There are a dozen conversations happening around me, and it feels like they've all been going on for years and years. I don't know how they do it, but I feel included, without being made the center of attention. This is a family.

There was a feast spread out on the table. Not just the sarmale, but an incredible soup DJ said was called Ciorba de Burta, a polenta dish they called mamaliga, and half a dozen others that she didn't catch the name of.

Also, if they eat like this every meal, how come none of them are fat?

When the meal was over, the men went out into the backyard to smoke, and the women and DJ cleared all the dishes. "You go sit down, Bunica," DJ said. "Ronnie and I will do the dishes."

The old woman didn't argue. She pointed out how she wanted the leftovers saved, then toddled off to a comfy rocking chair in the living room. She was asleep before the sink was full of dishes. His aunt and older female cousins sat around her, talking quietly.

"I know, I know," DJ said. "Kind of a crazy first date, isn't it?"

"Well, I don't think I could have gotten a better meal anywhere in Middle Falls, or maybe all of Oregon tonight. And, if my goal was to get to know you a little better, I think we've accomplished that."

"Ah," DJ said. "Then this is the part where you run fleeing into the night."

"This is the part where I say, when are we going out again?"

Chapter Forty-Seven

The next few months were heavenly for Veronica. She lived at home, spending time with her Mom, Dad, and Barbara; she got to work at Artie's; and best of all, she spent a lot of time with DJ. Although the two of them were often together, they rarely went on what would ordinarily be considered a teenage date in Middle Falls.

Once, they drove up to see a special traveling art exhibit in Portland, and another time they did go see *Cat on a Hot Tin Roof* at the Pickwick. Most of their time together, though, was spent either with his family, or hers, or going for drives and walks and talking. They never seemed to run out of things to talk about.

When autumn rolled around and Veronica had shown no forward progress in planning a life for herself, Doris began to inquire about what her plans were. One morning, as Veronica sat at the breakfast table eating a bowl of Cream of Wheat, Doris broached the subject.

"You've got three days scheduled at Artie's this week."

"Mmm-hmm," Veronica agreed.

"What else is on your agenda? And, before you answer, it should probably be something other than 'spend time with DJ'. You know we love him, but time is slipping away, and I don't sense much forward momentum for you. I thought you would enroll in City College."

Is time slipping away? It seems like it is just repeating, to me. "There was nothing I wanted to study at City. There's so few opportunities for women. I can be a secretary, or a nurse, right?"

"Or a teacher. If you don't get married right away, you'll always have that to fall back on."

Teaching. The third of the Big Three Career Opportunities for women in the fifties. I'll never get rich, but now I know how much I care about that. For a moment, Veronica let her mind wander over the idea. *I'd have a set schedule. I'd get to work with kids. It would give me a reason to get out of bed every morning.*

"I've never thought about teaching, Mom, but you're right. I could look into that."

Doris jumped at the chance to help. She had many superpowers. Chief among them was organization and planning, but she also loved to throw herself into a project for the kids. She had once spent an entire Sunday building a map of the Canadian provinces out of clay with Johnny because he had procrastinated an assignment.

Doris walked to where Veronica was sitting and hugged her. "I never told you this, but that's what I always wanted to be. I actually had two years of college toward it, but then I met your father. We got married, and then your brother arrived. I just never got back to it."

"It's never too late, Mom."

"No, it's not, but this is my life now, and it's a good life. Let's go down to the library tomorrow and see what we can find. It's too late to do anything for this semester, but I'll bet we could get you enrolled for Winter Semester."

AS SHE SO OFTEN WAS, Doris was correct. They were able to get Veronica accepted and enrolled at Pacific University in Forest Grove, a small town west of Portland. Doris and Wallace insisted she live on campus in the women's dorm. They couldn't imagine a young woman of only eighteen living on her own so far from home.

So, for the first time in five lifetimes, Veronica became a full-time college student, living in a dorm, surrounded by women who were ostensibly her age. Veronica attended classes, got a job as a waitress part-time to help make ends meet, and missed DJ terribly.

The third Friday of March, 1959, as Veronica emerged from her last class of the week into a pouring rain, DJ was there waiting for her.

"What in the world are you doing all the way up here?"

"What, Forest Grove? I went for a drive and the next thing I knew, I rolled onto campus. It's like the Coronet has a mind of its own."

"Well, your timing couldn't be better, or worse."

"You're confusing this simple brain of mine again."

"Better, because I've missed you terribly." She leaned into DJ and kissed him quickly. "And worse, because my professors take it as a personal challenge to load me up with so much homework over the weekends that I can't even come up for air."

DJ nodded. "I expected that. But, you've still got to eat, right? It's definitely worth a three hour drive to have dinner with you, any day. But, before we eat, I want to show you something. Game?"

"I'm always game with you, DJ. It's been too long since I've seen you. How long has it been?"

"Last weekend."

"Seems longer," Veronica laughed. "I'm surrounded by eighteen year old girls, and it doesn't feel like I have anything in common with them."

Neither of them had an umbrella—always a strategic error in western Oregon in March—so they were thoroughly soaked by the time they got inside the Corona.

Forest Grove was a small town, with a population of 6,000 in 1959. Over time, it would develop into a bedroom community of Portland, but in the late 1950s, it still retained its own distinct sense of community. The largest employer by far was Pacific University.

DJ drove out of the main parking lot and bypassed the down-town area, instead turning into the residential side streets. Less than half a mile later, he pulled up in front of a small, white cottage. The grass was overgrown, the paint was old and spotty, and the screen door hung at an odd angle.

"Much like this old Dodge, it ain't beautiful, but it is mine," DJ said, pointing to it.

"What? What do you mean?"

"I mean, I rented this house. Just got the keys. Wanna go see it?"

"Oh, DJ, you'll miss your family."

"I could either live in Middle Falls and miss you, or live in Forest Grove and miss them. I tried one for a few months, now I thought I'd try it the other way."

Veronica scooted across the bench seat of the Coronet and wrapped DJ in a hug. "You are the most foolish, gallant, wonderful boy."

"I try. Well, not the 'foolish' part. That seems to come natural."

The rain had let up, but they were still cold and shivering when DJ unlocked the front door and they stepped inside.

There were swirls of dust and dirt on the floor, a few yellowed newspapers thrown in one corner, and an overall feel that the tiny house had not been well-loved in some years.

"How in the world are you going to furnish this place?"

"Have you not met my family? They'll be here tomorrow with couches, chairs, tables, lamps, a bed, pots and pans, you name it."

"The endless benefits of a big family," Veronica agreed. "But, what about your job? Did you quit Artie's?"

DJ nodded. "I love Zimm and Artie's, but there's this amazing redheaded girl I love even more. And, you know the old saying, 'A good fry cook will never be out of a job.'"

"Is that really a saying?"

"It is in my world. I would show off my expertise in the kitchen to you at this very moment, but I am short a pan. And," he said, reaching into his pocket, "all the groceries I have is a stick of Juicy Fruit gum."

Veronica put her arm around DJ's waist and said, "Then we better go scout out your next place of employment, hadn't we?"

Chapter Forty-Eight

DJ was not out of a job for long. There weren't any drive-ins like Artie's in Forest Grove, but he caught on at one of the two diners in town, handling the breakfast shift.

Life was good for the next few months. DJ had his job, Veronica had hers, and of course, there was her school work. That meant they weren't able to spend as much time together as they would have liked. Veronica spent many evenings at DJ's house, studying, while he quietly read a book on the couch beside her.

Eventually, the school year ended, and Veronica faced having to leave DJ behind while she returned home. After the last day of the quarter, she drove to DJ's house to tell him goodbye before driving back to Middle Falls. The little cottage was unrecognizable as the slovenly mess she had first walked into a few months before. The lawn was trimmed, there were flowers planted in the flower beds, and everything was neat, clean, and organized. *Almost looks like Mom has been here.*

Inside, DJ was making them an early dinner, so she could get back home before full dark.

She snuck up behind him and wrapped him in a bear hug. "Usually, when I see you, it is the best part of my day, but not today."

"And why not? Have I lost my youthful good looks, my boyish charm?"

"No, and that's the problem. I'm going to miss you so."

DJ whirled around, grabbed her waist and lifted her in the air. "You know I'm going to miss you, too. I don't know anyone else in town. But, it's only for a few months, and I knew this was coming when I moved up here. When I get a few days off, I'll come back down there, and maybe you can come up and visit me a few times. We'll be fine, and it will be September before we know it."

"I could always stay," Veronica said.

"Where? Here? I think that if you moved in here, there would be nothing but a crater in the ground from the explosion your family and mine would make."

That's true, in 1959. Our living together would be an affront to the social order. We would be outcasts. Our families would be shamed. Nothing else for it, then.

She got to her parent's house in Middle Falls as it was getting dark. The streetlights had turned on and the glow of the porchlight looked warm and inviting. Inside, Doris was in the kitchen, as she so often was, Wallace was puttering in the garage, and Barbara greeted her at the front door.

"Come upstairs and look at my room! You won't even recognize it!"

"Mom, I'm home, " Veronica yelled. "Gonna go look at Barb's new room, then I'll be down."

Upstairs, Barbara bounced ahead of her, giddy and excited. She flung the door to their bedroom open, and it did look like a different room. The off-white walls were gone, replaced with a rosy pink paint. There was only one bed, now, and it had a matching pink bedspread. "Isn't it dreamy? It's just like I've always wanted it."

Veronica put an arm around Barbara's shoulders and said, "Yes, it looks just like you, kiddo. Did you paint it yourself?"

"Ha! No, of course not. Mom and Dad did it. Your bed is in Johnny's old room. Mom says you can sleep in there for the summer."

"Okay. Looks perfect, Barb." Veronica left Barbara, spinning with happiness, in her room.

Downstairs, Doris looked up from the pie crust she was rolling out and said, "I hope you're not too upset. She got so excited, and I didn't think you'd mind having Johnny's room to yourself over the summer."

"No, no, that's fine, Mom. It's her room now. Staying in Johnny's room will be great. I think Barb's been dreaming about having her own room since she was about four. Pretty sure I saw her counting down the days until I left for college. Did she wait until I pulled out of the driveway before she started the remodel?"

"Honestly, no," Doris laughed. "So, DJ moved up there to be close to you, now you're home. Is he coming back, too?"

"No, that would be silly."

"I think it was silly for him to move up there in the first place. There was some gossip about it."

The lyrics to an old Jeannie C. Riley song about the Harper Valley PTA popped into her head. *Small town America in the fifties, thank you very much.*

"Don't worry," Doris said, noting Veronica's expression. "I told those old gossips what's what."

The next day, Veronica went back to Artie's to see Perry Zimmerman. She found him sitting in the little closet that passed for an office, hitting the keys on a large adding machine with much more force than was necessary.

"Hey, Zimm," Veronica said, poking her head in. She didn't step inside, because there wasn't room. "I'm home from college for the summer. Need an experienced carhop?"

"I can always use you, Ronnie. What I could use at the moment is someone to balance these books." He struck at the keys viciously.

"You know hitting the keys harder doesn't give you better numbers, right?"

Perry gave her a severe look, but couldn't hold it.

"Look, you've got customers. You go take care of them and let me slide in there and see if I can organize things for you a little more."

"What do you know about accounting?"

"I took a class in high school," Veronica lied.

"The things they teach you kids in school these days. Well, I guess you can't make much more of a mess of it than I already have. Be my guest."

Veronica sat down behind the crowded desk, picked up a pile of receipts, another pile of accounts payable, and a third of accounts receivable. *Zimm, Zimm, Zimm. You are a great guy, and an absolutely horrible bookkeeper.*

Two hours later, Perry came back to his office and said, "Give up?" but the words froze on his lips. Where once had been chaos, order now reigned, and Veronica looked content.

"Voila," Veronica said, sweeping her hand across the now-organized piles. "It's not done, but now it's organized so you can find what you need to find. Your adding machine will thank you. It was never intended to be used as a weapon of war."

"They taught you how to do this in high school?"

Veronica shrugged. "I have a knack for it, I guess."

"I can put you on the schedule for three or four shifts a week, but how about working another ten hours a week handling the books for me?"

"How about an extra fifteen cents an hour?"

"Done," Perry said.

"That means I can have everything ship-shape for you when I go back to school, and you should be in desperate need of me by next summer."

"I guess this means I have to forgive you for stealing the best grill man I've ever had away from me, too."

Chapter Forty-Nine

As it does whether you are on your first life, or your fifth, time passed. Veronica studied hard and graduated in the spring of 1963 with her bachelor's degree in education from Pacific University. Her name got the biggest cheer when it was announced at graduation, thanks to the fact that in addition to her own small family, DJ's entire clan was there, too.

The question for both of them was, what was next? Veronica and DJ had been together every minute possible since their first date. Unlike her relationships with Christopher and Danny, the more she knew about DJ, the more she wanted to know.

But, it was the early sixties, and couples who had been together for four or five years typically got married. On the one hand, Veronica wasn't worried about it, but on the other, with each month and year that passed without a proposal, the more she thought about it.

Do I even want to get married? If I do, I can't imagine marrying anyone other than DJ. But so far, marriage hasn't been great. Christopher and Danny weren't DJ, though.

After graduation, both Veronica and DJ moved back in with their families in Middle Falls. After years of living away, being once again under a parent's roof felt chafing to both of them.

Veronica sent her resume to the Middle Falls schools, then crossed her fingers and waited. She wanted to work at Middle Falls Elementary, but if she didn't catch on this year, she thought she might spend the year making connections by substitute teaching.

It wasn't hard for DJ to talk his way back to working the grill at Artie's, and Veronica caught as many shifts carhopping as she could. The summer passed.

One night in mid-July, DJ and Veronica had dinner with his parents, then went for a drive.

They parked in the popular make out spot above the falls. It was deserted, except for them. They watched the falls for a few minutes in silence. Then, Veronica turned to DJ. "Why didn't you ever ask me out?"

"Four years, three weeks, two days, and," he glanced at his watch, "five hours. I wondered how long it would take you to ask me that question."

"You are never serious."

"I seriously doubt that."

"Fine. Don't tell me, then!"

DJ put his arm around her shoulder and drew her toward him. He kissed her gently. "I never asked you, because I didn't dare. I never would have. What mortal dares ask a goddess on a date? Not me. I didn't have the courage. I would have just gone on about my life, longing for something that I was missing, and never having the guts to reach out for it. I would have continued to worship you from afar, instead of from anear."

Veronica squinted at him. "That's not a real word."

"You college graduates, and your book learning."

"Can I ask you one serious question and get a straight answer?"

DJ's smile faded and he squinted out at the falls with a faraway look in his eyes. "Do I get extra credit if I guess the question? I'll bet it's 'Why haven't I asked you to marry me, when we're so perfect together?'"

"Yes," Veronica said, with a little tremble in her voice. "I don't want us to rush anything, or push you, but I wonder. We *are* so perfect together."

He nodded absently. "Sure. You deserve to know that. Hell, you deserve to know the truth about everything. Try as I might, I haven't been able to find the way to tell you. It will feel good to get everything off my chest, but I'm scared. The only reason I haven't told you is that I don't want to lose you. I figure that as soon as I do, you'll think I'm crazy and run. These past four years have been the best years of my lives."

"Lives?"

DJ nodded, sadly. "Lives. I've already lived this life before."

Veronica's heart leapt and her eyes grew wide.

"I knew that would be your reaction." DJ rushed ahead. "I've tried for four years to think of a way so you'll believe me, and I can't come up with anything. I mean, I can tell you that Ronald Reagan, the guy who made *Bedtime for Bonzo*, of all things, is going to become President in another sixteen years. I could have told you John F. Kennedy was going to be assassinated last November. That probably would have been the right thing to do, but I didn't have the nerve. I never have the nerve."

Veronica reached her hand out and laid it against DJ's lips. Tears welled in her eyes. "You don't have to say anything."

"I've blown it now, haven't I? I knew it. This is why I haven't wanted to tell you. I couldn't stand the thought of losing you."

"You haven't lost anything." Veronica's tears spilled as she lost her composure altogether and broke down sobbing.

DJ held her close. "Hey, hey, it's okay. I mean, honestly, I can't say for sure it's okay, but I *think* it's okay. I do know that when I'm with you, everything feels better."

Veronica pushed back from him, her face blotchy and a smile competing with her tears. She shook her head, frustrated at everything that had bubbled to the surface so suddenly. "I've just been so lonely. I never knew *how* lonely until this minute, now that I know I'm not alone anymore. I've been alone for so long."

DJ shook his head. "I'm so confused. I've been sure all along that when I tried to tell you this, that I would lose you. But, you're not freaked out?"

"No. I'm happy." Veronica drew a deep breath, then laid her head against DJ's chest. "You've only started over once, so you don't know it yet. If you had started over more than that, you would know you start each life in the exact same place. At least, I do. I wake up in the house of a couple I babysat for one time. The first time I woke up there, I felt completely lost, because I had just died, and then woke up in a strange place."

Now it was DJ's turn to feel an electric shock. "Come on, Ronnie. You're not being serious." He held her face in his hands and moved his own face until it touched her nose. "Are you?"

Veronica didn't blink. "I absolutely am."

DJ, deadly serious for once, shook his head slowly back and forth. "I can't believe this."

"Wait. You were sure I wasn't going to believe you. Now you can't believe me?"

"No, no. Of course I believe you. How else would you come up with something like this so fast? But, I have so many questions."

Veronica nestled back into his chest. "Me, too. I've only ever met one person who was going through what we are, and it wasn't a good time to talk about it."

"Okay, now I have one more question."

Chapter Fifty

Veronica and DJ stayed at the falls for hours, trying to figure out how this fit into the puzzle of their lives. DJ confessed that he wanted to ask Veronica to marry him right after their first date, but that he couldn't imagine keeping a secret like that from her.

DJ, you are a better person than me. I've always known that, but here is further proof. I rushed headlong into two marriages and was wishing for a third, and I never considered that I was holding a secret that would serve as a constant wall. And you, my Dimitri, you would never dream of asking me to marry you if there was something you couldn't tell me.

They decided they wouldn't ask about how each had died. That was information that neither wanted to give or get, particularly. They also agreed that when they were alone, they could be free to talk and think as they really were—people out of time. Around others, they would strive to continue to be period-correct.

"Did you ever make yourself rich?" DJ asked.

"Oh, yes. Last life, I was rich. I traveled. I saw everything I ever wanted to see, and I felt completely empty and unhappy. My turn for a question. Did you have children in your last life?"

DJ nodded. A haunted look played across his face. "I had a son, Maximillian. He was an adventurer. He had all the guts that I lacked. He traveled the world. He died in a rock climbing accident. That was the biggest factor in why I restarted. You?"

"Yes, two girls, Sarah and Nellie. When I woke up back here, I did everything I could to bring them back into the world. I married the same man, even though we divorced in my first life. I did everything I could to bring them back. I even got pregnant on the same night. I was so sure it was Sarah, but I miscarried. I haven't gotten pregnant since. My turn again. Did you have a good marriage?"

DJ shook his head. "Nah. You know her. Remember Lilly from Artie's?"

A memory flashed through Veronica's mind, the day she told DJ he had better ask Lilly out, or he was going to lose her. She nodded. "I remember."

"We got married pretty young. I guess it was okay early on, and we had Max. My family never liked her though, so I should have known. That may or may not be why I took you to meet my family on our first date."

"So, if your Bunica had looked me up and down with her evil eye and pronounced, "No good," we wouldn't be sitting here right now?"

DJ laughed. "Probably not! I knew they would love you, though. How can anyone look at you and not love you?"

"Believe me, plenty have managed that trick."

"Ronnie, you know what all this means, though, don't you?"

Veronica searched through her mind, couldn't come up with an answer.

DJ got out of the car, walked around the front and opened her door. He got down on one knee.

"Veronica McAllister, I am woefully unprepared for this moment, though I have had four years to prepare. I do not have a ring. I am living at home with my family. I have a pretty dead-end job working at Artie's. I hope I'm not overselling myself, but, will you marry me?"

"I have lived too many lives to know for sure if there are soul mates. If there is such a thing, though, you are it for me. I know this for sure—marrying you will be the happiest thing I have done in several lifetimes."

"So, is that a 'yes' then?"

"As much as I love you, you can be so frustrating. Yes, that is a 'yes.' Now get up here and kiss me."

He did.

VERONICA THOUGHT SHE had met all of DJ's family, but on the days leading up to the wedding, they began to arrive by plane, bus, and RV. The wedding was held on the first Saturday of September, 1964. DJ's family rented a hall so there would be room for everyone. Veronica, Doris, and DJ's mother, Maria, planned everything, and his Bunica oversaw the food preparation.

It was a joyous party. With DJ's family, there could be no other kind. Wallace McAllister found a new golfing buddy among DJ's uncles, and Doris and Maria found they had more in common with each other than just their children.

The wedding took on a distinct Eastern European flavor. DJ and Veronica both agreed it was easier to go along with that than try to persuade DJ's Bunica otherwise. That meant the night before the wedding, Veronica was kidnapped by DJ's uncles and cousins. DJ had warned her it was coming, so she was fully prepared.

The men whisked her off to a private house, where she was plied with liqueurs and desserts, while they negotiated with DJ for her release. In the end, the kidnappers settled for a bottle of whiskey and two bottles of wine, to be delivered at the wedding the next day. Veronica was delivered safely back to the comfort of her parent's house slightly tipsy, but none the worse for wear.

The next morning, Veronica got ready for the wedding in her parent's house, then DJ's cousins drove her to where DJ had spent the night. He was dressed in a blue suit he had bought for the occasion, and then he and Veronica walked to the church, surrounded by his family. When they arrived, they paused at the steps, and the wedding party formed a moving circle around them, singing a song Veronica couldn't understand. Still, the sweetness of the melody brought tears to her eyes and threatened her perfectly done makeup.

Inside, everyone else was already seated, and the wedding party led DJ and Veronica to the front of the church, where they said their vows. Immediately after, Veronica was led to a chair, where Bunica removed her bridal veil and replaced it with a white scarf. This symbolized her transition from bride to wife, from a girl to a woman who would take on the responsibilities of a household. While Bunica replaced the veil, DJ's mother, Maria, sang a song from their old country called *Say Good-bye, Dear Bride, to Your Father and Mother.*

The solemnness of this ceremony was the last straw for Veronica. Tears streamed down her face as she assumed her new role. *Five lifetimes and four marriages, and nothing has ever felt like this before. This isn't a civil ceremony, this is a lifetime commitment.* She looked into DJ's smiling eyes, standing before her, waiting. *And, this is the right man.*

She mouthed, "I love you," to DJ.

"I know," he answered, with a wink.

Chapter Fifty-One

Sitting at the head table, Veronica leaned into DJ and said, "If this isn't a little like *My Big Fat Greek Wedding,* I don't know what is."

"Two things. One, you and I are the only ones here who have ever heard of that movie, and two, we are not Greek. We don't think everything can be fixed with Windex."

"I think you know what I mean, my new husband."

"I do, I do. I know we can be a little overwhelming when you get our family together like this, but what a party!"

Just then, DJ's father, Constantin, picked up a microphone and turned to the small band, which had been quietly playing in the corner. "Hello, friends! It is time for the Bride's first dance. As father of the groom, I claim the honor."

DJ elbowed Veronica lightly under the table and said, "You're going to like this. Here, take this and put it around your wrist." He handed her a silk purse.

She walked out to the middle of the dance floor, where Constantin bowed deeply, then began a slow waltz in time to the music. After only a few seconds, DJ's Uncle Nicolae, who everyone called "Nicky" cut in. As he did, Constantin slipped an envelope into her purse.

The process repeated itself over and over, with men lining up to dance a few seconds with Veronica and slipping an envelope into her purse.

When the line finally petered out, DJ stepped into the limelight, bowed, and took Veronica on their first dance as a married couple.

Really, their first dance ever, as they had never had a reason to dance before.

"Do you have something to slip into my purse, too?"

"I have something much better to give you, but you will have to wait a few hours, until we can slip away."

Veronica laid her head against his shoulder and smiled.

WHEN THE MUSIC WAS finally done, when the food had all been packed away and every corner of the church's reception room swept clean, it was finally time for the happy couple to leave.

They drove straight to the airport and got on a plane to New York City. Veronica had told DJ she had gone there on her honeymoon with Danny Coleman, and how much she had loved it. She had thought it was best for them to pick another destination, somewhere new, but DJ disagreed.

"It's a place you love. Excitement. Broadways shows. Bright lights. Museums we will both love," DJ had said.

Veronica couldn't disagree with any of that, so they agreed that New York it would be. DJ had told her to pack two suitcases with everything she would need for a long stay, but had not told her how long that was.

When they got to their hotel—a nice hotel not far from Central Park, clean, but not gorgeous—he had told her why.

"You love this city, and there's too much here for us to see in a few days, or even a few weeks. We need time to absorb it. So, unless you strongly disagree, I want us to live here. Not forever, but for a while."

Veronica's mouth fell open. "Oh, DJ. There's no way we can. We don't have a place to live, and isn't it expensive to live in New York?"

"It is, but not nearly like it will be in another few decades. Eventually, it will be impossible for a young couple working modest jobs to live anywhere near where we are. We'd have to move out to one of the boroughs. But, in 1964, with a little bit of a head start, and if we both find a job, we can swing it. I've been going down to the library for the past few weeks and looking at the For Rent ads in the New York newspapers. We can do it, if you want. If you don't, that's okay too. Then, we can have a nice honeymoon here and go back home in a week or so."

"You said, 'with a little head start.' What are you thinking is our head start?"

"Have you looked in those envelopes in your purse, yet?"

"No, I just stuck them in my carry on."

"Go look."

Veronica rustled through the bag she had used for her carry on and pulled out the purse. It felt heavier than she remembered it.

"Here, bring it over here, we can open them on the bed."

Veronica sat down with DJ and emptied the envelopes out. She opened the first one and a fifty dollar bill fell out, along with a slip of paper that had writing on it that she couldn't read. She handed it to DJ with eyebrows raised.

"It says, "Many blessings on both your heads."

She opened another envelope. This time, two one hundred dollar bills came out, along with another blessing.

"I knew everyone was slipping money into the purse, but I thought it was just ones and maybe a five or two. Don't tell me every-one gave us money like this."

"Oh, yes. In our family, no one buys gifts. They do this. They would think they were cursing us if they only gave us a few dollars. It's great for us now, but believe me, it will all even out. I've got a lot of cousins, nieces, and nephews that will get married over the next few decades, and we'll be doing the same."

Veronica nodded. "Of course. What a sweet tradition. I love your family, DJ."

He shook his head. "No. *Our* family, now. We are all one."

Veronica continued to open envelopes and shake bills out onto the bed. When the last envelope was empty, they counted the bills and found it was a bit over three thousand dollars.

"Now, there's our head start, if we want it. So, what do you say? Is New York our new temporary home, or is it just our honeymoon spot?"

"Can we go look for an apartment tomorrow?"

"We'll have to! We only have one more night in this hotel."

Chapter Fifty-Two

Veronica woke up the next day as excited as she had been in several lifetimes. "C'mon, sleepy head," she said, nudging DJ awake. "One more night in this place, remember? We've got to go find a place to live!"

"What time is it?"

"It's almost nine o'clock."

"And we're in New York. That means it's only six o'clock back home." He buried his head under the pillow.

"If you are awake enough to do math, you are awake enough to take a shower."

He did. When Veronica put her shoulder into something, there was no such thing as an immovable object.

Forty-five minutes later, they were showered, dressed, and on the sidewalk in front of their hotel.

"Which way, my love?"

"Well, my favorite place, when I was here last time, was Greenwich Village, around Washington Square Park. It's probably too expensive, but New York University is right there, so there's got to be some kind of housing for poor students. Let's start there."

They elected to begin figuring out New York's mass transit system, and so rode a bus instead of paying for a taxi. They got lost, got on the wrong bus several times, and wasted several hours, but they didn't care. They met one of their primary goals—to get to know the city.

DJ had done some research before arriving, but when their feet were actually on a Greenwich Village sidewalk, things seemed loud, fast, and a little intimidating. Veronica had the idea to walk up to NYU and look for bulletin boards that might be advertising housing students could afford. It was a good idea, but the bulletin board system was not efficient. Every place they called was already gone, filled by NYU students.

They walked back toward the main business district that spoked away from Washington Square Park and realized they hadn't eaten anything since they arrived, so they looked for somewhere to buy lunch. They walked past record stores, head shops, and mod clothing stores. They finally saw a place called The Cellar Door, which appeared to be just that—a door that led down into a dark, gloomy cellar. What caught their eye, though, was the sign that said, "Help Wanted—Cook."

DJ pointed to it and said, "They're playing our song." When they walked down the stairs, they were pleasantly surprised to find a fairly large café. There were a dozen tables, a long bar, and a small stage at the back that was dark at this time of day.

"I think this is like the Artie's of Greenwich Village," DJ said, smiling. They approached a man who stood behind the long counter, wiping it down with a white rag. They took a seat at the bar, and DJ said, "We'll have two of whatever you've got for a special, and I'll take the job on the sign out front."

The man, who had a cigarette dangling from one lip, grunted, and looked them over. He leaned both elbows onto the bar and pushed his nose a foot away from DJ's. "I'll tell you what," he said, in a whiskey-stained voice, "you come back around here and show me what you can do on a grill. If I like what I see, you got the job, the food is on the house, and I'll hire your pretty girlfriend to waitress."

DJ said, "She my pretty wife, but, deal!" He stuck his hand out to the man, but he had already turned away and was walking to the grill.

DJ turned to look at Veronica with a look that said, "Now what have I done?" then followed the man into the cramped kitchen.

The man's cigarette had an impossibly long ash DJ watched with morbid fascination. "Here's some eggs. Make two eggs, over easy, a ham omelet, a side of bacon, and two side orders of whole wheat toast.

DJ went into a short warm up routine, cracking his knuckles, rolling his shoulders, even doing a deep knee bend, when he glanced at cigarette man, who was clearly unamused. "Right. Okay." DJ looked around at where everything was for a moment, then sprang into action. He cracked eggs with a dramatic flair, slapped bacon onto the grill, buttered bread and dropped it on the grill, too.

The man wandered back out to where Veronica was sitting. "Is he always a comedian?"

Veronica smiled a little sadly, and said, "Yes, he is. But, he's also the best fry cook I've ever seen."

They both watched DJ work behind the grill for another few moments, then said, "Okay, he knows his way around a grill. My cook quit yesterday, so he can start right now." He looked Veronica up and down. "Howsabout it? You want a job, too?"

"Yes, sir, I do."

"Apron's over there. After you two eat, you can start right in." He pointed to an older woman sitting reading a newspaper in a booth. "That's Margie. She thinks she owns the place, but really she just owns me. She's my wife. She'll show you the ropes. I'm Tony."

Veronica gave Tony her biggest smile and said, "You won't be sorry."

Tony stopped, considered, and said, "You know, that's what they always say when I hire 'em. Most of the time, they're wrong."

It took them a few days longer, and they ended up having to extend their stay at a hotel, but eventually, they tracked down an apartment they could afford. It was a small studio apartment directly

above a dry cleaners that smelled strongly of the chemicals from below. It was the size of Veronica's walk in closet in her beautiful home
in Falling Water in her third life.

It was essentially a one-room apartment that had the tiniest imaginable bathroom tacked on as an afterthought. The only way both of
them could be in the bathroom at the same time was if one of them
stood in the claustrophobic shower. There was a murphy bed that
converted their living room into their bedroom, and one corner had
a hot plate and old refrigerator.

They loved it. It was in the heart of the pulsing city they wanted
to explore, and the only time they ever went home was to sleep.

When they weren't working , they ate a sack lunch in Washington Square Park, listening to someone playing their guitar, or watching people play chess. The Frisbee had been invented by then, and
there always seemed to be kids on breaks between classes from NYU,
flinging the disc around. It was their favorite place in the city.

Because Veronica and DJ wanted to make their money last as
long as possible, they didn't go to Broadway shows as often as they
would have liked. Still, they went at least once a month. They learned
where the best bad seats were in each theater, and haunted the front
of the theater at show time, hoping a scalper might get desperate and
unload a pair of tickets at a discount.

There were also small movie theaters that played experimental
movies that didn't make a lot of sense to them, but they enjoyed the
experience of going. When they both had a day off, they made the
trek uptown and hit the museums.

More than anything, of course, they both worked. They started
off on the morning shift, but as soon as Tony saw DJ work the grill
and the way Veronica charmed all the customers, whether beatniks or
tourists, he moved them up to the evening shift.

Most of the entertainers were interesting enough in their own
right, but not destined to set the world on fire. The beatnik era was on

its last legs, and folk music was taking over Greenwich Village. They had been fortunate enough to catch a set of Simon and Garfunkel just as their first big hit, *The Sound of Silence,* was taking off.

One chilly evening in November, 1964, a long-haired, heavyset woman walked in and told Veronica that the rest of her band was running a little late, but that they would be right behind her.

Veronica gaped at her and couldn't help but blurt out, "You're Cass Elliot, aren't you?"

The woman took a half step back in surprise. "Do I know you?"

"No, no, I'm just a big fan."

"If you're a big fan of mine, you belong to the world's smallest fan club, but thanks, I appreciate it."

Right behind her, two tall, shaggy men walked in carrying guitars. "Oh!" Veronica said. "You're the Mugwumps." *Like in Creeque Alley, but that song won't even be written for a few years. You'd think I'd be used to this kind of thing happening by now, but I still get confused.*

Denny Doherty and Sal Yanovsky were still starving artists at that moment. Soon, Denny and Cass would go on to fame and fortune with the Mama's and the Papas. Sal would soon be a founding member of The Lovin' Spoonful.

DJ was stuck behind the grill that night, but Veronica spent every minute she could watching future folk music royalty toiling away in relative anonymity.

I should have thought of this last life, when I had all the money in the world. I could have traveled to Germany to see The Beatles play at the Cavern Club, or the Stones when they were still playing small venues in London. She let that thought roll around in her mind for a few moments. *No. None of that would have made a difference. When I was done seeing whatever I wanted to see, I would have still been alone in Middle Falls.*

DJ and Veronica had initially planned on staying in New York for a few months. By the following spring, they were still happily working at The Cellar Door and managing to get by.

That changed in April, 1965, when Veronica's biological clock, which had always been as steady as a metronome, skipped a beat.

Chapter Fifty-Three

Veronica didn't even realize she had skipped her period until she looked at the small calendar she carried in her purse. For many lives, it had been her habit for her to circle the day her cycle started on a small calendar. When she thought to look, it had been forty-five days.

Doesn't necessarily mean anything. I'll give it a few weeks. But, should I tell DJ?

Almost immediately, she answered that question on their short walk to work that same day. As casually as she could, she said, "I'm late for my period."

DJ stopped dead on the sidewalk. "You're always on time, aren't you?"

"You could set your watch to it."

"There aren't any home pregnancy kits yet, are there?"

Veronica shook her head, realizing this was a conversation she would have only been able to have with DJ. 'Not for a few years, yet."

"So, a trip to the doc, then?"

"I think so, yes. Beth Israel Hospital isn't far away, but it's big. I think I'll go to the little medical clinic here in the neighborhood. They can tell me if I'm preggers or not, I'm sure." She stared into DJ's eyes. "Would it be a good thing?"

"Two time travelers having a baby? Sure, what could go wrong? But, Ronnie, the chance to have a baby with you is worth any risk. Of course it would be a good thing. I just don't want to get too excited yet."

They worked their shift that evening, but DJ kept rushing out of the kitchen every time Veronica tried to pick up a heavy tray of dishes. Finally, she said, "I might be pregnant, but I'm not sick. It will be fine."

Or it won't, she thought, but didn't dare say.

The next day, they both went to the clinic that was a few blocks from their house. The waiting room reminded Veronica of the laundromat back in Middle Falls—humid, tile floors, and many people sitting in chairs, reading months-old copies of *Time* and *Newsweek.*

When they finally got in to see the nurse, she drew Veronica's blood and told her she could come back the next day for the results.

Twenty-four hours seemed like a long time to wait, so they went to see *What's New, Pussycat?* at the Bleecker Street Cinema near their apartment. The Bleecker usually only played more experimental fare, but *Pussycat* starred Greenwich Village denizen Barbra Streisand, so they made an exception.

They returned to the clinic the next afternoon and picked up the results. Once they had the envelope in hand, they were nervous to open it. Instead, they wandered by Washington Square Park and bought two dogs from a street vendor. They sat and listened to a long-haired man strum his guitar and sing a gorgeous, melancholy arrangement of *Mr. Tambourine Man.*

Finally, Veronica ripped open the envelope and read for a few seconds before she looked at DJ and said, "Your footloose ways are over. You're gonna be a dad."

AS SOON AS THEY CONFIRMED the news, they knew their time in New York was over. As much as they loved the never-ending excitement of the city, they both agreed it was not where they wanted to raise their baby.

"Not to mention that my Bunica will put a three-generation curse on us if we have a great grandchild three thousand miles away from her," DJ said.

"I can't tell if you're joking or not."

"That's the thing about Bunica. She's incredible, but she's still a little bit scary."

They put their notices in, both at The Cellar Door, and at the cramped closet they had called home for the previous seven months. Tony was sorry to see them go. He said that Veronica had been right. He wasn't sorry he had hired them. It was the nicest thing he had ever said to them.

Their landlord managed to rent their apartment sight unseen on the same day they gave their notice. Greenwich Village was still the place to be.

They counted their money, and to their surprise found they still had more than half of the three thousand dollars they had landed in New York with. That was more than enough to buy them tickets home and to set up a place of their own in Middle Falls.

They spent their last day in New York in their favorite places, all of which were within walking distance of where they had lived and worked.

Finally, Veronica said, "I have so loved this place, and I have loved being here with you. It's been a dream come true."

"For me, too," DJ said.

"But now, it's time to go home."

They didn't tell anyone they were coming back. They still only had their suitcases with them, and so hopped a Greyhound from Portland to Middle Falls.

They spent their first night at home in the small motel on the edge of town, too tired to see anyone. Early the next day, they took a cab to DJ's parent's house, where they had been storing his car and the rest of his belongings.

They did their best to sneak into the house, but DJ's Bunica was standing in the entry way waiting for them.

"Bunica, what are you doing here? Why aren't you home?"

"I knew you were coming," was all she would say.

DJ didn't bother to ask how she knew. He had learned as a young boy to never question his Bunica.

The old lady walked directly to Veronica, laid her hand across her stomach, nodded, then turned and walked away.

"See? I told you. Scary old woman."

Chapter Fifty-Four

It didn't take Veronica and DJ long to get settled back into Middle Falls life. After they had been back a few weeks, living in the non-stop atmosphere of New York seemed like a dream, or another lifetime.

DJ chose not to go back to Artie's. No matter how much they loved him, they still only paid minimum wage, which in 1965, was still only $1.25 per hour. Instead, his uncle got him a job working at a construction site. He was more exhausted every night, but they paid $2.25 an hour to start.

DJ thought Veronica shouldn't work while she was pregnant, but she thought that was crazy. Even though both families wanted to help out with getting things for the baby, she wanted to have some money to get what she wanted for him or her, too. So, as she had done so often, she made the trek back to Perry Zimmerman's small office and said, "Whadya say, Zimm? Got room for a middle-aged, pregnant carhop?"

Perry looked her up and down. "I guess maybe I can believe our man DJ has put you in the family way, even though you're sure not showing. I refuse to believe you're middle aged, though." He squinted, did some math in his head, and said, "You're what? Twenty-five? If that's middle-aged, I'm putting in for my retirement pension tonight. You know there's always a spot open for you here, Ronnie. Are you sure you want to work through the heat of the summer?"

She nodded. "You've still got that lifetime supply of salt tablets, right?"

He agreed that he did.

"Then we'll be good to go."

Veronica kept very few things from DJ, now that she knew they were both on the same unusual life path, but she did her best to hide her worry. The money from a part-time job would be helpful, but mostly, she wanted to work to keep her mind off her pregnancy. She had been three months pregnant when she had lost her baby in her second life, and she was anxious to get past that milestone.

So, DJ worked all day, hauling scrap wood and metal on the construction site of the new Safeway store right there in Middle Falls, and Veronica worked at Artie's. At night, they both collapsed on the used couch DJ's family had donated to their little rental house, both too tired to either cook or eat.

When Bunica saw Veronica next, she said, "Too skinny. Too skinny."

The next thing DJ and Veronica knew, their refrigerator was stuffed with casseroles and other easy to heat dishes.

When Veronica had her next checkup, the doctor told her that all looked perfect with baby and mother. Her due date was December 6th.

She decided to keep working at Artie's until a month or so before the baby was born. She gave her notice to Perry Zimmerman for the final time on Halloween, effective November 15. That gave her time to get everything ready for Thanksgiving and the baby without juggling shifts slinging burgers.

November 15th dawned overcast and unseasonably cold in western Oregon. By the time Veronica reported for her final shift at noon, the temperatures had dropped into the mid-twenties. When she came in through the employee's entrance, Perry looked at her stomach pushing her winter coat to its breaking point. "Ronnie, why don't we pretend like yesterday was your last day. I don't want you out there in this weather."

Veronica laughed and said, "I'm an Oregonian born and bred. No way a little chilly weather is going to keep me inside. I am going to enjoy my last day here, no matter what the weather looks like."

Perry shrugged and went back to what he was doing.

Veronica did her best to savor this last shift at Artie's. She knew that unless or until she started life over again, this would be her last few hours at the place she had loved so much. That thought—starting life over again—brought another pang to her.

I'd never found a reason to care about one life over another, but this one I do. I don't want to leave it. Carrying a tray with one hand, she unconsciously rubbed her stomach with the other. *This little one is a precious chance to truly start over. To be everything I've ever wanted to be—a wife, a mother, a part of a family.*

Veronica was daydreaming and not paying attention to where she was going. Crossing the parking lot, she stepped on a patch of ice. Her feet flew out from under her. The tray flew away from her, and even as she fell, she did her best to hold her stomach to protect the baby. She hit the frozen parking lot butt first, then slammed over backwards, hitting her head with a sickening crack.

OH, GOD, PLEASE DON'T let me be back in 1958. That would be too much.

Veronica opened her eyes and saw a strange man's face hovering over her.

"You've had a nasty fall. You're in an ambulance heading to the hospital. We're getting you there as quickly as possible."

Everything was spinning, as though she had been thrown in a dryer like a load of laundry.

No, no, please. This life is too precious. I love this life. I don't want to lose it. I don't want to start over.

She tried to shake her head, but the man reached out and touched her temple. "Try not to move. You've got a head injury. We'll be to the hospital in less than two minutes. We've radioed ahead, and they're ready for us."

"My baby?"

"Close your eyes. Try not to move."

Chapter Fifty-Five

Veronica opened her eyes.

The first thing she noticed was DJ, holding her hand, his face wet and strained with worry.

She moved her eyes and saw Doris, Wallace, and Barbara.

"I'm still here."

DJ leaned in close. "You're still here, my love."

"The baby?"

She closed her eyes. She didn't think she could bear to hear the news.

"The baby's fine," DJ said. "Whoever he or she is, they're a tough little nut. Don't try and move. You've had surgery to relieve pressure on your skull, but you came through it with flying colors."

He backed away a little and let Doris, who had been hovering over his shoulder, move closer.

"Lay still, baby. That was a terrible fall, but you're going to be fine now." She stroked Veronica's cheek like she had when she was a baby. "It's going to be fine."

INSTEAD OF BUSTLING around the cozy cottage she and DJ called home, getting the baby's room ready and helping with Thanksgiving dinner, Veronica spent the next few weeks in the hospital. She was never lonely, though, as either DJ, Doris, Wallace, or Barb was there with her around the clock. They were augmented by many members of DJ's family, including his Bunica, who came the first day and waved her hands over Veronica's head and stomach, blessing both her and the baby.

As soon as she began to feel better, Veronica complained about lying in the hospital bed. She wanted to be up and moving. The doctors thought it best for the baby if she stayed, though, so she did.

Doris and Wallace made arrangements with the hospital so they were allowed to bring Thanksgiving dinner to Veronica, since she couldn't come to it. It was as cozy a scene as any Thanksgiving could be in a hospital room.

The week after Thanksgiving crawled by. DJ ran to the library for her, but one symptom of the cranial bleeding and concussion was that she had a terrible time focusing on anything, including her beloved books.

Finally, on December 8, two days after her projected due date, Veronica's labor pains started in earnest. Shortly after, he water broke, and it was time. The doctors had discussed this moment in advance with both she and DJ, and they had all agreed that a Caesarean was the best method of delivery. They believed it would be safest for both mother and baby because the wound in Veronica's head was still healing, and could be damaged during delivery.

At 2:05 p.m., Veronica was wheeled into the surgical room.

At 2:45, the doctor came out to a waiting room as full of people as he had ever seen. "Who's the father?"

DJ stood up, the very picture of every nervous father ever. "I am." The man who had a joke for every occasion had run completely out of witty things to say.

"Congratulations, son, you've got a healthy seven pound, six ounce baby girl. You can see baby and mother in just a few minutes. A nurse will come get you."

His last few words were drowned out by cheering from all assembled.

In 1965, it was normal to keep mother and baby separated, but Veronica insisted that they bring the baby to her as soon as she was awake from the surgery. Doris, Wallace, and DJ were all in the room with her when they brought the red-faced, wriggling baby into the room. Veronica waited until everyone had a chance to hold her, then asked her parents to leave, so she could talk to DJ alone.

When they were finally alone with their baby, Veronica held her against her chest and cried. DJ laid his face against the baby and sang a gentle song she didn't recognize.

"What's that song?"

"It's the song my Bunica sang my mother, my mother sang to me, and probably the song my great-grandmother sang to my Bunica. It's like our family version of *Itsy Bitsy Spider,* or *you are my Sunshine,* I suppose. The lyrics are mostly, "We are glad you are here, you are loved, you are our blessing," that sort of thing.

"I want you to teach it to me, okay? We can't let a tradition like that die out."

Veronica unwrapped the baby and DJ counted her fingers and toes. They kissed her little face and told her how loved she was.

Finally, DJ looked at Veronica and said, "Do you recognize her?"

Veronica nodded, silent tears running down her face, but was unable to speak around the lump in her throat. She looked at the ceiling, frustrated by her inability to speak. She took a deep breath and finally said, "Husband, meet Sarah. Sarah, meet your Daddy."

Chapter Fifty-Six

Many babies, especially newborns, and especially newborns from the same mother look alike, so it was not surprising that this baby would match Veronica's memory from four lifetimes ago. Be that as it may, there are some things a mother simply knows, and there is no arguing with. One of those things was that first time Veronica held that little baby, she knew it was her Sarah. She recognized her spirit.

Over the next few weeks, months, and years, that was confirmed to her again and again. Every little habit, speech pattern, and peccadillo that this baby named Sarah had, was an uncannily accurate echo of the Sarah she had held so many years before.

Veronica became pregnant again two years later. This time, she gave birth to an active, always on-the-move little boy. They named him Maximillian. Veronica had never met the other Max, of course, but DJ knew him as soon as he saw him. There are things a father knows as well, and he knew his own son.

Nellie was the last to join the party, arriving just after Valentine's Day, 1969. This time, Veronica had every reason to believe she might recognize the baby when it was born, and it came to pass. She cried grateful tears when all three babies were born.

In between having babies, Veronica put her degree from Pacific University to good work and began teaching English at Middle Falls High.

In 1970, Veronica invested as much money as they had been able to save in one of her magic stocks that had been permanently added to her brain. It wasn't enough to make them rich, but it was enough to start a nice college fund for the kids. She also put enough away for them to take thrifty vacations around the country. She wanted Sarah, Max, and Nellie to grow up appreciating the beauty and majesty of this life they had been born into.

Just for fun, Veronica started a lady's investment club in 1972. She invited Ruthie, of course, a few friends from the neighborhood, and several of DJ's cousins. They called themselves the "Tea and Cookies Investment Club." Even though Veronica didn't use much of her knowledge of what was to come, the club's investments flourished. They had one simple investment philosophy. If they used it and loved it, they invested in it. It was a wonderful excuse to get together once a month, and it made a difference in their lives.

Once Veronica got the household a little ahead of their household budget, she sat down with DJ one beautiful Sunday morning in May of 1977.

They were sitting in their own house, in a neighborhood of other nice family houses. In fact, it was only a few doors down from where Veronica had woken up in what had been the Weaver's home in 1958. It was a neighborhood full to bursting with parents and kids. Just as the Village had been the perfect home for them as newlyweds, this was the same for them as a family.

At that point, DJ had been working in construction for almost ten years. He had risen from gofer to foreman, and was making good money. He was also spending a huge amount of his life doing something he didn't love.

"Let's take a drive, honey," Veronica said.

"Sure, let's get the kids together, we can be ready to go in what, two or three hours?"

"It's not that bad, and you know it. But, today, we are going without them."

Just then, there was a knock at the door, and DJ's mother, Maria, popped inside. She looked like she was holding a secret, but wouldn't be able to hold it for long.

Veronica pushed DJ out the door and into their sensible station wagon. "I'm driving," she said.

DJ narrowed his eyes at Veronica the whole time. He knew better than to try and get information out of her when she didn't want to give it. They drove the loop that the teenagers still drove, then turned into Artie's parking lot. Veronica pulled into the parking spot right in front of the door where she had carried thousands of trays to thousands of cars.

"The old place looks so sad," DJ said. "I hate to see it like this."

The paint was faded and cracked, and the overhead sign canted at a dangerous angle. Everything about the place screamed of neglected maintenance.

"It's been like this ever since Zimm died, though. No one else could ever run this place and make it work like he could, even though he was a terrible bookkeeper. He was a great boss, though."

"Let's get out and look in the windows."

"Why?" DJ said. "We already know every inch of the place."

"You could humor me every once in a while."

They peeked through the cobwebbed and dirty windows at the grill area, which looked sad and abandoned.

"I guess whoever owns it now will try to sell it again. I don't give them much of a chance, though," DJ said.

"Unless it's us."

"What?"

"I've been to the bank. Our credit's good. We've got enough money set aside that the bank will give us enough to buy the place, and a little more to rehab it. If only we knew someone who was handy ..."

DJ's eyes lit up. He took four steps back into the parking lot, looking at the place with new eyes.

"I think I smell smoke."

"That's what you always say when I'm thinking," he said.

"So, what do you think?"

"What do I think about signing up for many hours of back breaking labor, followed by years bent over a hot grill, watching my wife, and eventually my kids, schlepping burgers out to the hungry citizens of Middle Falls? Well, I think that's the about the greatest idea I've ever heard."

THE HARDEST DECISION they had to make was what to name the place. They considered calling it "DJ's, or "V's, but they didn't feel right. For the longest time, they talked about calling it "Zimm's" in honor of Perry. In the end, they wanted to keep the history of the place intact, so they left it as "Artie's."

DJ wasn't kidding about the long hard hours to get it back up and running. For the first few months, he continued working his construction job during the day, then putting long hours in at night. That saved their scant remodeling budget, but wore DJ down to a nub. He was still a young man—only thirty-six—but he was rapidly aging himself.

Finally, Veronica took him aside, reminded him that she had enough put away in their investment account to allow him to quit his other job, and he did. The work went faster, then, and Artie's re-opened in mid-November, 1977.

Veronica called down to KMFR and inquired if they would be interested in putting the old radio tower up and broadcasting live again on weekend nights. No one at the station had been there long enough to remember that, and frankly, they were a little doubtful it had ever been done.

As soon as Artie's reopened, it was a hit. *Happy Days* was on television, and the whole country was in the mood for the innocence of the fifties.

By the time that fad had once again passed, Artie's was back to what it had always been—a key part of Middle Fall's makeup.

Chapter Fifty-Seven

From an outside perspective, Veronica and DJ's life was an ordinary, if somewhat blessed, existence. All three of their children were healthy and bright. They all started work at Artie's at an early age. Sarah was retrieving trays, emptying trash cans, and restocking soda cups from the time she was eleven years old. When she turned fifteen, she became Artie's youngest carhop. Max and Nellie weren't far behind her.

Eventually, all three of the kids held their weddings right there in Artie's parking lot. Veronica and DJ made sure that everyone in town knew they were invited. There was no charge on those wedding days, and all tips went to the wedding couples. Between that and the envelope dance, they all began their married life with a nice head start.

Veronica and DJ became grandparents for the first time in 1989. Sarah blessed them with a beautiful dark-haired boy. She named him Dimitri, after the first man she had ever loved. Over the next dozen years, Max and Nellie chipped in with babies of their own. The crowds at family dinners grew.

Bunica lived to be over 100 years old, but finally passed away in 1990. At family gatherings, everyone agreed they could still feel her presence.

Both Wallace and Doris McAllister lived much longer in this life than they had in her first. Doris had a heart attack and died shortly after that in 2001. She was eighty years old. Not surprisingly, when Veronica went into her childhood home to comfort her father, he handed her an envelope. On the outside, it read, "For when I'm gone." She had made all the arrangements for everything well in advance.

Wallace was lost without Doris to tell him what to do, and wasted away over the next year. DJ and Veronica asked him to come live with them time and again, but he stubbornly stayed in the same house they had always live in. "It's the nicest house on the block, you know," he told Veronica, again. He, too, had a heart attack and passed away in 2002. He was eighty-two years old.

In 2004, DJ turned sixty-five and Veronica sixty-four. They knew they had run Artie's long enough, and sold it to Nellie and her husband Kelly. DJ couldn't stay away forever, though. He still came back to man his grill for a shift now and then, whistling along to the music and telling all the carhops they were beautiful.

In 2006, Veronica and DJ decided to travel while they were still young enough to enjoy it. They started in England and worked their way east across Europe, covering many of the same stops Veronica had when she rode the train across Europe in her previous life. They loved the trip, and Veronica particularly enjoyed seeing Romania, where so many of DJ's family traditions had begun. When all was said and done, they realized they loved their grandchildren even more than they loved seeing the world.

They built a swimming pool in their backyard, which made them a popular destination over the summer months. They added a massive playset for the times when the sun wasn't shining.

They lived a happy, fulfilling life that neither ever wanted to end.

When they were alone, they often spoke about what was next for them. Neither had any intention of leaving this life early, but when the inevitable time came, neither one knew what would be next.

One day in 2015, as they sat on their back patio, watching a grandchild do dive after dive into the pool. DJ said, "If we thought it would work, either of us could end our own life right after the other died."

Veronica shook her head. "No. I think each of us will start over and find the body of the other, but not the spirit. Not the soul. I can't imagine what it would be like to meet you all over again, but have you not know me. That would break my heart. This has been such a wonderful life, but I don't want to start it over again. Not without you."

"Luckily, we don't have to, any time soon."

THREE YEARS LATER, Veronica felt a familiar pain. That it *was* still familiar to her across so many years and lifetimes of not feeling it, shows how memorable the pain was. With sinking hearts, they made her an appointment with their doctor, who referred Veronica to an oncologist in Portland.

They felt they were only going through the motions, but they did it anyway. The news they received from the specialist was exactly what they had expected, and it was terrible. Veronica was told that she would need to undergo chemotherapy first, then radiation treatments.

DJ and Veronica thanked him, but told him she would not seek either treatment.

I've been down that road once, and I will never do it again. I'd rather die naturally.

The oncologist then referred her back to her family doctor, who would see to it she was as comfortable as possible.

Initially, she didn't even want to take the pain medications. She wanted to be as present as possible as she watched the final weeks, days, hours, and seconds of this perfect life slip away. Before long, the pain became too intense, and she had to give in and take the medication.

DJ arranged for all their living room furniture to be removed, and replaced it with a hospital bed. They didn't bother with all the monitors and paraphernalia that would have given readouts every hour. They already knew the story those machines would tell, and they didn't want to see it.

When Veronica's final day arrived, their house was filled with friends, relatives, and the sound of playing children. It was exactly as she wanted it. Everyone who had ever known and loved her, lined up to say good-bye. When that ritual was complete, everyone stood around her and sang the songs she loved. The songs were happy, but they all knew they were singing her good-bye.

At the end, DJ leaned in close to her and kissed her deeply. Her cheeks were sunken, her eyes set deep in their sockets. "You are my life, my love. In my heart, you will live forever. My life will be empty without you. But, I know it's time for you to go. I release you. If there's a way to find you when I follow, you know I will."

Veronica smiled and took one last look around the room, soaking up the love. She spoke her last words. "Thank you, my love."

Veronica McAllister died for the final time.

Chapter Fifty-Eight

Veronica McAllister did not open her eyes in the Weaver living room in Middle Falls, Oregon, in 1958.

She had completed her cycle. She was stuck no more.

She went on.

The Changing Lives of Joe Hart[1]

Typically, I have the cover of the next book in the Middle Falls Time Travel series in this spot, along with a link that you can use to preorder it. However, internet issues with my talented cover designer has resulted in me not having that cover just yet.

Instead, let me just tell you a bit about this book.

Joe Hart is a good, kind, lonely man. He is scarred from a horrible birthmark that covers most of his face. The scars he carries inside him are even worse. He lives a quiet, completely solitary life until he dies in 2004. His entire life barely made a blip on the world's radar.

But, Joe Hart lives in Middle Falls Oregon, so like Thomas Weaver, Michael Hollister, Dominick Davidner, and Veronica McAllister before him, he opens his eyes at an earlier point in his life, all his memories intact. Given a second chance, Joe decides to live a life in every way opposite to the one he just completed. He will make changes—both for himself and the world at large.

The Changing Lives of Joe Hart[2] will be available on July 20, 2018. You can preorder it here[3].

---

1. **https://amzn.to/2rYBqVh**

2.   *https://amzn.to/2rYBqVh*

3.   https://amzn.to/2rYBqVh

Author's Note

As is so often the case, the inspiration for this book came from different places and conversations and were ultimately poured into the large cooking pot that I call my imagination. In some ways, this book started in late 2008—before I had even published my first book. I had a long lunch with my oldest sister, Terri, that day, and for some reason, she chose that lunch to tell me many secrets from her past.

The fact that Terri and I were sharing secrets was nothing new. We had been each other's primary secret-keepers for more than thirty years. What was a bit unusual, though, was that there didn't seem to be a driving reason for choosing just then to talk to me about what it had been like being a young woman growing up in the late-fifties, and being a young working woman in the early sixties. I was saddened by the stories she told me that day, particularly by how offhandedly she told them—as if there was nothing unusual in them.

Those stories stuck with me. Even though I never had a chance to talk with Terri about those things again—she died just a month later—I carried them with me, and I knew that someday I would write a story about some of those very things.

The second inspiration for Veronica's story came from a review I got for the third book in this series. If you ever wonder if author's read their reviews, I can tell you that most do. I certainly do. I like to know what elements are resonating with my readers, and what, if anything, is taking them out of a book.

This particular review was for *The Death and Life of Dominick Davidner.* I thought it was a great review, although it was slightly negative. It's a great example of why I choose to read what my readers are thinking. This reviewer complained that Dominick was so single-minded in his goal of getting back together with Emily, his wife who he had lost at the beginning of the book, that he failed to see any other possibilities in his life.

I took that review to heart. I didn't mind that Dominick was so single-minded, because to me, that was the heart of the book. However, it got me thinking about a story where they character was more open to changing who or what they were chasing. Veronica McAllister was that character.

Did I successfully synthesize the diverse elements of what it was like to be a young woman in the Eisenhower/Kennedy era with that concept of being open to change? I hope so. I did my best. Ultimately, that's your call as a reader.

I do know this. I came to know Veronica in the months I spent writing her story, and I came to love her. I hope you did, too.

Up next in the Middle Falls Time Travel Series is *The Changing Lives of Joe Hart.* It will be the sixth book in the series, and for the moment, it's the last one I have planned. I have loved writing this series, but it's taken up every ounce of my creative energy for the last twelve months, and I'm ready to explore a few other ideas. Of course, if a killer idea that is perfect for Middle Falls comes barreling down my street, I'll return sooner rather than later. There are always tales of redemption to be told.

As always, I have thank-you.

First, to Linda Boulanger from Tell-Tale Book Covers, who designed this cover. Linda was the first person I added to my publishing team, way back in the spring of 2012, and she's still with me because she is wonderful. I give her a basic idea and she goes into her magic place and comes back with a cover that perfectly represents what I was looking for. I don't know where I'd be without her.

I owe a great debt to my two proofreaders, Debra Galvan and Mark Sturgill. It doesn't matter how many times I read over a manuscript, tiny little mistakes sneak through. It's like a cosmic law. Debra and Mark do a wonderful job of catching not only my wayward typos, but also in fact-checking me at every turn. You guys are the bomb.

I have an Advance Readers Group on Facebook. If you'd like to join, drop me a line. My Advance Readers often read the book as I am writing it, piecemeal. The rest of the gang waits until I am done, then gives me an honest review of the book. I appreciate you guys and want to say thank you for helping me put out a better book.

If you've made it this far in my Middle Falls Series, I hope you'll stick with me one more book. I have a few good adventures lined up for Joe Hart. Thank you so much for reading. You are the reason I write.

Shawn Inmon
Seaview, WA
May 2018

Other Books by Shawn Inmon

The Unusual Second Life of Thomas Weaver[1] – Book one of the Middle Falls Time Travel Series. Thomas Weaver led a wasted life, but divine intervention gives him a chance to do it all over again. What would you do, if you could do it all again?

The Redemption of Michael Hollister[2] — Book two of the Middle Falls Time Travel Series. Michael Hollister was evil in Thomas Weaver's story. Is it possible for a murderer to find true redemption?

The Death and Life of Dominick Davidner[3] – Book Three of the Middle Falls Time Travel Series. When Dominick is murdered, he awakens back in his eight year old body with one thought: how to find Emily, the love of his life.

The Final Life of Nathaniel Moon[4] – Book Four of the Middle Falls Time Travel Series. Nathaniel Moon gains perfect consciousness in the womb, but when he tries to use his miraculous powers to do good, difficulties follow.

Feels Like the First Time[5] – Shawn's first book, his true story of falling in love with the girl next door in the 1970's, losing her for 30 years, and miraculously finding her again. It is filled with nostalgia

1. https://www.amazon.com/Unusual-Second-Life-Thomas-Weaver-ebook/dp/B01J8FBONO

2.   http://amzn.to/2wyUfCH

3.   http://amzn.to/2yTgHnk

4.   https://www.amazon.com/gp/product/B078H3376R

5.   https://www.amazon.com/Feels-Like-First-Time-Story-ebook/dp/B00961VIIM

for a bygone era of high school dances, first love, and making out in the backseat of a Chevy Vega.

Both Sides Now[6] – It's the same true story as *Feels Like the First Time*, but told from Dawn's perspective. It will surprise no one that first love and loss feels very different to a young girl than it did for a young boy.

Rock 'n Roll Heaven[7] – Small-time guitarist Jimmy "Guitar" Velvet dies and ends up in Rock 'n Roll Heaven, where he meets Elvis Presley, Buddy Holly, Jim Morrison, and many other icons. To his great surprise, he learns that heaven might need him more than he needs it.

Second Chance Love[8] – Steve and Elizabeth were best friends in high school and college, but were separated by a family tragedy before either could confess that they were in love with the other. A chance meeting on a Christmas tree lot twenty years later gives them a second chance.

Life is Short[9] – A collection of all of Shawn's short writings. Thirteen stories, ranging from short memoirs about summers in Alaska, to the satire of obsessed fans.

A Lap Around America[10] – Shawn and Dawn quit good jobs and set out to see America. They saved you a spot in the car, so come along and visit national parks, tourist traps, and more than 13,000 miles of the back roads of America, all without leaving your easy chair.

A Lap Around Alaska[11] – Have you ever wanted to drive the Alaska Highway across Canada, then make a lap around central Alaska? Here's your chance! Includes 100 photographs!

---

11. *https://www.amazon.com/Lap-Around-Alaska-AlCan-Adventure-ebook/dp/B0744CVWT4/ref=sr_1_4?s=digital-text&ie=UTF8&qid=1506966654&sr=1-4&keywords=shawn+inmon+kindle+books*

66630521R00156